PRAISE FOR

Sputnik Diner

"*Sputnik Diner* is so appealing because it holds nothing back.... Maddocks carves out his characters craftily and succinctly, leaving you rife with anticipation when the plot is left hanging.... You'll start to miss it after you've finished it, and wonder when you'll have a chance to read it again."

Books in Canada

"[An] impressive talent.... Like Alice Munro, whose works share the common terrain of late-20th-century Ontario, Maddocks' skill lies in turning out vivid and compelling characters. [His] detailed observations speak of a warm affection for the mess of family life and the rhythms of small town living."

Quill & Quire

"The quirky humour in *Sputnik Diner*...makes the book an enjoyable read.... Maddocks' attention to detail leaves a powerful impression upon the reader."

Kingston Whig–Standard

"*Sputnik Diner* is a bona fide gem—a deeply felt suite of short stories that chronicle a Welsh family's dislocating arrival into the strange new world of a small Ontario town. Maddocks is a calmly lyrical talent."

Vancouver Magazine

Sputnik Diner

Rick Maddocks

VINTAGE CANADA
A Division of Random House of Canada Limited

VINTAGE CANADA EDITION, 2002

 Published in Canada by Vintage Canada, a division of Random House of Canada Limited, in 2002. First published in hardcover in Canada by Alfred A. Knopf Canada, Toronto, in 2001. Distributed by Random House of Canada Limited, Toronto.

Some of the stories in this volume were previously published in the following periodicals: *Prairie Fire* ("Plane People" and "The Birthday Boy's Song"); *Prism International* ("Lessons from the Sputnik Diner"); and *Fiddlehead* ("The Blue Line Bus").

National Library of Canada Cataloguing in Publication Data

Maddocks, Rick
Sputnik diner

ISBN 0-676-97379-5

I. Title.

PS8576.A3235S68 2002 C813'.6 C2001-903817-8
PR9199.4.M34S68 2002

www.randomhouse.ca

Printed and bound in Canada
This book is printed on 100% recycled,
100% post-consumer waste paper.

2 4 6 8 9 7 5 3 1

for Phil, Fran and Sa

And he saw a tall tree by the side of the river, one half of which was in flames from the root to the top, and the other half was green and in full leaf.

—*The Mabinogion*

But what I would really like, when the time comes to break away and jump, is to jump not backwards, not down, but forward to something higher.

—Andrei Tarkovsky,
quoting *The Glass Bead Game*

Contents

Plane People

IN THE SUMMER OF 1981, two months before my family landed here, a man fell from the sky over Nanticoke and hit the roof of the mall seconds before his parachute blossomed out of his pack like a red and white silk handkerchief. The rest of him pollinated the employees' parking lot—A&P cashiers' hatchbacks, managers' sedans, a dumpster—but the whole county felt the aftershock. When Dad took up a job offer from SteelCan, packing up me, Mam and Sal and leaving South Wales for the north shore of Lake Erie, the skydiver was still falling. Always in the same rehearsed, hushed tones from the locals' lips: *Nice guy. Good friend of the De Konnings who run the airport. Had a wife, couple of kids. Gave lessons out there, real safety-first fella. Packed his own chute every time. Said he was even in the running for the national team. Wouldn't you just figure, eh? Made the same jump a thousand times.* These words were wrapped up by a quiet nod and a stare that left your face slowly before it settled into space. Later we'd hear how the skydiving school was in financial trouble, how Nanticoke Public Works guys were busy out back at the mall for weeks afterwards. Steamrollers, mops, sprayers. Gallons of paint and tar. Yet in early August, when my sister Sal and I walked our brand new Supercycles over the yellow lines of the employees' parking lot, the blood still showed there.

My family didn't *land* in Nanticoke exactly. We were in an Oldsmobile travelling west on Highway 3, crossing the upper lip of Lake Erie through a moustache of tobacco fields and sky. My head was still full of the exotic cars I'd seen since landing in Toronto. Back on the 401 they hissed under street lights that bowed over the superhighway like sunflowers of steel and glass. But gradually, over two flat hours and a series of exits and off-ramps, cars gave way to pick-up trucks gave way to open road, until we encountered only the odd blare of headlights every few miles. Wind was a blow-dryer through the back window. And I was drunk on countryside, the flatness and ragged symmetry of it, the names of the small, foreign towns we passed through—Caledonia, Garnet, Hagersville, Jarvis—which, index and all, were nowhere to be found in my *Collins Illustrated Atlas.*

Twenty minutes west of Jarvis, our driver pointed over the steering wheel at a blush of pink on the horizon. Pink street lights that, though miles ahead on the flat highway, flared up into the darkening sky. "There she blows," he said.

His name was Tom Gadd and he'd driven us a hundred and forty kilometres down from Toronto in the plush burgundy interior of a Delta 88. "There's your new home."

Sal, curled up on Mam's other side in the back seat, surfaced from sleep and panicked at the fields outside the window. "We're lost, aren't we?" She broke into tears. "We're lost. We're lost."

"No, Sal. No." Mam smoothed down my sister's long dark hair, the soft melody of her voice leaning. "Bad dream, that's all. We'll be there soon."

Gadd looked in the rear-view, then laughed amiably at Dad sitting beside him. "Cute," he said. Dad laughed politely back.

After a minute Sal fell back asleep, her cheeks still damp. She was only nine, a year and a half younger than me, and because of her birth defect, I was never allowed to forget I was her big brother. When she was delivered her left eye swung inward so her pupil was facing the bridge of her nose. Mam and Dad waited till she was three—for her skull to grow, I figured—to okay the operation. The doctor plucked her eyeball clean out of its socket, set it on a metal platform at her cheekbone, pivoted it around and placed it back in her head. *Voilà.* In memory I was sitting at the foot of her hospital bed watching the whole procedure, Sal's eye staring back at me from its own little steel podium. But Dad said no, I was at Nana and Grampa's house watching wrestling. Even he wasn't allowed in the operating room, he said.

He was in there for Sal's delivery though. When Mam was in labour with me, Dad was off in the north of England with his Swansea rugby team. He was almost famous back home. He played twice for Wales back in 1971, and swore he would've got a string of international appearances except he broke his leg in the first half of his second match. "Your father missed your infancy playing that bloody game," Mam said. Dad said she was bitter; rugby was always the other woman.

But afterwards he made it up to her through Sal. He was there to hear how, during her surgery, Sal's retina was jarred a little by accident, stretched, so that later in life she could lose sight in her bum eye altogether. And how six years later the eye acted up whenever Sal got overexcited or, as Mam said, "all of a doodah." Not only did her eye swing back to its old haunt like an alcoholic, but her hands shook as if drying nail polish and her mouth tightened and froze in a severe pucker. It was a sort of giddy trance. Embarrassed the hell out of me. But Dad said, "Just pretend she's sleeping," like she was now, in the back seat of a fancy American car purring down a black crickety Ontario highway with Mam singing "My Bonnie Lies Over the Ocean" into her hair.

⁂

When Sal, Mam and I followed Dad out of gate number five back at Toronto International Airport, Tom Gadd was a tall stranger standing under the arrivals screens. His mirrored glasses threw back the light. He was holding a sign that, beneath a SteelCan logo, said ALIAS in black marker.

"I think that's us, Dad."

"No," he whispered. "You're having me on."

"No, really. They spelled it wrong." I was a good speller.

"Duw, Duw," Mam tutted. "There's bloody cheek."

Dad waited, just in case anyone else would show. The man nodded our way unsurely. The gate slowly emptied of people.

Finally Dad approached him, his smile tentative, strained. "Pardon me," he said, in a polite, almost English accent, "but I think you're waiting for us. We're the *Eliases*, from Wales."

"Oh, the Aliases!" the man said brightly, rolling up the sign like a newspaper and clapping it against his leg. "Hi there!" he said. "I'm Tom Gadd, industrial relations. You must be David. And you must be Sian. And here's little Salwyn and Luke." When he shook my hand, his ringed fingers swallowed it whole. His face was happy and tanned. He made two of Dad.

"Sorry," Mam said, "we would have approached you sooner, Mr. Gadd, but we weren't sure if—"

"You buggered our name up," Sal said.

"It's Elias," I said, "with an E."

"And his name's not *Luke*," Sal snapped. "It's Lucas. *Luke* is common."

"Geez," Gadd laughed, his hands up in surrender. "Guess I'm the one should be sorry!" As we followed him toward the automatic doors his stride was easy and generous. He pitched the sign into a garbage bin. "Close but no cigar, eh?"

Dad laughed to be nice. "Yes," he said, trying to keep pace. I felt an empty plash in my stomach.

Now, past the male hum of conversation in the front seat, I saw farms, lone petrol stations flickering signs that said Gas, rural concessions, and more farms. I watched gravel and hydro wires unravel along the highway, threading us toward the pink lights. Gadd was talking SteelCan again. "We're projected to replace tobacco, the traditional economy, as the major source of revenue and employment here, David. Ninety per cent of the tobacco produced in Canada is grown right here in Nanticoke County. It's enjoying a peak year in terms of production, but speculators say the market's going to take a beating the next few years. Place needs a shot in the arm," he said. "Otherwise we're talking dying economy." Dad nodded intently. All I knew was he was getting paid three times as much as back home.

"See that?" Gadd pointed into the fields at a clump of buildings. "Kilns. They pick the leaves, then hang the tobacco leaves in there to cure." I watched the strange, boarded-up houses hiss past in the fading light. Inscrutable, alien. "Just about harvest time," he said.

"It's so flat," Mam said. "Are these prairies?"

Gadd slapped the wheel. "Ha! Well, no there, ma'am. These are definitely *not* the prairies."

He traded laughter with Dad. I leaned my head on Mam's shoulder; she smelled of Charlie perfume.

"They're in Alberta," I said, quiet and humiliated. I pointed at page 17 in my atlas, but it was getting too dark for her to see.

"This is just a sliver of the country, guys," Gadd said. "You can multiply what you've seen by thousands and it still wouldn't add up to Canada."

"The land mass of Canada totals three million, eight hundred and forty-nine thousand, six hundred and seventy-four square miles," I said. "That's forty times bigger than Britain."

Gadd turned to Dad. "He's a bright bulb, this one."

"Aye," Dad said. "A proper clever clogs. Soaks it all up." He spoke over his shoulder at me. "Don't you, *bach*?"

I blushed.

"I just love that accent," Gadd said, and I was going to tell him it was a language, not an accent, but he never gave me a chance. "They might bump your *bach* up a grade here, you know." I soared with pride at these words, smiling through my reflection as darkness worked over the friendly monster of land.

"What the hell have we come to?" Mam whispered.

Dad crooked his neck. "What's that, love?"

"Nothing."

On the outskirts of town the highway widened to four lanes. We passed a modern Baptist church surrounded by sparse patches of grass, then what appeared to be a local makeshift airport hangar, a giant Dutch barn with NANTICOKE painted in yellow on the red spotlit roof. Small planes were parked here and there on the grass, shiny black ribbons tied flapping around the trees. But Gadd pointed at the opposite side of the highway. "There's the Nanticoke Mall," he said, leaning his voice back toward Mam. "That's where you'll be doing most of your shopping."

"Hmm," Mam said. "That's nice."

We stopped at a red light. A car dealership, MacMorgan's Pontiac Buick Chev Olds, shone brilliantly on the corner, the lot all aglitter with gaudy red and silver streamers. "You can rent a car there, David. I'll take you first thing tomorrow."

My eyes drank in the cars, luminous and perfect beneath the lot's bank of spotlights. Sports cars, convertibles, luxury sedans, in all colours and sizes. They were parked in trim regiments, by model, and above each model flapped a sign bearing its name. Firebird, Parisienne, Skylark, Camaro. "Look, Dad," I cooed, my finger jabbing the window. "Can we have a Firebird?"

He laughed, awkward. "I think we'll opt for something

more sensible, Lucas. Something maybe your mother can learn to drive."

"Yessir," Gadd said. "Everyone drives here. It's the only way of life."

When I looked at Mam for a second Firebird opinion, her eyes were closed behind the streamers and pink light that danced on her glasses.

The Oldsmobile purred through Nanticoke—a rough, unfinished exhaustion of fast food joints, gas stations, doughnut shops and motels—until it left the last of the pink lights behind. Finally, Gadd flicked the Oldsmobile's indicator and turned into a gravel driveway. A big yellow sign, with bold black letters that read Surf and Sand Cottages, welled in the headlights.

"Where's the beach?"

"Oh," Gadd said vaguely, "about twenty miles due south."

In the front a swimming pool glistened through a chain link fence, its still water gathering leaves. Beyond it an arc of small, whitewashed cabins squatted under a wall of trees. "Look, Sal," Dad said as he opened the back door for her. "A pool. Remember your dream on the train this morning? You must be psychic, love." She held out her arms, too old for that, but Dad picked her up anyway, her legs flopping down and him groaning, "Solid as a brick shithouse, you are!"

Tom Gadd went toward the office. "I'll get the key for you guys. Then you'll have to come pay up front." He ran up the steps, change jangling. "It's reasonable, just a hundred bucks a week."

Dad raised his brows at Mam. "Not bad," he said. "Fifty pounds."

"I thought SteelCan was paying for it," Mam whispered. Then to Gadd, "Excuse me!"

"Yup?" He stopped at the top of the steps.

"I thought the company was paying for it."

Gadd looked back down on her with a tired face. "I'm sorry, but I thought it was understood that SteelCan booked the room for your family, to allow for smooth integration into the community, but we did *not,* at any time, state we were going to pay for the room."

Mam's voice was shaking. "Well, back home I was always led to believe that when you booked a room, you were in fact paying for a room."

The man looked up at the stars, then regarded us as if from a distance. He put his hands on his hips and sighed through his nose. "Well, that may be so in Wales, you guys, but it's not here. I thought I made it very clear—"

"Obviously, you didn't."

"Now, Sian," Dad said placatingly, still holding Sal. She was starting to sag in his arms, as if by will. Her pale, creased face stared dully at me. She rubbed her eyes. "It's just a misunderstanding, Mr. Gadd," Dad said. "See, Sian thought—"

"We haven't got the money to pay now," Mam said.

"Look," Gadd said. "I'm sorry folks, but it really isn't my problem. You're going to have to take it up with the management here."

Dad shrugged at Mam, as best he could with Sal in his arms. "I'll have a word with them at work next week, whoever's responsible, love."

"I know you will," she said angrily.

Gadd opened the office's screen door. "Now, I'll get the key while you take care of your luggage, okay? Cottage four.

And please, come meet me back here." He blustered inside. That was the last I would ever see of him.

"Lucas," Dad said, keeping a smile. "Help us with the bags, *bach*."

I lugged a suitcase out of the trunk, dragging it out with all my weight, then struggled with it across the gravel using both hands. A red sports car was parked out front of the cottage next door. "Look, Dad. *They've* got a Firebird."

"Shush now. People are sleeping." He spun around so Sal could look over his shoulder at the whitewashed cottage. "See that, Sal?" he said. "That's our new house."

"I don't like it," she mumbled. "It's too small."

"Tough," Dad said. "That's where we're going to spend the rest of our days."

"Nooo!" She buried her face in his jacket. "It looks like Grampa's tool shed! I want to go home."

"Oh, no, no, I didn't mean it, love!"

He turned back around so Sal couldn't see the cabin any more. He flashed a warm, knowing look at Mam, but it was lost in her tutting and brushing Sal's hair. Her voice was angry but loving all at once. "Your father's having you on. It's in jest, love."

"Where's Jest?" Sal said, suddenly panicking, looking about. "I thought we were in Canada!"

Dad laughed and then, in spite of herself, so did Mam. But Sal was pouting, rubbing her eyes, her chin on Dad's shoulder, until they stopped laughing and she stared sullenly at me trailing behind, alone, bent on feeling nothing, as Dad's tired arms carried her weight across the gravel to the cabin.

The next morning rumours of thunder grumbled low above the tobacco fields. Rain ploshed the roof. Bacon spat and crackled, mosquitoes laughed in my ears and a bright, crystalline game-show theme crackled from a television. But it was real human voices that woke me.

"Don't be so soft, Dai. Why are you making excuses for the man?"

"He's harmless," Dad said, sitting at the tiny table in the middle of the one-room cabin. "He's just got a job to do, that's all. He took me up to the mall first thing this morning, didn't he? Helped me rent a car. He didn't have to do that."

"Aye," Mam said. "And you didn't have to blow all that money either."

"We've got to eat, don't we?"

"It's not the food I'm talking about," Mam said, her shoulders busy at the two-burner stove. She was trying to flip over strips of bacon and fried bread with a white plastic fork. "*Iesu mawr!* You think they'd provide cutlery at least."

"Smells lovely, Sian," Dad said. He sat back and sniffed luxuriously, then he rapped the table. "Come on now, sunshine," he said softly. "Time to get up from there, or you won't get your prezzies."

"I'm up," I said, kicking back the covers.

"I wasn't talking to you," he said.

Confused, I rubbed my eyes and regarded the empty pillow beside me, then surveyed the one-room cabin for Sal. No sign of her. I got up and walked to the table; it was strewn with strange new clothes. I picked up an American football shirt and held it before me. Dad smiled. It was blue, with little holes all over it and a big red number eight on the front.

I tugged it hungrily over my head; it fell against my skin baggy and strange. As soon as my arms threaded through the three-quarter sleeves, Dad shoved a pair of white canvas tennis shoes into my hands. The word *Sparx* was printed along the sides in red and yellow letters.

I grimaced. "White shoes?"

"They'll only get dirty, Dai," Mam said. "Give him a couple of hours and they'll be black as tar."

"Hsst!" Dad said, annoyed. "They're all the rage over here, see." He took another pair off the table and set them down gently on the floor beside his chair. "Here's some for you too, Sal. And—oops!—don't let me forget *this,*" he sang, holding up a flimsy pink band of elastic cloth. "It's what all the pretty Canadian girls are wearing. The lady in the shop said so." He spoke softly, right at the bowl of fake chrysanthemums in the middle of the table. "A tube top, they call it."

Thunder rumbled over the cottage. On the portable TV, happy American people clapped and jumped up and down around a multicoloured spangled wheel until static slashed across their bodies. A fork of lightning blazed under blue-black clouds outside, over tobacco fields, flaring the kilns brilliant red and green. Thunder then, unforgiving thunder, the likes of which we'd never heard before. "It's bloody unnatural!" Mam hissed. She set the charred meat down on the table. Then she rapped the tabletop impatiently. "Come on, Sal." Her face was shiny sweat. Through her glasses I saw dark bags. "C'mon, love. Come and have a look at your new togs."

Sal's voice gruffed from under the tablecloth, "Bollocks."

"You're pressing your luck, Salwyn!"

"Come on, Sal," Dad said softly. "You can't stay under there forever, love."

A second later the white tablecloth shivered about the edges and two small hands appeared. Nails chewed down into redness, strips of skin peeled back. The hands took the plate off the table and quickly retreated under the cloth.

Dad's forehead nettled over. "You're not making it easier, Sal," he said. "Especially for your brother."

I shrugged. "I don't care."

Mam jabbed a dripping triangle of bread toward me, impaled on a plastic knife. "Say *I don't mind,* love. It's nicer."

I took the fried bread, set it aside, and bit into a piece of bacon; it tasted of coal. Mam crunched hers, resentful. "They call this bacon." She pushed up her glasses and rubbed at her temples, leaving shine on skin.

"It's nice, love," Dad said.

"No, it's not," Mam laughed in spite of herself. "On your own, you are." She gently touched the back of his hand, fingerprints left there too.

"It's shit," Sal said.

Silence.

"Pig shit. Arse shit. Fuck shit."

Mam's hazel eyes narrowed. "Salwyn Elias, get out from under there and eat proper or there'll be hell to pay." Dad looked at me and his eyes said, *Go on, now. Be a big brother.*

"Get up, Sal," I said. "Don't be a twat."

Mam reached over and hit me hard in the temple. "Lucas Elias!" she shouted. "Don't you ever say that word again!"

"What?" I pouted. "It just means twit."

"It does *not* mean twit!"

Mam turned to Dad, exasperated, but suddenly he was miles away; a smile painted, wistful, on his lips. He pointed at the window behind her and, in an excited whisper, said,

"Look, love! By there! A Canadian robin!" Mam didn't budge. Through the window pane I could see a sad, wet and bedraggled bird. It was hunkered down in a bush under the eaves, its brownish feathers ruffled and soaked through. Beads of water dripped from its beak. "Well, well," Dad shook his head in amazement. "It's twice the size of the ones back home."

"David Elias," Mam closed her eyes, "why must you always, whenever there's anything even close to—"

"Hsst!" Dad waved her off, on the edge of his seat now. The robin shook its drenched wings and lit off the branch, the bush smattering down a shimmer of raindrops in its wake as the bird flew low and clumsy toward the wet green fields, then after some moments lifted itself up and disappeared into the dark sky to the west. Dad slumped back in his chair, smile fading. Mam was reaching across the table for my hand, her eyes sorry, when another mammoth bang of thunder shuddered the window panes. The TV cut out, quick and dead. Rain rattled the roof harder, drummed at the eaves. I could even hear it dance on the hide of the car that I knew wasn't a Firebird sitting outside. Pock-pock-a-pock-pock. We sat silent at the table for some time, nibbling at our food, our hearts beating small and foreign under the rage of our first Ontario storm. Faintly, in the next cottage over, a baby started to cry.

"It'll pass," Dad said. "Blue sky on the horizon."

Mam just stared into the bowl of fake flowers. "My father grew chrysanthemums," she said. "In his old glasshouse. And when they grew, I don't know, so high, my mother made him dig them up and plant them in the front garden for show. Big and beautiful, she said they were. Unearthed parasols."

The tablecloth lifted again and we watched Sal's little hand flutter around, a ratty five-winged bird. It patted the tablecloth, snatched up her tube top, and vanished under the table once more.

Dad was right about the storm. By the time we'd finished breakfast and cleared the table, the black-bellied clouds had rumbled over the fields and across town to the east till all we could hear was the hiss of highway traffic, the still-dripping music of the eaves. Mam, at the sink again, was using her bare hands and nails to scrub guck off the dishes. She stared out at a sky of perfect deep blue. "We're in the middle of nowhere," she said to herself, blowing a stray hair from her cheek.

Done clearing the table, Dad stared at her for a long time, then motioned me to the door.

"Aw," I moaned. "Do I have to?"

"What do you mean," he said, laughing, "*Do I have to?* It's our new car, mun."

"I know it's not a Firebird."

"You don't know you're born."

It took him a couple of tries at the screen door before it stammered open. "That's for mosquitoes," I said, stroking the wire screen.

"Aye, aye. Clever clogs."

Outside, the weight had lifted from the air. Steam licked slowly off the tarred shingle roofs. Leaves were larger here, more elaborate, their broad green faces bowed down with rainwater. Gaggles of mosquitoes teemed in clumps here and there across the glistening lot. Dragonflies the size of small birds whizzed by our heads and Dad ducked, laughed a bit eagerly. Beyond the swimming pool and the highway's haze, a rickety grocery stall wore the sign Paradise Market on its roof. Everything was prehistoric and new at the same time. Even the car, which Dad was now proudly leaning on, seemed fashioned from a bigger, simpler age. Its grille smiled all its teeth at me. Perfect beads of rain sat quivering on its aquamarine paint job. A polite, boring family sedan. My heart slumped.

"Chevrolet Malibu."

"That's right," Dad said. "A Chevy. Your mother likes this sort of thing, see. Comfortable. Sensible. Nothing fancy, like." He changed his tone then. "You can have a Firebird of your own in a few years, Lucas, if you play your cards right. You can drive when you're sixteen over here, see."

"Can I go back inside now?"

"What?" he laughed. "You haven't even given it a look, *bach.* Go on," he nudged me. "Go give it a walkabout."

Behind his smile his eyes were serious, insistent. So, huffing, I dragged my new white shoes around the car till I stumbled into a pair of bicycles around back of the trunk. One a black-and-white checkered BMX, the other a blue girl's bike with a water bottle. I whispered the brand name: "Supercycle." Dad smiled at me, his eyes twinkling. Such were his means of magic. I jumped on my Supercycle, its handlebars stretched out ready for my arms, as if to hug me. "It's excellent!" I shouted. The seat was too high, so I bounced from one tiptoe to the other, the seat doing a number on my balls. "Excellent!"

"Bloody painful, more like." This was spoken by a man leaning in the doorway of the Firebird cottage. He had a happy face behind his glasses, paunch swelled over his belt, and even with his grey-flecked hair, he must've been a good ten years younger than Dad. Beyond him, through the screen door I could see a woman lying in bed, still under the covers, her arm draped over her eyes. Beside her a baby kicked and grasped at the air.

The man stepped forward, screen door clattering behind him, and shook Dad's hand. "Bryn Llewelyn," he said, "from Seven Sisters. Electrician. Landed here three days ago. *Bore da.*"

"Bore da," Dad said. "Dai Elias. Swansea. Fitter. Last night." Then he razzled my hair. "My boy, Lucas."

"Bore da, bach," the man said.

"Good morning," I said tightly, and nodded at his Firebird. "Nice car."

"Aye," he said. "Not bad, like. Lots of horsepower under the bonnet." Bryn then regarded our car and said quickly, "Oh, yours is nice too though, Dai. Very practical."

Dad raised his brows at me—*see?*—but I ignored him, pushed away on my Supercycle. I didn't get far; I'd never ridden a bike in my life.

"Well, boyo," Bryn said quietly. "Hope you last longer than the others." He nodded at cottage number one beside the pool. "The Reeses weren't here a day before they were fed up."

"They've gone already?" asked Dad.

"No, they're still here. Flying back tonight, they are, after midnight. They've got a boy too, bit younger than yours, Dai." Bryn shook his head and sighed as we followed his gaze to the cabin, set apart from the rest. "Imagine that," he said. "Sold everything they had back home, just like us. Didn't give it a chance. What do they have for the boy to go back to, I want to know?"

Dad said nothing. He just stared at the tiny building, its door and windows shut tight, curtains drawn, dead leaves brittle and rustling on the tarred roof. There was no car parked outside.

Bryn was muttering to himself—"Dai Elias, Dai Elias, Dai—" then he snapped his fingers and stepped back and pointed at Dad. "I thought I recognized you! David Elias! I saw you play against England at Cardiff Arms Park!" he said. "Went with my father. Good God, what was it, eight…?"

"Ten years ago." Dad laughed, humble. "You're making me feel old."

"Having a scorcher of a first half, you were too!" Bryn's eyes were big and bright as a little boy's. "Shame about the injury," he said wincing. "Nasty, it was. Could hear the snap clear as day in the stands."

Their eyes drifted till both men stared down at the patch of gravel between them. Dad rubbed at his whiskered chin, fingers cracked and permanently blackened. Bryn fixed him with a serious, tender look. "Whatever happened to you, Dai?"

"Oh, you know, got married, got my apprenticeship at British Steel, raised a family—" As Dad spoke, Sal came scuffing out across the driveway in her pink tube top, her shoulders ghost-pale in the sun. She walked past her Supercycle, chewing her nails, and stared instead through Bryn's screen door at the woman and child upon the bed. "Sal," Dad said. "Leave your fingers alone now." My sister carried on gnawing with abandon. "Salwyn Elias!" he shouted, harsh as he could amid company. "Stop chewing at your fingers or I'll put shit on them!"

She paid him no mind. "Love her heart," Bryn smiled. He bent towards her and said softly, "Are you coming to try out your new bike too, love?"

Sal was still staring through his screen door. Spitting out a strip of nail, she said, "Can I play with your baby?"

Bryn kneeled down beside her. His greying hair thinly laced the crown of his head. "Sorry, love," he sang in a high, soft voice. "Morgan's Mammy and Daddy have got to get ready for a meeting with the SteelCan and real estate people, just like your Mammy and Daddy."

"I'm not *two,*" Sal snapped.

"Salwyn!"

"No, no." Bryn chuckled. "She's right. You're a big girl, aren't you, love?"

Sal wouldn't dignify that with an answer.

"How about after tea?" Bryn said.

Sal peeled a strip of finger skin away with her teeth, then turned brusquely and marched away across the grass toward the creek. "Love her heart," Bryn chuckled. Dad smiled and nodded, small and wiry beside him, but I could see his eyes were pained as he watched Sal's clumsy progress across the lot.

"Well," Bryn sighed. "I suppose your boy won't be following in your footsteps, Dai."

"How do you mean?" I mumbled.

"Nope," Dad said, mussing my hair. "Soccer is Lucas's game. Rebelling against me early, he is. What was it you said to me yesterday, boyo…?"

"Nothing."

"Ah—" Dad snapped his fingers "—that's right. He said, *I was mediocre back home, so that means I'll be a star in Canada!*" The men laughed till I turned beet red and Dad tried to muss my hair again but I ducked.

"Well, he's not short on confidence," Bryn said. "I'll give him that much. No matter how good he is though," he sniffed, stepping back to his cottage, "there's no money in it over here. Better take up baseball or ice hockey if he wants to fit in."

I glared, not at Bryn, but at my father nodding at his words. I hated how he humoured the man. Just like I hated Bryn's broad back and the way sweat spread across it like time-lapse photography, the baby kicking and gurgling on the other side of the screen.

"Tea!"

Dad waved back at Mam and then smacked his lips. "Keep an eye on your sister, *wus*," he said absently. I stood silent and watched his gnarled fingers run along the Malibu's trim as he crunched back over the gravel to the cottage.

Sal sat in the knuckly grass beside a creek choked with reeds. A wall of tall, thin deciduous trees rustled just beyond her. I walked my Supercycle across the lot, past clumps of maple saplings and a pair of horseshoe pits. When I reached the creek she was bent over in the reeds, chin on hands. Mosquitoes swarmed about her, some landing to drink from her pale shoulders. Sal swatted lamely at the air.

"Oy," I said. "You're getting eaten alive."

"Hsst!" She pressed a ragged finger to her lips and nodded at the ground before her. A turtle had crawled out of the water, parting the reeds. Steam flamed softly off its green shell. Sal reached to pet it.

"Don't touch it," I said. "You don't know where it's been."

She stroked the ragged hexagons on its back. "Where have you come from, then?" She gazed east into the trees, then west over the endless tobacco fields. "Have you come a long way too?" The turtle craned its wrinkled bullet head at her, ducked back into its shell, and after some seconds, its red- and yellow-flecked eyes surfaced shy once more. "You're beautiful," Sal said. "Aren't you? Aren't you beautiful now?"

"Don't be daft," I said. "Talking to a turtle. They don't even have ears."

"Of course she does," Sal sang. "Don't you, missus?"

I nudged at it gently with my Supercycle's front tire. "How do you know it's a she?"

"Leave off!" Sal shouted. When I rolled away she quit scowling at me and nodded, as if to convince herself. "I just know, that's all."

Then the turtle, after swaying back a moment, stepped forward slow as summer, its claws digging into the wet grass. "It'll take forever," I yawned, though I couldn't take my eyes off the thing. "You'll be an old woman before it gets ten yards." But Sal didn't care. Her eyes danced as the turtle slowly left the reeds behind. Here, in sunlight, its shell was large and bulbous. Greens and yellows and browns shimmered on its back.

"Lucas!" Dad shouted from our doorway. He crooked me with his finger. "Oy! Boyo!"

"What?"

"Come inside for a cup of tea!"

"I don't want a cup of tea."

He stared me down. "Come on! You're old enough to drink tea now!"

"In a minute."

"Now!" he said, stern.

I pouted and, with some effort, climbed down off my Supercycle. "All *right.*" I headed back sullen to the cottage, my wheels tickering over the grass.

"You can have mine too," Sal said after me.

"Your what?"

"My bike." She rested her chin on her folded arms and stared at the turtle's slow, inevitable progress across the grass. "There's nowhere I want to go except back home," she said. "And I need a plane for that."

A week before we left Wales, a Sunday, Sal got up at five in the morning, dressed herself and sat on her bed with her spangly red plastic purse looped over her arm. She'd taken some Liquid Paper and fashioned a white maple leaf on the front of the purse. It was the first thing I saw when she woke me up. I mumbled for her to turn off the light and go back to bed, she was too early. After she stormed cheerfully out of my room, I couldn't sleep. I listened to traffic, stared into black until the dawn's cold light washed in slow, brought my old wallpaper into clarity. Cream birds, flowers, leafy vines on a hushed backdrop of green. I'd always played at birdwatching with this wallpaper: a barn owl here, a nuthatch there, identifying the various species in my pocket-sized *Guide to British Birds.* But this morning in the stark light I noticed the pattern of the print. Every fourth bird was the same. The vines took calculated turns at regular intervals until they hit a new roll of paper. I half expected my birds to start falling, one by one, from vines suddenly shrivelled and brown.

Sal sat prim and proper on her bed till nine o'clock, when Mam came in to wake her up. She cried for hours after she found out she was a week early. "I want to go to Canada," she shouted, "now!" That night Mam took us to the summer pantomime in Aberavon instead. *Hansel and Gretel.* Sal kicked giddily in her seat as Welsh celebrities sang and danced in the lush forest onstage. Mam leaned over and whispered that it looked just like Canada. Trees everywhere. A funny man with hairy red armpits played the witch and I laughed because I knew it was all fake, but Sal got scared so Mam had to take her outside for a walk. She was petrified of Canada from that moment on.

That same night Dad attended a "This Is Your Life" in his honour. Swansea Rugby Club culled all the figures from his past—family, childhood friends, teachers, teammates—and set them up behind a curtain with a microphone and funny, humiliating tall tales. He came home plastered, with a red leather-bound book of his life, complete with pictures, and a beer tankard with autographs etched into the steel. In the days remaining, while Mam packed and readied us, Dad floated about the house, a glaze over his face, sometimes stopping to stand alone in empty rooms for what seemed like hours. Once, catching me stealing past the doorway, he pulled me aside into the sparse, echoing master bedroom. "Canada's a big country," he said. "All the more room to be a big brother." When I left, his words still bounced unfettered against the pale blue walls.

We left Swansea first thing the next Sunday. I'd never been in a taxi before. Mam and Dad told everyone *not* to come to the train station to see us off. But Mam said, "The Eliases have two unfortunate features. One: eyebrows that meet in the middle, and two: a bit of the showman in them. Worse than Mick Jagger, they are." We got on the train pale and baggy-eyed, and just before it pulled away they came out under the stone archway on the platform, all of Dad's side of the family, Grampa and cousins and aunts and uncles, even Uncle Wilf, the best pool player in Swansea, flapping his one empty shirtsleeve. They held Welsh dragon flags and big banners that said Bon Voyage and *Cymru am Byth* and at that moment I believed Wales *would* last forever.

Dad just shook his head, said, "I knew it." I opened the window and we shouted goodbyes, but our voices were swallowed up by their chorus. They were singing the opening words of "Myfanwy," the sad, slow longing of its melody filling the platform like steam, rising clear and pure above the noise of the train engine. Dad started singing, but Mam laid her hand on his rough fingers and told him to stop. She was dry as gravel behind her glasses. Her family had stayed home, never ones for spectacle. We waved silently as Dad's family sang us out of the station, following the train to the end of the platform, the Welsh words fading behind us down the tracks.

Sal slept almost the whole way to Heathrow Airport, waking only to tell us of her dream about Dodger, her cat she'd left behind. "He was leaving Nana and Grampa's house and he was coming over the valley to Ynysygerwn, down the hill, over the stones in the river, up Main Road to our house but we're not there, there's strangers there. And he takes a plane over to Canada but when he lands there's a bugger of a man out in the fields with fire for hair and he wants to kill us. But I'm all right 'cos I'm sitting at the top of a big blue slide wearing water wings and there's lots of boys and girls down in the water below me." Sal's eye turned in at her good fortune, her hands began tremoring. And there I was in my new crew cut, holding tight to my *Collins Illustrated Atlas,* promising myself I wouldn't cry. Flipping to page 10, the map of England and Wales, I circled Swansea and wrote "The greatest place in the world" down along the margin. A minute later I scratched it out. I remember Dad's eyelashes shining when he blinked. He kept waving till his family was long gone, around the bend, till he didn't have anything to do but hold Mam's hand. When he squeezed, he pushed all the tears out of her eyes.

⁎

Mam stirred the pot of tea. Dark moons of sweat were blooming under the arms of her summer dress. "Four bags over here," she sighed. "Four bloody bags it takes to make a proper pot."

Dad was at the table, in his own world, gently leafing through a Dylan Thomas book of poems. "No worries," he sniffed. "Besides, we're in the money now."

"Don't be so *twp,*" Mam said. "Waving money around like that in front of the others. It's embarrassing. You don't even get your first paycheque for another fortnight."

"Positive, Sian," he said. "Think positive."

"You shouldn't overcompensate by spoiling the children, love. And I'm telling you this now: they are *not* riding those bikes on that motorway."

"Sal doesn't want her Supercycle," I said casually from the door.

They both looked at me, startled. Dad's eyes sank back down to the poetry, his chin rumpled and sorry. Mam's cheery voice was a high, brittle bubble. "Well, at least they get you outside," she said. "It's no good being cooped up all day, staring at all that dumb American TV, is it? Pale enough already, the both of you. You look anaemic compared to these Canadian kids. They're all so healthy-looking it makes me sick. Do us a favour, Dai, and get us the milk."

Dad gently set down his book. He cranked the old-fashioned lever handle of the fridge and took a bag of watery milk off one of the rusty shelves. He placed it on the counter and stared at it. "How do they expect you to do this, then?"

"You have to put the bag in the jug," Mam said. She opened the only drawer in the kitchen and handed a pair of scissors to him, blades first. Then she went outside after Sal. Her hand, warm from tea steam, soft on my cheek as she passed.

Dad watched her trudge across the driveway, then he pointed the scissors at me. "Now," he said quietly. "I got you and your sister those bikes because I want you to do things *together*." His voice lowered to a whisper. "I was talking to the salesman up at MacMorgan's. He says if you go up to the mall, to this Canadian Tire shop, his boy's hanging around there all day. He'll teach you how to ride your bikes. Just wait till after we go to the SteelCan meeting, all right?" He took a bill out of his wallet. A dead politician's crumpled blue face stared up at me. "Here's a fiver, get some pop or something. If you get lost on the way, follow the skydivers. And don't tell your mother or there'll be hell to pay."

I pocketed the money. "How will I recognize this kid?"

"Paul. He'll be playing a video game. And he won't be wearing any shoes. And if he gives you any trouble—"

"Oh, great."

"*If* he gives you any trouble, tell him his dad, Chuck, sent you, and he'll teach you how to ride your bikes.

Together, all right?" He pulled the bag and jug close together, gingerly, introducing them. "You got to start thinking beyond yourself, Lucas. Sal doesn't know what to do with herself half the time. She's chewed her fingers raw already. And the Llewelyns will only let her play with their baby so long." I watched his calloused hands fumble with the milk bag, propping it up before him with one hand. Its bottom corners sagged over the edge, pale little legs kicking. He did a couple of practice cuts with the scissors and then snipped off a corner of plastic. For a moment his grey eyes gazed past the still-dripping eaves to the tobacco fields. His eyes misted over and then, waking, he carefully aligned the bag with the milk jug. "At least with the bikes you're in the same boat, like. You can help your little sister along."

"I've got better things to do than—"

"You...!" He shoved the bag down into the jug and milk spilled out in all directions, glugging over the counter, into the sink, down the front of his trousers. "Ah, *Iesu mawr!* What the hell would possess them to put drinks in bags?!"

I pointed at a teatowel. He whipped it off the tap and dabbed roughly at his trousers. "You," he said, quiet and breathless, "have got *nothing* better to do than help your sister. She's not like you, Lucas. She's going to have a harder time adjusting than you. You can make friends easier. Sal's...unique. Like her mother. She's a bit awkward and, I don't know—"

"Awkward, is it?" Mam said. She was leaning against the door frame, smirking at the stain establishing an empire across the front of Dad's trousers. "*I'm* awkward."

Dad threw the rag in the sink. "How is she? She warming up to it yet?"

"No. There's a turtle out there. It's digging a hole. She thinks it's having babies. Told you she didn't need TV."

Through the open screen door we saw Sal crouched down in the middle of the driveway, hair falling brown about her face, watching the turtle scrape away at the stones before her. Slowly, methodically, it scuttled aside several large hunks of gravel, shovelled one and, after a slow second, another off to the side with its scooped claws, then it kicked the gravel dust back and out with its hind legs, as if doing the breaststroke. Sal tucked her hair behind her ear and smiled absently, engrossed in the turtle's work.

Beside me Dad stirred the tea, lifted the steaming tea bags out of the cups one by one into the sink, then touched the back of the spoon to my hand.

"Ouch!" I rubbed.

"Hurts, doesn't it?" He nodded at me blankly.

"Aye!"

"Look after your sister, Lucas," he said.

"Aye," Mam smiled. "Because we're all alone in this big, flat country now."

Dad shook his head at her. "Positive, woman. *Positive.*" He blew at his tea, took a sip, then spat it automatically onto the orange shag carpet. "That's bloody awful."

A gaggle of kids was playing ball hockey in the mall employees' parking lot. Sticks scraped, clacked and chattered on cement. There were six or seven boys in all. They wore yellow-and-black T-shirts that said Nanticoke Minor Hockey Association across their chests. As Sal and I wheeled our

Supercycles past, a couple of the boys quit playing to watch us, their chins resting on the nubs of their sticks. Sal stared right back at them. I felt my face burn red, concentrated on the ground. But when I caught a glimpse of our shadows moving over the dark, blobby patches on the tarmac, my stomach caved in. So I focused on the Supercycles instead. Magic things, iridescent in sunlight. Sal had grown quite fond of her bike too, especially her water bottle. She stopped to hike up her tube top, then unfastened the bottle from the Supercycle's frame and offered it to me. "Want some?"

I took it and drank it and spat the warm, plasticky liquid out. "*Ach!* Cat's piss."

She snatched it back and took a long gulp. "Dad told me to tell if you weren't nice."

I propped the Supercycles against a large dumpster by the employees' back entrance. There was another, older bike leaning against the wall. A dilapidated red mongrel of a bike, with mismatched wheels and no seat.

"What happens when he wants to sit down?" Sal said.

"He doesn't."

She nodded gravely then stared at the hockey players again as I locked the bikes to a bracket on the other side of the dumpster, facing the wall. One of the hockey kids, the lone goalie, stepped out of his net and stared back at her through his mask. He was smaller than Sal, must've been all of seven years old. You couldn't see the boy for the gear strapped to him. His pads looked like two shanks of beef strapped to his legs. "What're *you* looking at?" he said.

"You bugger," Sal spat.

The boy gaped at her long enough for a tennis ball to tear into the net behind him. "He shoots, HE SCORES!!!" a big kid shouted, his arms raised theatrically, stick rising and then clattering to the ground behind him.

"No fair!" The goalie shouted back, pointing at Sal. "Interference!"

"Come on, Sal," I hissed. "Let's go."

She sullenly fastened the bottle back to her Supercycle and strode ahead of me, opening the big steel door as the hockey kids shouted *Car!*

⁂

In Canadian Tire, under a fake neon sign that read Atari Entertainment Centre, a boy wrestled a joystick, his thumb manic on the fire button, his eyes passionate. He was dressed in a muscle shirt and cut-off jeans. His greasy hair shucked up at the back, a rooster tail. The rest of him was tanned and dirty. Knees hacked up and scarred pink. Black dirt webbed on his bare toes, caked under his toenails.

"Paul?"

He acted like I didn't exist. Up close his eyes were two convex screens, flickering, full of space. Blip. Squawk. Blip blip.

"Pardon me," I said, "but are you Paul?"

"So you want me to learn ya how to ride a bike, eh?"

I was speechless.

"Shit," he said without peeling his eyes from the screen. "Any foreigner kid comes up to me knowing my name, I figure he can't ride a ve-hicle to save his life and he's staying at that shitbox out there on Highway 3."

"The Surf and Sand Cottages."

"Surf and Shit Cottages, more like. Yup, just a couple of days ago I learned this little guy called Rice or Russ or—"

"Rees," I said.

"Whatever," he said. "I was learning him pretty good on my ve-hicle. He was English like youse guys."

"We're Welsh," Sal snapped. "And we've got our own Supercycles, thank you very much."

"*Super*cycles?" He winced. "Four words: Major. Pieces. Of. Crap. Frames'll warp on ya in two months tops, I bet. I coulda gotcha a ve-hicle good as new through my brother. He could getcha a Redline, original parts and everything. Fifty bucks." He stressed *bucks* so hard it riddled the TV screen with spit.

"I like my Supercycle," Sal said, looking at his feet, "dirty *mochyn*."

Paul ignored her. His eyes were lost in the screen and I couldn't blame him; the game was magic, a dream. "What is it?" I whispered.

"Asteroids," he said, pride shimmering in his eyes. He flexed his hand and looked at us blankly. "Wassamatta with all youse guys, anyways? Don't you got bikes back in England?"

"*Wales,*" Sal snapped again.

"Same difference."

"Is not," Sal said. "In Wales there's woods everywhere with dirt paths up through the trees into the mountains but we're not allowed to cross Main Road it's so busy and at the bottom of the garden there's blackberry bushes and—" she dragged in breath and closed her eyes "—on a nice day Dad says you can even see Nana and Grampa's house."

"Whoopee shit." Paul snorted, like a donkey. "You want me to learn ya how to ride your Supercycles or not?"

"Aye," Sal said. Her eye wavered a little; her hands started to shake.

"Well," Paul said, "it's gonna cost ya."

Hesitating, I looked at Sal. All of a doodah. I had no choice. I fluttered the five-dollar bill at Paul, but he waved it away. "Just play Asteroids with me," he said. "Okay?" He flicked the game to two-player before I could say boo.

Nine games later, Paul's face was still serene. His hands worked the joystick like heaven. After spelling out his name on the high score board for the tenth time, he flexed his wrist and sighed. "I'm history. You go."

He wasn't history. I knew history and it was the Battle of Hastings, 1066. The signing of the Magna Carta. I read about it all in my *New World Treasury Encyclopaedia*. Paul was now. He was Canadian Tire and Atari and a BMX bike with no seat. He was saliva and a donkey when he laughed. Paul was Canada. But my thumb was sore and my eyes were sandy tired. And Sal was rubbing her goose-pimpled arms against the air conditioning as she paced back and forth. She stopped to tug on my sleeve. "Can I play now?"

"Next game."

"That's what you said last game. It's been three hours. When's he going to teach us?"

I swivelled my ship around a blue asteroid. "See that, Sal? Excellent, that was."

"I'm going back," she said, folding her arms.

"Suit yourself."

"You'll be late for tea," she said.

"So I'll be late for tea."

"Tea?" Paul sang in a high voice, somewhere between Irish and Chinese. "Tea?"

Sal seared a look right through us and then stormed away down the aisle.

After a sweet tumble of minutes, while I was into my best game yet, the hockey kids came clacking and scraping their sticks over the plastic floor. They stood behind us, reflections looming yellow in the screen. The little goalie still wore his mask and pads. The big kid wound up and took a mock slapshot at my back. I flinched; my ship got shattered by a bright pink asteroid. The hockey kids cackled. When Paul, silent, clicked the fire button to start his turn, his hands were shaking. The big kid promptly jabbed him in the back with his stick.

"Hey, treefucker."

Paul ignored him. This time the boy speared him up between the legs and Paul winced. "D'you fuck a tree today, treefucker?" The boy had sun-bleached hair and a big untouchable smile and a way of moving his head that seemed practised. The others leaned toward him and circled him like neutrons. "No shit, guys," he said. "Seen him this morning through the fence, whipped out his little pecker and fucked the cherry tree right in his back yard. Does it every day. Finds a knot-hole and just starts giving her! Don't you, treefucker?"

In the mirrors of Paul's eyes luminous rocks fell through space. When he got speared again he stammered, "W-why don't you just bug off, huh, Thane?"

"'Cos we like you, treefucker." Thane turned to me lazily. "Who are you, wimp?"

"He's English," Paul said, taking my arm. "C'mon, Luke, let's go."

"Who asked you, treefucker?" Then Thane nodded at me. "You live around here?"

"Yeah," I said, shaking off Paul. "The Surf and Sand Cottages."

"Surf and Shit Cottages, more like."

"We won't be there long," I said. "Our father's got a job with SteelCan. He says there's better opportunities here."

"Well, *my* dad's been working at SteelCan since before I was born and *he* says there's too *many* Limeys finding better opportunities here."

"I'm not a Limey," I said. "I'm Welsh."

"Same difference," he said. "D'ya bring enough limes with you on the boat?"

"We didn't come over on a boat. We came over on British Airways."

"Oh." Thane paused to spit. "My Dad says you Limeys all came over on boats."

"No, that's boat people," the goalie said. "These guys are plane people."

"Hey!" Thane said, slapping the kid's mask askew. "Budder made a funny!"

They were still laughing when Sal returned, followed by a mountain of a man wearing the name tag *Duncan* on his brown uniform. He had big brown doe eyes. Sal pointed to the Asteroids. Duncan nodded and parted us like ferns. I came up to his ribcage. He ratcheted a knob on the machine. Sal tugged on his shirt and pointed at Paul's feet.

"They're dirty," Duncan said. He spoke to Paul, heart-breakingly earnest. "You should clean those feet." Switching the game to one-player, he pointed a well-fed finger at Sal and said, "She plays," in a sad, high voice before he disappeared again into the sporting goods section.

Sal snatched the joystick from my hand. Her eyes were fevered, big as bowls. Her tongue stuck out the side of her mouth and her sad, tattered little fingers worked in manic unison, twirling the ship round and round in drunk circles. I felt a big wash of pity for her. But for a moment I thought I saw a light grace her shoulders. Even if it was the fluorescents, it was the happiest I'd seen her since she woke me up a week early to leave Wales. A smile soothed her face; she started humming a little tune. Her spaceship spun in tight circles, smithereening rocks into black endless space. The hockey kids crowded the Atari for a better look. Asteroids exploded delirious in our eyes. Sal's eye began to drift. "Calm down, Sal," I said. But before long the excitement got too much for her.

"Sal!" She was hopeless. Her fingers tremored at the joystick till they left it entirely and shook in the air before her with a force I hadn't seen since back at Toronto airport, when we lost each other in traffic near the automatic doors and I walked off and stood beside a mirrored column, apart from the bustle, where after a while I could see Sal striding ahead with her red purse slapping against her legs, her hands frantic, till she came up alongside Tom Gadd and, thinking him Dad, took his hand, and when Gadd stopped and looked down, surprised to see this little human on the end of his arm, Sal looked up into his foreign shaven face, his mirrored glasses, and jumped back and it was hard to tell who shook off whose hand but Sal ran back through the throng of people until she found Dad's side and took his smaller, familiar grip, and then Mam caught up and they all walked easy ahead of me out of the automatic doors and into the humid Ontario air.

"That's enough, Sal." Her dead ship was a fizzled mess of white dots now, but her hands still flapped about her face, mutilated birds. Then her tube top slipped down, far down. The hockey kids giggled. "Quit it!" I slapped her ruined fingers. "Game's over." Sal stopped dead. Her eye swung back to normal and she scowled at me with silent, refined hatred.

The hockey kids were doubled over now, laughing embarrassed into their hands. I was frozen to the spot. My new white shoes were anvils on my feet and my holy football shirt, still rife with store smell, chafed my skin. Suddenly I was absurd. Over the store intercom a woman's monotone voice crackled: *Attention Canadian Tire shoppers, the store will be closing in ten minutes.* And there, scowling up at me from under her bangs, stood Sal. Her left eye nudged out a tear. A single, lonely pink nipple poked out of her tube top.

"So," I said, turning away. "Do you guys want to play?"

A wall of yellow and black swarmed the Asteroids. Sal reefed up her tube top and stormed away. She stopped at the discount album racks and started leafing fakely through albums, glared at me over the seventies titles. "Sorry, Sal," I sang, hollow, but it was too late. She dropped an album and started running, wailing like a siren down the aisle, just as Thane body-checked me from behind, so hard I fell down, history. Anne Murray's milk teeth smiled up at me from the floor. A rose in her hair. "$3.99. The Nice Price." Then a pair of dirty feet stood on her face.

"So," Paul said. "You want me to learn youse guys now?"

"Bugger off," I muttered.

"Don't worry about it. Those guys, they're all assholes. We don't need 'em, eh Luke?"

He extended a dirty hand to me. I ignored it, scrambled up and then glared at him. "Treefucker."

"Hey." I bolted past him down the aisle, laughter still rich in my ears. "Hey, Luke! Wait up! I'll learn youse guys with my eyes closed! Luke!" I didn't look back. My heart sang and wept down aisles stacked to the rafters with hockey sticks and pads and pucks and skates.

When I shoved the door open, Sal was standing in the parking lot gaping up at the blue sky. Her face was blank, unbelieving, her tears perfect on her cheek. A hulking black shadow fell across her. She was staring at our Supercycles, hanging fifteen feet in the air, shiny and beautiful and new and still chained to a dumpster which was now being lifted by the great steel forks of a refuse truck. We stood mute. Sal took my arm. It was an awful, awe-inspiring sight, and I was torn by horror and joy, watching our Supercycles ascending so effortless into the sky, then clattering hard against the dumpster as it rose above the cab of the truck, reaching its zenith, and in the blink of an eye descending toward the bed with a Niagara Falls of garbage bags tumbling out of it. The Supercycles flopped over and slammed against the dumpster's wall.

Paul burst out of the back entrance. "Holy tits!" he shouted. He shoved past us and ran at the truck, jumping up and down, pantomiming a forklift. "Bring them down! Bring! Them! Back! Down!" Smiling, the driver waved back at him. Paul picked up a rock and threw it at the windshield. The trucker glared and rolled down the window, but as he opened his mouth to speak, the dumpster arced back over the cab and the Supercycles swung at the end of the lock's chain and hit the roof. Startled, the driver rushed the forks straight to the tarmac. The Supercycles swung and crashed against the outside of the dumpster, then came to rest. Sal stood beside me, not all of a doodah, but strangely silent.

The truck driver turned off the engine, climbed down from the cab, hiked up his overalls and strode over to the dumpster. He kneeled down and surveyed our Supercycles, us, then our Supercycles again. He scratched his red head, scooped up a handful of stones, thoughtfully flicked them one by one at the dumpster. Ting. Ting. Ting. Then he came at us with his thumbs crooked through his belt loops. His face was ruddy and satisfied. "You kids," he said, in a surprisingly high voice, "are lucky you didn't get hurt."

"Why'd you do it?" Sal said quietly. "Why'd you kill our Supercycles?"

"He didn't see them," I said, unlocking the bikes. "He didn't mean to kill our Supercycles, Sal."

"Good idea, there, son," the trucker said. "Get those things unlocked pronto."

"Besides, he didn't *kill* them. See?" I made my voice painfully happy and propped up her Supercycle. But both of them were tangled together, fused. Her bike's frame was scratched badly, the handlebars warped, the front forks bent irreparably. And the rim of her back tire was so twisted that two spokes had been torn out and still quivered in the air, rattling against mine. Sal's mouth drooped, a circus tent collapsing. A low whine snaked out of her mouth just as the hockey kids came out of the back door.

"No, Sal. Please. Aw, no."

She sobbed. Great gut-wrenching gusts of sobs. She hugged herself and squatted down on the concrete and sobbed more. Her voice echoed throughout the parking lot. The hockey kids stood with their equipment, staring dully down at her. "Look," the goalie said quietly. "The Limey girl's crying."

Thane punched his shoulder. "Shut up, Budder."

Employees were filing out of the back entrance now. They slowed and watched Sal bawling—a pink lump on the tarmac—then got in their cars and drove away. The parking lot gradually emptied until there was only one sky-blue car left. A Buick Skylark. A semicircle of us stood, baking silent and stupid under the sun, around Sal. The truck driver took a rag out of his coveralls, mopped his forehead, squinted at the sky. I was humiliated. "Aw, come on, Sal."

"Bugger off." She curled tighter, into a silent heaving ball.

The trucker went to pat her back, and she squealed so loud he pulled away as if burnt, with a pained expression on his face. He walked gingerly around her in a circle until he stood just behind her, listless. He had a white oval crest sewn on his overalls: *Noel.* He mopped his head again, then turned to me. "Listen, son," he said. "Is your sister going to be all right? 'Cos I gotta get back to the yard otherwise that's all she wrote. I'm outta there, history."

A woman wearing an A&P uniform bustled out of the employees' entrance next. "Come on, guys," she snapped her fingers. "Load 'em up." The hockey kids peeled their eyes away from Sal, picked up their gear and followed the woman silently. On their way to her big blue car, the woman stopped and, for the first time, acknowledged our presence. Her face was soft and sorry. "She all right?'

"Yes, yes," Noel said, "she'll be fine, ma'am."

Sal blubbered, "That's not my Mam!"

"Come *on,* Sal," I tugged at her sleeve. "C'mon. Let's go."

"No," she snuffled. "My water bottle first. I want it."

"This one's ruined, Sal. Garbage. Mam and Dad'll get you a new one."

"It's not the *same* one," she cried, her face a tomato with a hole in it. "I want *mine!*"

"My brother can getcha one," Paul said, "for a buck, buck-fifty, tops."

Sal howled, "Shut up, you dirty *mochyn!*"

"All right," I muttered. I stormed over and snatched the water bottle off the bike and then walked back and extended it to her. "Here." When she reached for it I lobbed it into the dumpster. Sal screamed, hunkered on the ground, her wretched voice racking out, but I was far away and cold as steel.

Across the lot the hockey kids bungled their equipment into the trunk and climbed into the car, all five of them. The big one, Thane, was the last to get in. He stood beside the passenger door for a spell, squinting back at us. "C'mon, honey," the woman said. "Let's hit the road." He clambered in the front seat then and the cashier drove them away in her blue Skylark, slowing enough for the kids to catch some final bovine glances as the car purred across the lot, its fan whirring confidently, its hood ornament catching sun every few feet, the whitewalls swerving slowly to avoid the dark splatters on the tarmac. Sal's voice was a low, steady moan now. She stopped only to gulp back the odd gob of phlegm.

"So." Noel sniffed. "You happy?"

"What?"

He mopped at his forehead, studied the rag, then squinted back at me. "You proud of yourself, son?"

"I'm not your son," I mumbled.

"No, you ain't. 'Cos if you were I'd of kicked your sorry ass around this lot before you could piss yourself crying for your mother."

"Shit, if *my* dad was here right now," Paul said, "I'd just have three words for youse—"

"Shut up, tree—"

"Hey, come on, son." Noel spat in his palms, rubbed them back and forth. "C'mon, I'll give ya a boost." He laced his meaty fingers together. I looked down at Sal, her head buried between her knees, her burnt shoulders riddled with mosquito bites. She rasped in a long, shaky breath and slowly moaned it out again. "Come *on,*" Noel said, stepping toward me, his red hair furious in the sun.

"All right, all *right,*" I pouted.

"Atta boy." Noel laced his fingers together and I stepped into his hands and then—"Oopsy daisy!"—he vaulted me up and into the dumpster. I landed hard on the metal floor, felt it shock up through my heels and shins. The air inside was thick and swarmy. It reeked of dead milk, plastic, cheese, rotten apples, motor oil and a thick metallic smell that tickled the back of my throat. My breath was amplified till I held it. I picked up Sal's bottle, some red and yellow guck on it, but otherwise it was surprisingly clean. Above me all I could see was a blue serene sky, big as all Canada. A plane shone overhead, then its engine suddenly whirred down. A figure fell out of it, free falling, the body an asterisk tumbling through the air. Soon it was joined by a second, a third, a fourth jumper, tumbling out of the side of the plane. I could hear them, thousands of feet up in the sky—"Yeeeeeww!! Yeeehaaa!!"—their arms and legs stretched out, those screams of fear and amazement and joy trailing and merging. I leaned back against the wall of the dumpster and watched them draw in closer to each other and for a fleeting, magical moment join together, a tiny flower, their voices travelling down through low wisps of cloud, toward earth, until the circle broke and they all pushed out streaming into their own pockets of sky. Petals exploding down to earth.

"So." I heard Paul, outside. "How many gears she got?"

Noel spoke to him in a slow, emphatic voice. "Well, twelve originally, son, but they can strip them down in such a way, see, that—"

"Converted her, eh? Down to four?" I heard Paul smack his lips, pictured him surveying the truck.

"Uh, that's right."

"Bet she's a bitch to drive sometimes, huh?" Paul said. "Covering for all those missed gears."

"Uh huh."

"And then she's got a separate set of hydraulic gears for the forks, eh?"

"Yes, that's right."

"So does she got a Pitman hydraulic rig like they use on flat beds, or is she more like, say—"

"How old are you, son?" Noel said.

"Eleven," Paul said.

The parachutes blossomed open. I could hear the sound, a buckle of silk, even from here. Drops of food colouring in water. Red. Yellow. White. Green. In the short minutes it took the divers to fall to earth, the sky shifted behind them. Dark clouds drifted over the mall and for the first time I saw purple blotches spattered and dried like strange birthmarks all the way down the orange bricks from the roof, and I remembered the blackberry bushes at the bottom of the garden back home in July, how our fingers were stained purple after we picked them and how Sal, whenever she found the odd one being eaten by a maggot, would throw it down in disgust and, with a pickled face, say, "*Ach!* Magnets!" And after tea Dad would take me out birdwatching into the woods that buzzed and chittered across Main Road, the sun flapping through the leaves. How he'd teach me the various bird calls, the difference between chaffinch and willow warbler, and I couldn't whistle so I sang them. Once he went ahead on the path with his binoculars and I just gazed up into the thatched ceiling of trees and whirled and whirled till I got dizzy and landed in a bed of bluebells and Dad came back and picked me up and, pressing his finger to his lips, handed me the binoculars and pointed into a clump of trees where a hidden song thrush was twittering: *He's telling all his friends about you.* And going to Porthcawl on weekends, Sal fumbling after me on the rocks, barnacles and shells rucked onto them, shush and lap of the water, the fizz in the little pools. Our bare feet crimped over the rough rocks, seaweed lacing them like thin hair. Weeds shocked up green against a dark blue sky. Sandpipers crying. Moss on the rocks farther out. Rotted-out pier, only shards of black wood poking up out of the sand. Fish-and-cockle smell at the market later. Taste of laver bread, which I hated: black boiled seaweed dipped in oatmeal and fried, like eating a bowlful of salt. Mam would say, *I used to hate it too when I was your age, but I just grew into it.* Me and Sal running across the empty beach at twilight, the tide gone out, only the footprints of the day left, jellyfish like half-buried umbrellas, the saltwater smell and a dog barking over by the rocks, sniffing rumours the tide washed in, a sandy stick in its mouth, its spraying wet tail. How, living in Canada, I would never grow up to like laver bread.

*

When we got back to the Surf and Sand Cottages, Bryn Llewelyn was bobbing in the shallow end of the pool. He waved a can of beer at us. "D'you make any new friends today?" he asked.

"Lucas did."

Bryn grinned at me. "Champion, that is. Champion." Then he shouted at our cottage. "The prodigals return!"

They were sitting just outside the doorway on white plastic chairs. They stared at the gravel in front of them, talking quietly, as if they hadn't seen us. We jumped the creek and walked past the maple saplings and across the driveway, our shoes, laced with wet grass, crunching over the stones.

"And where have you two been?" Mam said. "I made your father drive up to the shopping centre three times. We were worried sick. Called the police, we did." She hugged us both then, desperately, tight as fists. Kisses, kisses.

Dad regarded me with gravity. "Where's your bikes, boyo?"

"They're dead," Sal said, matter-of-fact. She set down her water bottle and crouched beside the turtle. It was scraping rocks back down over six soft, pink-white jellyish eggs.

Mam smoothed Sal's hair, her voice a breeze. "She started laying just after we got back, love. Been at it for hours. I made your father stand in the way whenever—Oh, look out!" She pointed at the highway and slapped his arm. "Here comes another one, Dai!"

A taxi, a Chevy Impala, pulled off the highway and crackled over the gravel toward the swimming pool. Dad jumped up from his chair and stood akimbo over the turtle, but the cab swerved and skidded over the stones before stopping outside cottage number one. The cab driver popped the automatic trunk and seconds later beeped the horn and then, after some more seconds passed, the cottage door opened and from out of the darkness pale white hands began lifting suitcases and travel bags onto the gravel outside. The cabbie got out of the car, his pockets jingling, and walked to the luggage. He said something through the cottage door and then shrugged and slowly began to load up the trunk. The Llewelyns' baby cried next door.

"All right," Dad said tightly, settling back down in his chair. "Where are your bikes, Lucas? We're still waiting."

Before I could muster an answer, Mam rescued me. She nudged Dad and nodded at her feet where the turtle was filling in the last stone over the eggs. It walked back over the stones, packing them down, like a dog's prehistoric habit of tramping over imaginary grass before it lies down to sleep. Done circling, it slowly walked away and, blocked by Sal's water bottle, tried climbing over it but fell down. It tried again but toppled over, this time onto its back, its head and legs sucking back into its shell. "Do something," Mam said quietly.

"It's all right, Mam." Sal gently lifted up the turtle by its shell and set it right side up. The head slowly emerged, with its yellow-red flecked eyes, and then the legs padded the ground once more. Sal rolled the water bottle aside, clapping her hands clean, and we watched as the turtle made its slow, ponderous way back across the gravel. The sun was low in the west now, clouds hummed pink and blue behind the tobacco kilns. Mosquitoes sang in the air around us. Over at cottage number one the cabbie had loaded the last of the luggage and slammed the trunk shut and walked to the driver's side with keys jangling in his hand. He beeped the horn again. After a minute the screen door shuddered open and the Reeses, dressed all in beige and white, bustled to the car, their eyes fixed on the ground. The man was dark-haired, nervous. He said something harsh over his shoulder and then got in the front, and the woman and boy, both fair-haired and gentle-looking, climbed silently into the back seat. The cab sat idling for some time.

"Nanticoke to Toronto," Dad whistled, settling back in his chair. "That'll cost them a fortune. Eh, gang?"

But no one answered. We were watching the turtle now, how it crossed the narrow strip of grass and then, without looking back, disappeared into the reeds and swished into the creek. Mam took off her glasses and her face was wet. Dad's arm was already around her. Sal kissed her knee and then patted it, her face frumped in a smile beyond her years. Suddenly, the taxi reversed recklessly, sending up a cloud of dust over the lot, and then pulled out of the driveway, passing Bryn Llewelyn who, on his way back from the pool, waved a half-finished six-pack at the car.

"Au revwa-ah!"

He didn't bother turning to watch the taxi speed toward the pink lights of town. He just came swaggering across the lot, a towel wrapped around his waist, his flip-flops slapping. Up close his silvery hair glistened with water. Black hair matted over his arms, his gold bracelet. I could smell the chlorine coming off him. He looked quizzically at the ground we were huddled around, but his smile stayed broad. "Evening, pioneers," he said.

Mam turned away and, in shadow, wiped at her face. But Dad perked up, a chameleon. "Hiya, boyo," he said.

"Fancy a Newcastle Brown, mate? They had 'em down at Brewers' Retail. Cost you an arm and a leg, like, but you can't be choosers, can you?"

"No thanks, Bryn. Not tonight."

"Not good enough for you Swansea boys, eh?"

"What's this 'eh'?" Dad laughed. "You're a right bloody Canuck, aren't you?"

Bryn cracked open his beer and leaned, smiling, against his door frame. "Well, you know what I say about the colonials here, don't you?"

"What's that?"

"If you can't beat 'em, take the bloody mick out of 'em!"

They both laughed, Bryn loudest.

"I'll have some beer, Bryn," I said.

"No, you won't," Dad said. "And it's Mr. Llewelyn to you."

Bryn grinned at me then bent forward and, looking past Dad, said in a softer, higher voice, "What about about you, Sian? Want a pint of Brown, love?"

Mam put her glasses back on and smiled timidly. "No thanks."

"Suit yourself, love," Bryn vaguely raised the can at her.

"She's not feeling well, Bryn."

"Aw," he said. "Don't blame you, with the sodding food over here. Joanne's got some Anadin if you want," and he whispered, "uses it for the time of the month, like." Then he called inside, "Joanne!"

There was a mumble from the cabin. Mam stood up, hastily. "On second thought, love," she said, "I think I will have a pint. It'll help me sleep it off, like."

"Champion," Bryn grinned, cracking open a can and handing it to her. "Champion, that is, Sian."

Mam sipped at the froth and gave Bryn a hurried smile. But on her way inside, she couldn't open the screen door. She pulled and pulled at it, but the door didn't give and she just stood there till finally Sal had to tug on it with both hands to stammer it free. Mam hurried inside and Sal followed, hand at the small of Mam's back. The screen door clattered behind them.

"Feeling bad, she is," Dad said, apologetic.

"Ah, love her heart." Bryn sipped thoughtfully on his beer and stared at the highway. "No news to me though, Dai. Joanne's pretty much been in bed ever since we got here." He licked foam off his moustache. "She was under the doctor before we even came over. Nerves. Didn't want to leave her mother. That meeting today didn't help either."

Dad shook his head and smiled at me. "Should've seen it, Lucas. They had this promotional film about Steelford, the new community out by the SteelCan plant, right? They showed a bunch of drawings—"

"Artist's representations," Bryn corrected him.

"Aye," Dad nodded. "And then they showed a film promoting this new community they're building. They say it's going to be bigger than Toronto in thirty years, but all you saw was a water tower that said Steelford, a petrol station and then, for miles around, nothing but tobacco fields. And then this narrator came on and said"—he put on a low, booming, Americanized voice—"'Steelford, City of the Future.'" His shoulders hunched with laughter.

"What's so funny then?" Bryn said. "They say it'll be a good investment, buying one of those new homes out there. No, it was the people at the meeting Joanne didn't like. All those SteelCan bigwigs."

"Aye, aye," Dad said. "Sian's the same way. She wants us to look on our own. Do it private, like. Trusts SteelCan and the real estate people as far as she can throw them. Says they're all out to get rich off us."

"How about you, Dai?" Bryn said. "You're the man of the house. What do you think?"

"Don't know," Dad said, scraping up a handful of stones. "I wish... ah, I don't know."

"I don't know either," Bryn said. "I was all set to go for a foreman's job when I got here, work my way up through the ranks, like. Thought the colonials were all probably backward." He smiled, then downed his Newcastle Brown. He slowly crunched the can in his fist. The pub smell of it. "Know what I *do* know though?"

"What's that, Bryn?"

"Right now I'd give it all back—the contract, the relocation money, the City of the Future—-just to be at the Angel Arms after a Seven Sisters game with a set of darts in one hand and a pint of Welsh bitter sweating in the other, and some boys at the bar striking up the opening notes of 'Myfanwy.'"

Dad scraped up another handful of stones and flicked them at the highway, the chirping fields. I watched them trail into darkness. "Ah, don't say that."

"Already did." In Bryn's voice I heard the faintest tremor. "I've got it on tape, if you want to hear it." He pointed his thumb back in his room. "Pontardulais male voice choir. All the best, like."

I pictured a hundred red-faced Welsh men in suits crammed into their one-room cottage.

"Don't think I could stomach it," Dad said. "Not tonight. If I heard 'Myfanwy,' that's it, pfft! I'll be on the next plane home."

"All right, Dai." Bryn looked at Dad with wounded eyes. "*Nos da,* then."

"*Nos da,* Bryn."

"*Nos da,* Lucas."

I said nothing.

"*Oy,* Lucas." Bryn smiled, serious. "*Nos da.*"

I looked at Dad, nodding me into Welshness, and I froze inside.

"Lucas," Dad glared.

"No, no, the boy's right," Bryn said. "He's not back home any more, is he? His life's here now. No sense pretending."

He opened the screen door and went inside, but before the door shut, he'd pushed it back open, lingered there a minute. "Know what the most popular beer's called over here, Dai?"

Dad shook his head.

"Blue," Bryn said. "It's just called Blue." He sniffed a dull laugh and shut the door silently behind him.

⁂

That night we sat under the covers with American TV flickering at our feet. WICU, from Erie, Pennsylvania, right across the lake, so close and confident. On the newsflash they talked about an air-traffic controllers' strike. Ronald Reagan said the union had to go back to work for the good of Americans everywhere or else they'd all be fired. Dad called him a bastard. Then the station returned to its regular programming. The show was *Family Feud.* Sal was the only one really watching. I looked up from my *New World Encyclopaedia* from time to time and watched the host kiss women extravagantly on the lips. His bejewelled hand pointed behind him at the big blue board, a bell rang and the answers flipped over, old-fashioned carnival style. A family jumped up and down, hugged each other. White teeth, California skin.

"It's just like *Family Fortunes* back home," Sal said. "They copied it."

"No, Sal," Mam's voice was muffled. She was bundled under the covers, facing the wall. "We copied it. The Brits always copy American game shows. They copy our comedies."

"Why?" Sal said, frowning at the screen.

"Because British comedy is superior," Mam said.

Sal chewed at her thumb, regarded me blankly and turned to the next bed. "Are we superior, Dad?"

But our father was miles away. He was reading his Dylan Thomas. His rough fingers held the book gently, with reverence.

"Dad?"

"Hmm?" He looked up, startled. "Oh. Aye. Your mother's right. Go to sleep. Early night tonight," he said. "Going out to Steelford tomorrow with the real estate agent."

Groaning, Sal got up and switched the TV off and circled their bed. Under her kiss, Mam shrugged warmly beneath the covers, brushed Sal's hair, gentle as lace. "G'night, love."

When Sal kissed Dad he said, "*Nos da,* love," and put his calloused hand on her burnt shoulder. She closed her eyes and smiled in the soothe of it. When he let go, white finger ghosts stayed on her skin. She was always his favourite. Within minutes she was already asleep beside me, her tattered thumb in her mouth, stubborn even in sleep. And for a moment I saw her alone in a field, a sturdy tree that could break in a strong wind, and me swaying beside her, a willow that knew in its veins to bend back.

"What you reading about, Lucas?" Dad said.

"Asteroids," I said.

"Oh, aye?" He smiled vaguely, focusing back on his book.

"Yeah," I said. "It says here there's some with orbits that look like horseshoes, so they're referred to as horseshoe objects."

"Hmm," he said.

"And then it says there's asteroid families, and that family members were created by the spontaneous fragmentation of a parent asteroid in the distant past."

"That's interesting," Dad nodded. "But here's a line for you. *It was my thirtieth year to heaven.*" He smiled at me wistfully. "Isn't that great?"

"I don't know," I said. "I suppose."

"He could've just said, *I was thirty years old,* but not Dylan. He made it beautiful instead, see, from another world. He made it..." and I saw him searching for the word, his mouth ready to shape it, then his eyes twinkling when he stumbled upon it. "*Welsh.* He made it *Welsh.*"

"Don't be so daft," Mam grumbled. "You never even opened that book back home."

"I've always loved the bard. He was a Swansea boy, from the Mumbles. Lived not five miles from us."

"Bard, my foot," she laughed, suddenly. "He was a drunk and a womanizer. On your own, you are."

Dad looked back at the stanzas, then stared across the room at the mosquitoes batting at the light, the small TV up on a chair, with its countless numbers notched into the changer knob, the windows the size of unopened newspapers, the plastic flowers on the table. He closed his eyes suddenly and whistled in a breath, as if in pain. And I heard something low, quiet, barely distinguishable from the summer drone outside. A solemn, drawn out hum, so low I wondered if I was just imagining it. But Dad soon started humming a slow melody and I heard, below his voice, the low mournful sound of a hundred male voices from next door, the harmonies graining against each other, ebbing and flowing. Slow, pronounced words that, save for salutations and place names and swear words, I didn't usually understand. But these words I knew. My father got out of bed and stood in the darkness, frozen in the middle of the room. He stood up straight, his arms at his sides, and he started singing "Myfanwy." His clear tenor voice sang the warm, elegiac sadness at once beautiful and strong and frail. He sang of things about which I knew nothing, of loves both faithful and foolish, of blushes cooling over years only to burn once again with anger, of dark eyes and voices no longer full of sweetness.

"Don't be so soft, Dai!" Mam said, turning over gruffly. "It's depressing."

But Dad sang on, sang past the peeling wallpaper to the black fields and the lake, sang across the North American sky, the Atlantic, sang louder, his voice coming from somewhere deep and beyond him. And at the climax of the song, with the voices rising and swooping like great black birds into my ribcage, flapping up my spine, struggling past the base of my skull and exploding joyous and knowing and infinitely sad, he stood on his tiptoes and I could feel the hairs stand up on the back of my neck.

"That's it!" Mam said. She sat up, her pale face creased. "We're going back," she said, her eyes frail and full of home. "Lucas, start packing, love. Dai, you go to the office and call a taxi."

I kicked off the covers. "Shut up," I said. "I'm never getting in a taxi again!"

"Lucas," Dad said quietly, lost in the act of himself.

"Don't talk to your mother like—"

"Shut up, the both of you...you Limeys!" I sprang up and knocked him out of the way and winged the door open and kicked at the screen door.

"Lucas! What *are* you talking about?" Dad laughed, reaching for me, but I was already out across the gravel in my bare feet, across the wet grass. "Lucas!" he shouted.

And I could hear Mam behind him. "Dai!" she hissed. "David Elias! Get back…a scene…" And I laughed spitefully with tears cutting my eyes and I didn't look back but instead kept running past the maple saplings and swimming pool until I crossed the highway and ran into tobacco, the sharp smell of it, the leaves lashing my skin, the sandy soil wet and spraying from my feet. I ran past the kilns with their soulless boarded-up windows and doors, my feet hitting the earth to a dull, inescapable rhythm: *Canada Canada Canada Canada.* I ran until I collapsed to the ground, then I kicked and scrambled up and ran some more, my heart lunging in its tight quarters, until I fell down again with my face full of earth.

"Lucas!"

I sat there breathless in the wet, the tobacco plants about my head, and looked back across the highway at the cottages. Their little white frames squatted, insignificant, under the blue-black trees. "Myfanwy" was no longer playing, or if it was I couldn't hear it. And there, in the doorway of the cabin one from the end, was my father, standing in a rectangle of light, somehow straighter than before, a taller man who let the night wind blow against him, illuminated from behind by a naked bulb. Unable to see me but still shouting my name, a name that got caught up in the wind and swallowed itself whole.

The wind swooned and then, after some seconds, kicked up again, making the pink lights of the town blink and twitter in the near distance. This Is Your Life, I thought. A place where there were as many gravel roads as tarmac, where the currency was half as valuable as that from whence we came. Where people drove pick-up trucks and said "same difference" with a straight face and where a meal was "good" instead of "nice." Where you could sit half-naked in a field, not knowing what to do, not knowing anything at all, because you were only a child and the dark land all around you was ragged, flat and faceless and full of strange insects chirping messages you couldn't understand.

Wind cut the humid air, goose-pimpling my skin. My father didn't call my name any more, he just stood. After a minute, he walked inside and shut the door. The night above was black as pitch save for only the massive foreign constellations overhead, their dim pinpricks of light, a star falling here, there, and the mosquito hum of a plane, its red and blue lights flashing on/off, on/off. When it faded somewhere in the sky to the east, I walked out of the tobacco and back across the highway to the cottages.

Dad was reading when I came in. He looked up from his book and blinked pleasantly at me, as if I was a surprise and welcome guest. "There he is," he smiled. "There's my boy." For a moment my heart raged all over again, at him, at Mam bundled back under the covers, at the small boy with tobacco gum and earth smeared over his body who stood in the cheap filigreed mirror hanging between the beds. But from how Mam's shoulders trembled and the way Dad's eyes were, the hurt behind them, the slow circuit they travelled from my face back to his book, I knew somehow it was just their way, it had to be. Without a word I circled my bed and climbed between the clammy sheets. Sal was still out cold; she hadn't budged. Save for saying she wanted a game called Asteroids for Christmas, she'd told them nothing about the day's events. Five dollars or no five dollars, I felt a grudging respect for her.

I opened my *New World Encyclopaedia*, flipped back to astronomy and stared at the pages without reading.

"Lucas."

"What?" I said it harshly, regretting it.

"I saw a blackbird today."

"Bigger than the ones back home, right?"

"Nope," he smiled. "Half the size, looked like. And it had red wings with a splash of yellow on them. Pretty," he nodded to himself.

"Dad?"

"What is it, *bach?*"

"The Supercycles, they—"

"Hsst!" He waved me off and nodded at Mam, her suffering back. He reached to touch her but brought back his hand and twirled the hairs on his chin slowly. Then he smiled and shut his book, without ceremony, and flicked off the lamp. "*Nos da,* Lucas."

"Good night," I said.

He began to say something, but his mouth stopped halfway and turned it into a yawn. Traffic hissed in the afterimage of his face. A baby's hoarse cry rose from next door, but it soon waned back into silence. After a minute Mam whispered, "It was for you, love."

"What?"

"You," she said. "We came here for you and your sister. Your father and I want you to have all the things we never had, love. That's why we came here. You and Sal. All the possibilities..."

"Aye," Dad said softly. "You, Lucas, you've got so much going for you. You've got all on a platter, see. It's all up to you from now on. Your mother and I left everything we had, everyone we knew, so that you and your sister—"

"Don't be so soft, Dai," Mam hissed, tugging the polyester covers violently over her head. "Telling the poor boy that, love his heart. You go too far sometimes. On your own, you are."

I shut the book and held it tight to my chest in the dark. Dad sighed heavily. "My thirtieth year to heaven." After that there was only the sound of skin against damp sheets, the engines of mosquitoes whirring in the black, circling above us. A pair of headlights swathed the walls of our cabin, sweeping over the silent, resolute shape that was Mam. When, for an instant, the crisp light washed over Dad, it showed a man whose hands were folded behind his head, a man smiling up at the ceiling. His eyelashes shone when they blinked. It was his first day of thousands in Canada. He was thirty-five years old and he would never be so young again.

The Birthday Boy's Song

THE BOY KNOWS the way from Nanticoke to Hamilton in a blue '79 Skylark. He knows his mother will drive him and Budder, his younger brother, east on Highway 3, past the skydivers and Baptist Church, to Steelford, where she'll stop at Bellow Brothers Self-Serve, so the boy can pump the gas himself. After he's done, his mother will put it on her Mastercard along with a Tab and, for the boys to share on the trip, a Pepsi. She'll let the boy go in and pay by himself. Him leaning on the counter, chin on hands, wondering if the stubbly man with the baseball cap and glasses sitting behind it is one of the brothers on the sign. The boy won't ask, even though he's in here twice a week and every time, before he is fully in the door, the man stretches his hand out, smiling but without looking, ready for the card. As the man runs it through—ch-*ching!*—the boy will have the sudden urge to stick his hand in the machine. He'll sign the receipt "T.F.," a little flourish at the end even though he's printed block caps with periods.

Carrying the pops, credit card and receipt back to the car, a wave of feeling will hit the boy, like he's fully grown inside, chock-full of years, and the rest of his body is just playing catch-up. Though anyone will tell him he's big for his age, like his father was before him.

"Thane, don't slam it!"

"Okay, o*kay*."

He'll ease the passenger side door shut gently: watching his mother turn over the key, apply the brakes, put it in D. Clumsy, he'll think. The air inside the car is thick with her perfume and a strawberry air freshener that hangs from the mirror, verging on fart smell, which he'll notice more now since the gas has cleaned out his nostrils.

"Why can't I have a whole pop?" Budder will ask.

"Because you'll pee your pants," the boy will say flatly.

He knows they'll travel east to Jarvis next, then hook left onto Highway 6 North. Same old, same old. Whenever he's offered different routes in the past, she's turned him down. "I don't need any variety, honey. We're going from point A to point B, no fancy stuff." This time he'll use an Ontario road map for proof, not even talking, just pointing out the kilometres they'll save on the backroads. She'll wave him off, flick the indicator down, and pull away slow and deliberate as history. "No surprises. I'll just get flustered otherwise. We're late anyways."

The boy's always been good with directions. Later, at a Caledonia traffic light, shrugging off another of his suggestions, she'll say, "In four years you'll be allowed to drive there yourself, Thane, any newfangled way you like." She'll laugh then, a little too loud, and Budder will chime in from the back, his small eight-year-old body jammed in there with the sticks and the big bag of hockey equipment. There'll be no reason to go there in four years, the boy will think. Except maybe for Ti-Cat games. Or the dinosaurs. But he'll say nothing. Due to the four fresh stitches over his upper lip, he has trouble talking without being asked to repeat himself, and he doesn't feel much like talking anyway.

In Hagersville, twelve kilometres north of Jarvis, they stop at Dixie Chicken for sandwiches. Budder wants to stay in the car, but their mother says, "I'm not leaving you here with the window down a crack just so's you can stick your muzzle out like a dog."

She says sorry as soon as she's said it, but Budder's already crying, even more when Thane punches him on the shoulder. "Shut up." Budder whimpers in behind them, shoes scuffing over Dixie Chicken's brown tiles. Thane offers him the can of Pepsi. "This'll help."

"None left," Budder pouts.

"Sure there is," Thane smiles, stitches pulling, and shakes the can. Budder's face brightens hearing the swish, fizz.

While their mother orders two regular chicken sandwiches, Thane watches his brother tilt back his head and down the last drops of Pepsi, theatrical, one arm out at his side, keeping his balance. The girl at the counter clears her throat nervously, telling his mother, "Sorry, ma'am, but he can't bring his own drinks in here." Thane shakes his head at the girl—pimples, skinny, equals unpopular, lonely—and walks to a window table and sits down. He prides himself on seeing things clearly.

Outside the sky is a heavy grey but without rain. A caravan of tractor-trailers clatters past, chains holding down huge coils of steel on the flatbeds. Each chain link as big as Thane's fist. He feels their noise buckle in his stomach.

"Bud," he hears his mother say, "give me that." And to the girl, sharply, "There. He's done. Garbage. Now are you ready to take my order?"

A minute later she sets a red plastic tray down on the table. She unwraps one of the sandwiches and cuts it, actually presses it, in half with a white plastic knife. "Here, Budder." She hands him his half and Budder dutifully chomps. A smaller male version of her. Tongue smacking, he looks over his half sandwich at his brother's whole one and then follows his gaze to the window. There are white grids in the glass, creating little squares that Budder counts between bites of his sandwich. "One. Two. Three. Four. Five. Six. Seven . . ."

"Shut yer yap, Bud."

"Not now," the mother says into the tray. "Please."

"He was talking with his mouth full!"

"So are you."

"But I could see like mayo and lettuce and stuff swirling around in there all mushy and—"

"Finished?" His mother shoots him an electric charge of a look before she continues, "Do you remember how I said you better start looking out for him instead of beating up on him?"

"Yeah." Thane slouches under the weight of her eyes and decides to stare through the window's white grid again.

"Coulda fooled me." She wipes some mayo from her lip, then waves her half-sandwich for punctuation. "Pretty soon there won't be any time to whine about if his mouth's open or not. You'll have other things to worry about. He's all you've got."

Under the table, Thane counts off on his fingers the number of times he's heard this. He stops somewhere on his second hand, then says, "I got *friends.*"

"It's not the same."

"What about you?"

"What do you mean?" she says, taken aback.

"I got *you,* don't I?"

"Well, yes, you've got *me,*" she says. "Of course you've got *me.*" She takes a big, comical bite of her sandwich: jaw muscles bulging, food showing. "Whether you like it or not." She's hoping for a laugh, thinks Thane. Her make-up is shiny.

"Why didn't we wait to eat till the dinosaur place?" he says, knowing these words will hang in the air a good while before she's done chewing.

"Because this is halfway and we like eating here," she says, swallowing. "And we're not stopping at the dinosaur place."

"They got hot dogs at the dinosaurs. Smokies."

"Mmm. Smokies," Budder says, legs kicking happily.

"Well, that's good for the dinosaurs," their mother says. "Now eat your sandwich. We've got to hit the road." She says this just as one of Budder's swinging legs kicks Thane under the table. Thane shoots him a slapshot look and even before that Budder's face sprouts red, ready to cry.

"It was a accident."

Thane counts to five in his head and peels his stone-blue eyes away and out of the window. Another truck grinds by. Steel. He bites down on the sandwich. His stitches smart, opening a little, a drop of blood trickling down over his upper lip and mixing with the dry flakes of chicken and stale bread. When he first got the stitches, almost a week ago now, he was in the habit of covering his mouth whenever he smiled or ate, trying to keep them from opening. But gradually the pain has become bearable. He tests himself now, stretching his mouth more and more. Pain its own reward.

"Mommy."

"What is it, Bud?"

"It was a accident."

After Dixie Chicken they play count the blue cars. Thane has counted four, so has Budder, who now shouts out, "Blue Caddy," a second after his brother. A transposed echo.

"No fair." The mother laughs. "You've got to spot your own cars, Bud. Defeats the purpose."

"But Thane's in the front seat. He gets first dibs!" Budder's chewing on his straw; he's chewed it down flat, teeth holes at the ends.

"Ah, forget it," Thane says. "I'm bored anyhoo."

His mother gives him a double-take, then strokes his head, though because she's concentrating on the road she nearly pokes out his eye with her thumb. He pulls away and looks out past his reflection at a tire yard, rusted-out cars, the front of a truck with weeds growing out of the engine.

"Oh, I forgot," she says, stung, "you're too cool now." She turns on the radio and flips the dial around until she finds a bad country station. The man singer tells them, "I caught a keeper when I caught you." His mother sings along out of tune. Thane, sullenly watching a cow's tail flick the air, is convinced she sings like that on purpose, to get a laugh, but lately he just ends up being annoyed.

The Skylark passes the blue Six Nations sign. An arrow pointing: *5 km west. Ohsweken.* Thane fingers his stitches, barely touching. He looks back at the ragged fields, horse bent over a creek. Yet he can only picture the Six Nations arena, more like a glorified shed, its roof and parking lot draped with Christmas lights year round. Where the ceiling is so low the taller visiting players, Thane being one of these, have to remember to duck when they skate over the blue lines or else be decapitated by the water pipes. The native boys using this to their advantage.

"Penny for your thoughts." His mother has been watching him, sad smile quivering. Thane thinks it a wonder she took her eyes off the road. To him her new perm resembles a wig. He remembers feeling a wash of pity for her when she came home, trying to keep busy, avoiding mirrors so she wouldn't cry.

"Nah," he says. "Fifty bucks."

His mother clicks her tongue. "Too rich for my blood," and then is silent, fingering the chain around her neck, contemplating her crow's feet in the rear-view mirror. The radio blabs, stupid. Thane watches his mother's face twitch in the corner of his eye. There's Budder, she's thinking, still chewing on that damn straw, splintered at the top now.

"I've got thoughts! I've got thoughts!"

"Okay. Shoot, Bud."

Bud's smile is a collection of pale freckles stretching chaotically outwards from his nose. He sticks his hand between the front seats, palm up, clapping itself. "Slip me some coin."

His mother pulls out the ashtray under the radio and slides out a penny with the tip of her finger. When she holds it up, Budder grabs for it but it's not there any more.

"Uh-uh-*uh,*" she says. "Give us the goods first; then you get your coin." Saying this, she rolls her eyes in conspiracy at Thane, but he makes like he doesn't notice, just stares ahead at the road. Yet he is careful to *almost* look at her face, knowing this makes things worse. He feels the anger buzzing off her, though he knows full well that his own anger hums louder.

There. Beyond a cornfield's bleached stubble on the other side of the highway, he spots the sign. Red on white and, unlike everything else on this drab strip of road, freshly painted. As they pass the DINO PUTT sign, the dinosaurs come into view. From here they are brilliant but blurry at the edges. Colorized characters in a black-and-white film. Orange diplodocus with its head lost in a big tree's branches. Lime green stegosaurus with red back plates, looking nonchalantly over its shoulder at the highway. Blue *Tyrannosaurus rex* looming over everything, razor teeth a-snarling. Before he knows it, Thane's shouting and pointing across his mother's field of vision. "There! Mom, there they are!"

"Dinosaurs! Dinosaurs! I wanna see them dinosaurs. Pleeease?" Budder is shaking his mother's shoulder. And with Thane tugging at her arm, trying to force her into a left turn, even straining to reach the brake, she's losing control. The Skylark starts bleeding into the oncoming traffic, weaving in and out of the lane. "C'mon, can we go, mom? C'*mon!*" Horns swooping *wah* bleating around her, their mother cranks the wheel right and slams on the brakes and the next thing they know they're sitting at the end of a farmhouse's long driveway, a cloud of gravel dust lifting and settling back on top of them like a tablecloth. The hockey sticks chatter against each other in the back seat.

"This isn't where the dinosaurs are," Budder mutters.

Thane's stomach sinks. Beside him, his mother's breath is locomotive. She lifts her head from the steering wheel, eyes shut tight. "Enough!" she screams. Then she repeats it one, two, eight times, leaning on the horn each time the word is screamed. Thane's lip trembles for an instant, hurting, then settles down and once again he's iron ore inside.

"Is that it, Bud?" she says, arm slung across the back of Thane's seat like she's reversing. "Is that your thought? Dinosaurs? Haven't you got a single dumb thought of your own?"

Bud scowls up from under his bangs.

"*Don't* you?" Her face is unforgiving.

"Thane started it."

"I know he started it, Bud. That's the point." Then she softens. "Just think for your*self*, Bud. Try. Thane's not always going to be able to be your brains, you know. You're going to have to grow some of your own. You're going to be a big boy before you know it. Okay?"

Budder nods, still red in the face. "Thane was bad too."

She laughs. "I'll get to *him,* don't you worry." But when she catches Thane's eye—a dime flashing—she hurriedly shoves the change tray back in and runs the same hand through her tight new curls. Her rings look cold, Thane thinks, looser than normal around the finger skin. They are coming over at him now, fast. He ducks, but her nails merely comb through his brown thatch of hair, scratch at his scalp. He closes his eyes against it and, in spite of himself, bows his head toward her like a horse. A sigh through his nose only he can hear. "You're too old for stuff like that," she says softly. When he opens his eyes and looks, the dinosaurs are two fields back and across the highway. Minuscule. But their skin is still luminous, their colours sing in his eyes. His mother's now holding Budder too, her lips pressed against his hair as he leans forward between the seats, rocking.

"Sorry, chumps. No dinosaurs today. Anyways, there's a mini-putt back in Nanticoke, and it's better too, even without all that fancy-schmancy stuff."

"Dinosaurs are cold-blooded," Budder says. "I saw it on the TV."

"I guess that makes two of us, eh?" she says.

Thane wants to tell her he doesn't care about the miniature golf part, but he lets it slide. He checks his watch, pressing the light button not because he has to but because the watch is new. Visiting hours are over soon, he thinks, and we just passed Caledonia. His mother puts her hand to his cheek, her thumb lightly dabbing the stitches on his upper lip. He winces and pulls back—reflex—and, as if a mime's hand has passed across his face, his features go blank again.

"Hurt?" she says, cautiously backing up onto the highway.

He checks for traffic behind. "Yeah. It hurts well enough."

Orange. Green. White. Pink. Red. Blue. Yellow. Black. These are the lines painted on the University Hospital's floors that tell people which way to go. Thane prides himself in knowing he doesn't need these lines. He's the first out of the car, through the automatic doors, the first to press the elevator button. He folds his arms and taps his foot, textbook impatient. He watches people file into the elevator while his mother and Budder are only now coming through the main doors. The elevator closes before they catch up. Thane shakes his head and in doing so feels that credit card emotion again.

Budder finally gets his jacket on, now that he's inside. By the fourth floor he will have the shiny black-and-yellow thing off again, twirling around, a dog after its own vinyl tail. Thane knows this like he knows his mother will take her compact out of her purse and make fish puckers when she's done with her lipstick. He knows Budder will look up at her, beatific, and say, "You look pretty, Mom." His little teeth white as Tic-Tacs. In the steel of the elevator door, Thane will regard his reflection as if from a great distance. He'll see himself as something melted and welded back together. Sandblasted. Pounded with hammers. Family. When the door opens to the eighth floor, his reflection disappearing sideways into the walls, his mother will say, "Don't forget what I told you to keep shut." Thane will nod, remind himself not to look down.

As soon as they enter his father's room, Thane wants something to hold in his hands. His mother's got a stack of photo albums under her arm, autumn leaves and mountains and oceans on the covers. Budder's carrying the puck ahead of him as if it's a small, fragile animal.

"Half an hour, Mrs. Fearie," the nurse whispers, slipping out the door.

Their mother follows the nurse out into the hall, and doesn't see the need to whisper. "I don't care what *regulations* say. We just drove an hour from Nanticoke. Rush hour even. They're staying with their father till *I* say." The nurse's face is a trap shutting. His mother stares her all the way down the hall. Thane can hear the nurse's starched dress scratching against nylons.

Turning back to the room, his mother is all smiles. She must have put more rouge on while I was waiting at the elevator, Thane thinks. She guides Budder around one side of the bed, hands on his shoulders, while Thane finds a seat over on this side. Despite the ruckus, his father is sleeping. His face is drawn but, when he breathes out, puffy. Above his collarless green gown, bones push at skin. Tubes come out of him like science fiction. And although he probably weighs only half of what he was, from the way his shoulders almost span the entire width of the metal headboard and the size of his hands folded upon the sheets, any stranger could walk in here and see that he once was a big man. An athlete maybe. Perhaps even able to swing both his sons at once, with one hand, under the apple trees in the backyard, at least until Thane hit nine and started sprouting.

When she leans over to smooth out the sheets, Thane sees his father's nostrils flex, then twitch. "Mmmm, the expensive stuff," he says, eyes rolling out of white. His gaze finds Thane before anything else—"Look at you!" he whispers—then slowly pans over to the other side of the bed. His eyes are lashless.

"Chanel Number Five," she says, kissing his forehead and sitting back down stiffly. "Wore it special."

"Nice." Still the slow, deep voice. Yet even this smacking of lips is epic, painful. "But you don't need anything fancy, Ruth. I'd take a bottle of your sweat and keep it right here on this table if I could..."

She laughs. "Jake! What a thing to say!"

"...take a whiff of that bottle every once in a while," he carries on, oblivious, "like smelling salts."

"Grody!" Budder makes a face.

The father looks at his youngest son, squinting, as if he is looking through frosted glass. "Well, hey there, Budder. How goes it, little man?"

"Goes okay." Budder kicks happily in his chair, freckles spreading. "Broughtcha present."

"What the puck is this?"

"Jake! Don't press your luck."

Know that word, Thane thinks, the real word he meant. Used it.

The father laughs quiet, well below cough threshold, and takes the puck gently, tubes pulling at his skin. In his hand the puck looks like a chocolate cookie.

"It's from Six Nations," Budder chirps. "Thane got two goals and two ass—ass—"

"Assists," Thane humbly says to his shoes, sniffing.

"And he almost got a hat-trick, Daddy! But then they called the game."

His father rolls his head round to Thane now, eyes slow to focus. "I told you guys to keep your cool this time around. Knocking those Indian kids around like you're in some John Wayne movie or something. Geez." He sits up, sweat beading. "It was opening game of the season too. And I bet Buzz belted around the ice like some half-jacked-off dog and hauled off on one of those kids like there was no—"

"Take it easy there, hon."

"They're not kids," Thane says. "Some of those guys got moustaches. They got babies even; I've seen them carrying them in the parking lot after the game. And that goalie—I saw him take his mask off once and he had a full beard, for Chriss—"

"Hey, hey."

"Sorry. But it's like playing against you or something!"

His father laughs silently. "You'd be kicking serious butt if you were playing me right now." He closes his eyes, folds his white hands over the puck. Thane knows he laughed because his chest went up and down. The man mumbles, "I thought those native boys didn't have facial hair."

"Huh?"

"Your stuff's still in the car," the mother says quickly, flashing a cautionary look across at Thane.

"We're keeping it there for when you get better." Budder, smiling.

"Take it out," the father says.

"Don't, Jake."

"I'm telling Thane to take my Koho stick out."

"Why?" Thane says, leaning forward, ignoring his mother's eyes.

His father points the puck in his direction, waving it loosely with every other syllable. "You take that Koho stick, the one with the yellow tape, and you put it under your bed. You hear a bump in the night, there's your weapon. Burglar won't know what hit him. You know the things you can do with a hockey stick? The damage you can do to a guy's face?"

Thane looks at the man's knuckles, white on white, clasped around the black rubber disc, and remembers how he'd walk into the dressing room before every game, puck in hand. And just the size of him when he came through the door would make the guys' blabbing shrink to a mumble, shrink to nothing. And he'd hold the puck up and say, "This is what we're playing for, remember." Pause. "You're hitting a guy to get the puck, not to get him. Keep your heads up and your sticks on the ice. Don't let me see you lift your stick up more than a foot off the ice unless you're passing or shooting. Else I'm benching you." Then he'd announce the first line, Thane included—centre. By the time he grinned and said let's have fun out there, the Pee Wee Reps were already a swarm of yellow and black clopping up the stairs, hissing away across the ice, their socks striped busy, their blades flashing.

Thane nods and says, "I guess."

Budder jockeys himself back into the conversation. "Thane knows about sticks and faces!"

"Shut up, goof."

"—he got those stitches from a Six Nations stick."

The father squints at Thane, who's fidgeting, working on his stone-wall face. But from his father's tired smile, he knows he's failing, miserably.

"That right, Bud?" his father says. "I was waiting for your brother to tell me about it himself." He speaks again to his eldest son. "You caught a high stick?"

"Yup."

"So. How's it feel?"

"Not too goodly." They both say this phrase out of habit, though Thane can't remember when he picked it up and has no idea why or where or when his father found it. He grins darkly. "You should see the other guy."

"Thane!" His mother snaps, stern face. "He's kidding, Jake. He didn't lay a finger on anybody."

"Uh-huh," his father's still squinting at his son. His eyes are the same: light blue, except there's no shine, someone's got to polish them up, Thane thinks, take a rag to them. "Did you retaliate?"

Blank-faced, Thane looks at his mother, the bricks of photo albums waiting on her lap, the certainty of this visit quivering at the corners of her mouth. Her eyes are sparkling encouragement. "Nope."

"Atta boy."

She beams at him, and in his head he's saying every swear word he knows.

"Buzz MacMorgan got his nose broke," Budder says. "It was crazy. Mommy covered my eyes. Everyone was screaming and swearing. Mommy was the loudest!"

She blushes through her rouge. The father laughs and squeezes her hand. Her fingers bulge around her rings like fruit. "You're S.O.L., kids." He smiles, sad. "Italian mixed with Irish. S.O.L."

I know what S.O.L. means, Thane thinks. Used that a few times too.

"So how'd Buzz break his nose?" his father asks.

"Well." Thane clears his throat, conscious of his mother's face draining on the other side of the bed. "You know how low the ceilings are in that arena," he says, deadpan. "Buzz had just gotten a cross-ice pass and he was crossing the blue line when he tried to deke out this guy charging up with a mean hip-check brewing. Had Buzz lined right up. Buzz, genius that he is, decides to jump. And his face slams—*bang!*—right into one of the water pipes."

"Ha ha!" His father coughs. "Bet it's an improvement over that little pug excuse of a nose he had! Cocky bugger!"

"That's not what happened," Budder says, frowning.

"How would you know, little man?" His mother laughs,

patting his head. "I thought I was covering your eyes the whole time!"

"Well, that's not how I was 'magining it happened."

"I swear," his mother says, sighing, "Budder and his imagination. And then there's Thane here, telling his hockey stories like some old-timer on the TV. Like he's an old legend or something!"

They are all laughing now except for Thane, who tries not to smile too painfully at his good delivery and watches the room light up for a moment, the fluorescents giving way to human light. His mother's eyes catch his and there is a spark, something fleeting and electric, that he can't articulate. The same sharp sensation from his brother and, when he spends a second inside his father's eyes, something from a similar species, stranger and knowing things the rest of them don't yet.

"It was great, Daddy! You shoulda been there! There was blood all over the ice!"

Budder's words sink the room into machine silence. Thane prays for his mother to smooth out this minute like his father's sheets, but she's staring at the floor through her mascara.

His father lets go of her hand and leans back on the pillows, smile cracking. The fault lines in his skull are naked under the lights, his temples dug out. His Adam's apple is large, solitary. And his face has suffered in the short time they've been here. There's a ghost of blue around it, as if someone has given it a once-over with scouring powder and neglected to rinse it off. He's failed all his blood tests, Thane thinks, got F's on them all. He knows they'll sit the rest of the time here battling the silence. His mother breaking out the photo albums, pointing at the pictures of him and Budder, from babies to boys. He knows his father will look up from a picture, always the same picture—Thane frowning, pushing Budder's hand off his shoulder while posing on the beach in Turkey Point—and remind them how Budder got his nickname. "You were so excited to get a brother, Thane. When Brian came home from the hospital you just kept saying, 'I got a brother, I got a brother!' But you couldn't pronounce it right, so it just came out, 'Budder, budder!' You remember that?"

Thane will strain a smile and nod, not sure if he remembers it for real or from the endlessly rehashed story. Budder will ask his father to sing him a song. "You know, Daddy, that one about me and butter."

"Sorry, little man, I don't have my guitar with me."

The pages of the album will be flipped, flipped. Relatives will be mentioned, weather, hockey again. Thane will swing in and out of the tired chatter, watch the machines blip and bubble and he'll figure he could plug in a joystick and play them. Or else tear their insides out and keep fish in them. He knows just before they leave his father will say, "It looks fine, Ruth, just fine," when she fusses with her perm, self-conscious, and tells him they loused it up down at Misty Rose. He'll sigh and nod and smile off and on until he drifts into sleep. And Thane knows Budder will already be asleep in his chair by this time. That he'll mumble, resentful, when his mother wakes him up. And just before hustling the boys out of the room she'll tell them to give him a kiss, and after Budder's wet smacker, Thane will bring his lips an inch from his father's pale blue cheek before making a small kissing sound and pulling slowly away.

He knows she won't notice. From the doorway she'll be looking back at her husband and whispering to herself,

"Not *his* face. I know his face and that's not it. Nowhere near it."

But now, out in the hall, nurses shuffle past in their sandpaper skirts. "Well. . . ." His mother sighs and slaps her lap, running her hands up her sheeny pants as she gets up and gathers the photo albums quietly from the bed.

On the way back home they pass the Six Nations sign in silence, though Budder, who's now in the front seat, starts punching an imaginary opponent. Pow. Pow. Pow. Thane's slumped against the massive hockey bag in the back, still looking out the rear window. The dinosaurs have long faded behind them, but in his mind he still sees their bright multicoloured skins lit up against the sky's dark belly. "It was still open," he says.

"Not tonight."

"When then?"

His mother sighs. "Don't press your luck, Thane. You're too old for that stuff, and it's too late anyways."

"*Dad* let us go there."

Her eyes pin him down in the mirror. "That's a lie and you know it."

"They got floodlights," Thane shrugs.

"That's enough! You've been good till now. Don't spoil it."

Thane feels a surge behind his ribs and says, "Does *good* mean what *you* think is right?"

But she's clicked on the radio, the chorus to "Superfreak" funking through the Skylark. She sings along, a thin wavering voice, and Thane closes his eyes, embarrassed and angry. Budder forgets about his invisible sparring partner and jumps around to face her. "Sing a song like Dad, Mommy."

"What?" She laughs.

"Do one of those songs Daddy sings for us with the guitar, you know, like 'Budder's Eating Butter.'"

She clicks her tongue. "Sorry, Bud. No guitar in the car today."

He looks slyly out of the corner of his eye. "*You* don't play guitar," he points at her, *clever me* painted all over his freckles. "Don't matter," he chirps, "I'll sing it myself:

Budder, Budder, he's got butter
Now what's he doing with the butter
Is he gonna sell it? No!
Gonna kiss it? No!
Gonna hit it? No way!
Gonna eat it? Okay!
Watch it, 'cos Budder's eating butter
Budder's eating butter."

They all know he's singing it wrong, out of key, with wrong words and bum notes, and that's what makes them laugh. Even Thane. His mother singing along worse than usual to keep Budder company. Thane stares out through the black hole that's his reflection. Thinking of his eighth birthday party when his father came home from work, gave his mother the daily ritual kiss—"In front of everybody!"—and picked up the old guitar. The kids gathered round him, Budder bossing them into a semi-circle. Kids resisting, already trying on new cool attitudes. He sang a song for every kid there—Buzz, Adam, John, Matt, Andy, Geoff—plucking the words out of the air like apples. His fingers cracked and blackened from years of coke ovens' dust, nails splintered. Squeaking against strings, along frets. "Now here's a song for the birthday boy:

> Thane, Thane, he's got a pain
> Now, where on earth is that pain of Thane's?
> Is it in his ankle? No!
> In his elbow? No!
> In his shoulder? Hell, no!"

Etc., etc. A tour of the body until they found the region in question. Relieved, satisfied, proud. Now, when he follows the verses and chorus through in his head, Thane's stumped. Each time he gets to the end he can't see around the song's corner to where the pain was. He smacks Budder's head rest, with little effect since Bud keeps singing, his head halfway down the seat.

"Hey, Bud," Thane says, leaning in between the seats. "I don't think you're ever going to hear those songs ag—"

He's silenced by his mother's hand which snaps, a wrist shot, against his temple. "Don't *ever* say that again!"

"I was just—"

"I don't care what you were *just,*" she says tightly, eyes fused to the road. "If I hear you saying something that stupid to your brother again I'll cuff you so hard—"

"You just did." And he mumbles, "Dad always said you got to be honest, no matter what."

She says nothing but her glare burns him. It keeps flashing back until the second set of traffic lights in Hagersville. Her hair curled so tight. Ready to explode like bottle rockets. Imagine them going off in here. *Tssss! Tssss!* Thane wonders how that would look from a house on the side of the road as they go whizzing past at eighty klicks an hour.

"You look in the mirror more than Dad."

"Don't be a smartass."

"No, I'm serious. Dad looked in the mirror every once in a while, but not as much as you. You do it all the time."

"I guess I'm just vain then, huh?"

"No, you're nervous. You don't have to be though. You don't have a target painted on you or anything."

"And where'd you hear that little piece of wisdom?"

"Dad."

Save for Budder, they say very little the rest of the way home.

⁂

"Do you guys really need that TV on?!"

Thane and Budder are in the basement playing Trouble. Bud's winning but ignorant of the fact. He's absorbed in the *ABC After School Special,* sipping Pepsi in between turns. He pushes down on the Popomatic bubble in the centre of the board, rubbing his hands as the dice skitter over each other, coming to rest at five and three.

"One-two-three-four-five-six-seven-eight. Same as me!" He moves his orange playing peg nine spaces and spreads his freckles at Thane. Then he's back in the TV.

"Go back one," Thane says, monotone.

"No-*oo,*" Bud whines.

"Does that look like nine?" Thane points at the dice. "You say, *Eight! Blah blah blah!* And then you go nine spots. Goof."

He jabs Budder's shoulder—"Geez, Thane"—then moves the peg back one and presses the bubble.

Their mother shouts from upstairs, "Be nice!" Then, "Thane, come help your mom for a minute!"

Bud smiles at him. "My turn, 'member," Thane says. "*Don't* touch anything." Rising directly to his feet from a cross-legged position, he jogs upstairs, slightly bow-legged.

She's in front of the bathroom mirror, cream silk blouse half done up. Thane turns his head away as soon as he's in the door. "Jesus."

"Language." She's busy with her nail polish. "Don't be silly," she says. "You're not in the locker room with your friends now." She blows at her fingernails, then shakes her hands frantically at her sides. "Now, help me with these buttons. Started my nails before I was done getting dressed. Pretty smart." She turns to him, her back to the mirror, hands still flailing. "Nice colour, eh?"

"I guess." He doesn't know if she means the nail polish or blouse. He's looking at the floor tiles, embarrassed, as he takes hold of the first button.

"Come on, Thane. It's not the end of the world." Her voice stern now. She starts impatiently humming a tune he knows but can't place. Fumbling with the buttons, he stares over her shoulder at his own face. Big eyes, like Bud, like her. Stitches bulbous and sore under these dressing-room-style lights, bruising around them, the rest of his face made ghost pale in comparison, except for the bluish half-circles under his eyes.

"You might have to get used to it," she says.

He sees the full picture of them again. She shaking her hands manically, his face floating like a moon over her shoulder. He feels his toughness fall. Snow from eaves. He frowns at her ear. "What do you mean?"

"I mean as long as your father's not here to look after

these little things, then I'll be depending on you. Same for the not-so-little things."

Thane hears the TV blab downstairs. He sees his Adam's apple working the circuit in his throat. "I know." He slips the last button through. His mother's hands quit flapping and come to rest at her sides.

"You do know, don't you." She's looking at him now. Her face is still, indelibly still. "Sometimes," she says, "I look at you and I think you're old. Older than me sometimes. Other times..." Her eyes are somewhere else. We are the same height, Thane thinks.

"Where are you going?" he says, stepping away, casual.

"Thought I told you. Hamilton. With your Aunt Marnie."

"Marn's coming down?"

"Yeah, just for a night or two." Her eyes flit around the room, catching his in a second of mock busy emptiness. She pats her pants pockets. "Now where'd I put my keys? I had them earlier." Off, down the hall.

"Marnie drove all the way down from Timmins just to stay a night or two?"

She shouts something muffled from the bedroom, head in a closet. She comes out, scrambling through her purse. "Be a hon, Thane, and go fetch me your dad's keys from downstairs. They're on the bookcase."

He doesn't move. "Can I come?"

"No."

"Why not?"

"Girl stuff. Shopping, you know. Clothes, perfume, gossip. Things like that."

"You're all dressed up. You're going to see Dad, right?"

She walks past him, deaf. Then, as if snapping out of it, she stops and looks at him square in the eye. "We'll be seeing your father, yes." She's exasperated, smaller than real life as she walks into the living room, rifling through her purse again. "Well?"

"What?"

"How's about them keys?"

He wills the red from getting to his face. In a burst of movement he storms down the stairs, mumbling, "Whatever."

Budder's engrossed in a Green Giant commercial. Miming the *ho-ho-ho* at the end while absently popping the Trouble bubble over and over. Thane kicks Bud's arm out from under him—"Geez, Thane!"—and strides over to the bookshelf, not missing a step. He picks up a set of keys that were resting, along with his father's wallet, on a casually askew copy of *The Hockey Sweater.* Budder sulks at him, red-faced. "What you do that for?"

Thane shouts, whirling on him, "'Cos you're an idiot! 'Cos I told you it was my turn and for you not to touch anything and you did anyway, about eighty friggin' times!" He's standing over Bud now, hands on his hips, nudging his brother with his knee, so that the kid rocks back on his heels, repeatedly pushing himself back up, like a toy.

"Do-*ooon't!*" Budder cries. Thane stops knocking him down. Instead he slams his heel down on the Popomatic bubble, shattering it. Budder screams beyond language, his lips working but useless, face unbelieving.

"You guys! Cut it out down there!" Her head hanging over the banister, sharp.

Budder squeals for more effect.

"Quit picking on your brother, Thane!"

And he quits nothing because he's just standing there now, a lit flare in the room, aware only of a plastic die pressing hard against the bone in his heel. Budder chokes back a glob of tears and shouts, "It's his temper, Mommy!"

Their mother's feet thump away across the ceiling and, after a moment of silence, come back to the stairwell. "Forget about the keys. Found mine!"

Thane considers the weight of the keys in his hand, then slips them into his jeans pocket.

There's a beep in the driveway. Engine whirr. She's grabbing her coat from the front hall closet, threading it onto silken arms as she runs down the stairs. "Mmm-*wa!*" She kisses the top of Bud's head, ignoring his tears and the broken board game. Thane next. "Mmm-*wa!* Don't do anything I wouldn't do, 'kay?" She ruffles his hair—"Don't worry, Mr. Navigator. Us girls won't get lost"—but as she goes back up the stairs, she looks past the bruised pout that's his mouth and significantly, slowly, looks back and forth between him and Budder, giving Thane an exaggerated nod for punctuation.

"Yeah, yeah," he says.

It takes her five minutes before she's actually ready and out the door. But not before Budder has left the basement and trundled up the stairs, socks flapping into the front hall just as Aunt Marnie steps in the door. "Well, hello there, Bud!" Leaning over the banister, she sings, "Hiya, Thane, honey!" Marnie's a slightly larger, more made-up version of their mother; tonight the likeness is doubled because she's rushed and breathless too. Thane says hi back, but makes a point of not smiling. "Well, fine then," Marnie sighs. "I'll talk to you guys later, okay?" She's gone before Thane can think to say another word. Collapsing back on the couch, he listens to the vinyl hiss of his brother's jacket, his mother hurrying back down to the front hall.

"What do you think *you're* doing?" she says.

Budder's voice is sheepish. "Coming with you."

"Uh-uh," she says, "not this time, Bud."

"But—"

"But nothing. Just me and Aunt Marnie this time. Sorry, little man." When she goes "Mmm-*wa!*" again, Budder offers nothing back but a low whimper. "Shit," she sighs, oblivious, "my purse." She thumps back upstairs. After a moment of silence, Budder's jacket hisses away and a door closes. Thane, staring at nothing on the TV, hears the out-of-tune plang of an unchorded guitar being slapped.

Here she comes again down the stairs. Here she is saying, "Bye, guys," her voice not all there, and shutting the door behind her.

"See you later," Thane says, blank as he can.

After the car whirrs out of the driveway, Thane jumps up from the couch. He gets a plastic bag from the stowed away pile in the laundry room, then returns to the Trouble board. He flicks the channels on the TV till he finds a sports highlights reel. Baseball playoffs. No Jays, no Expos, who cares. He picks shards of plastic from his socks and the floor, scooping them into the cup of his hand, then dropping them into the bag. From upstairs he thinks he can hear the unchorded guitar again, but then he's lost in the sound of plastic and Pepsi cans clattering into the bag, the sportscasters' patter. He packs up the Trouble board and loose dice into the box and slides the game's remains under the TV trolley. When he flicks off the tube, the sportscaster's mouth is still smiling. Thane takes his father's wallet from the bookcase and slides it into his back pocket. Thinner than it used to be, he thinks. He ties up the plastic bag and carries it into the front hall, where he drops it on the floor, threads on his black and yellow Nanticoke Minor Hockey jacket—wincing against the hiss—and steps into his running shoes. He can hear the Fisher Price radio blabbing up in Budder's room. Forgetting the garbage, Thane slowly opens the front door, locking it behind him.

The garage door is already open. Thane walks around to the Skylark's driver's side door and opens it quietly. But he panics into the front seat and slams the door behind him, his elbow accidentally sounding the horn. "Shit," he whispers. "Shit shit shit." He waits, staring through the windshield at the chaos of hockey nets, sticks, baseball gloves hanging from nails on the back wall. No sign of Budder, although for a moment he almost senses him close: sulking down the stairs maybe, lingering just on the other side of the front door, jacket and all. Thane breathes against the thick smell of fake strawberries. He can see his breath. He counts to twenty, slowly, in his head. Still no Budder.

Spreading the keys like a fanned-out deck of cards, he passes over the round trunk key, selecting instead the square-shaped one. He slips it into the ignition, but before turning it all the way over, he catches the glint from his dad's key chain. A miniature gilt frame and inside it a family photo he's seen a thousand times, if not on this chain then framed on the living room wall: their mother back when she had that dye-job and hoop earrings, her face smiling but unimpressed, like the photographer said something rude instead of cheese. Their father when his body still worked, that faded old red lumberjacket, shirtless underneath. When his hair was long and his bushy moustache made their mom sneeze when he kissed her. Budder and Thane in front, dressed like twins. Striped shirts, corduroys. Blond with promises of brown poking through underneath. In normal light, their large, seemingly unblinking eyes would be gazing out with their mother's open, catch-all look. But here in the sun, thanks to hard-faced squints, they are carbon copies of their father.

He blinks and the picture twirls on its chain, a faded price tag on the back. He turns the key over full, and suddenly he is in the belly of a blue shark, the engine amplified against the garage walls, the exhaust pluming up and over the trunk, rear window, roof. He inhales deeply, then lets it out in staggers. He can still see his breath and he's shivering but not from cold. He knows the seven things he will do next:

1. *Fasten seatbelt.* If only to shut up horse-fly buzzer.

2. *Check rear-view mirror.* Perfect, because he and his mother are the same height.

3. *Check brakes and accelerator.* Comfortable, both pedals surprisingly easy to reach. Though when he revs the gas, his foot cocks back, alarmed at its power. He whispers "Jesus" through his teeth.

4. *Shift into Reverse.* Foot flooring the brake, he grips the automatic shift and pulls it back and toward him, carefully guiding the orange marker on the dash display from P to R, going too far and slipping into N before bringing it back up, making sure it sticks in the R notch. Surprised at how much the car lurches with each capital letter visited.

5. *Reverse.* Stares over his shoulder at the driveway and

road, right arm around the back of the passenger seat, left hand at twelve o'clock on the steering wheel. Eases his foot off the brake, his Adam's apple humming like a bee in his throat. The Skylark slowly rolls backwards into fading daylight.

6. *Back up onto road.* Once the front wheels roll back to the lip of the curb, he turns the wheel to the left, his open palm making slow, anti-clockwise circles as if he's washing a window. This technique he remembers from his father, along with the smell of lumberjacket armpit when he'd drape his arm around Thane and the passenger seat on their way to morning practice.

7. *Shift into Drive.* Same as "4" but different, since P is now R and R is now D. He must brake smoothly, pull back through N all the way to D, be sure not to cause lurching or, worse, squealing, and thus draw attention from neighbours and Budder, whom Thane pictures spooning with the old guitar on his bed. When he switches his foot from brake to accelerator he's a trapeze artist in mid-air. But the Skylark merely purrs in a different key and, after he tilts his ankle, pulls away lazily with him floating on velour seats inside it. He glances back at the house: the windows blank, indifferent. He coasts down Ironwood Crescent, his foot fluttering on the gas pedal, wanting only to reach the stop sign undamaged and unseen.

The only person he sees outside is the new neighbour, Mr. Elias, trimming his lawn with an electric mower, holding the extension cord out at arm's length as he awkwardly pushes the machine forward with the other hand. Should be wearing steel-toed boots, Thane thinks. There are still empty boxes piled high on the porch behind Mr. Elias, and his daughter Sal's riding her bicycle up and down the driveway.

Thane recalls how when they first moved here in the summer she and her brother couldn't ride at all, they just pushed their bikes wherever they went. Now, as the Skylark passes, Mr. Elias glances up and smiles and, with great difficulty, waves at the car. The extension cord flaps dangerously above the mower. Thane waves back quickly as he glides past, does his best to act like he's doing the most normal thing in the world. But his hands are shaky, gushing sweat. In the mirror he sees Mr. Elias's smile fade, the bright orange extension cord brought down to half mast. Through his teeth Thane is hissing all the swear words he knows.

8. *Drive.* Once he's past the Nanticoke Mall and turned right onto Highway 3 after a rolling stop, Thane's in two-lane territory. He does as he's studied: keeps right, checks the mirror every ten seconds, keeping count in his head. The town's pink street lights have already kicked in—the sky darkening, a beer gut sagging over the tobacco belt. He passes the skydiving school, the Baptist Church, obeying the 60 km/h speed limit. Tonight the yellow rent-a-sign on the church lawn says Prepare to Meet Thy God in big black letters. The pink lights fade behind him now, almost audible, a breeze. He passes the Town of Nanticoke sign, a pentagram spray-painted on the back of it. The traffic is thin here, more people driving into town than out of it. He checks his mirror, then shoulder, and merges into the 80 km/h lane, headed for Steelford and, beyond it, Jarvis.

Tobacco fields stream past the windows, a green and brown liquid. Thane's eyes snap back and forth between the ribbon of tarmac and the speedometer. Every time a car approaches his insides cringe. A vintage candy-apple-red pick-up flashes its lights at him twice, three times. Thane's heart lunges but then, fumbling only slightly, he finds the headlight knob on the dash and pulls. Pictures himself peering over the wheel: badass kid with a blue-blossom mouth. He snatches another look in the mirror, imagines Mr. Elias with the extension cord tangled up in his lawnmower, shouting for his daughter to pull the plug before he's fried. Thane laughs, but not out loud. He laughs so it is only breath stammering through his nose. Laughter, real laughter, would feel like battery acid in his throat. He has not laughed out loud since the Six Nations game. He reminds himself he will have to work the high beams soon. Check: bingo. Proud, he clicks on the radio and within seconds is drumming the steering wheel along to a Mr. Transmission jingle, thinking nothing sounds bad when you're driving.

On the short flat stretch to Steelford, he's taught himself to look slightly to the right whenever headlights approach. He's learned to picture all oncoming drivers, not naked, but completely invisible. He's also realized the gas tank's nigh on empty. Nothing in the mirror except a faint binary shimmer, he flicks the left-turn indicator and swerves into Bellow Brothers Self-Serve. Seven out of ten this time around, since he misjudges the power brakes and stops a few feet shy of the unleaded pump. Car now running in P, he climbs across both seats so that he opens the passenger door as usual, hip-checks it shut. The man in the baseball hat is a flicker in the window, absorbed in a portable TV, his feet propped up on the counter, his back to his business. Thane unhooks the gas nozzle, presses the lever down, but finds he has to wrestle the hose and pull it taut in order to reach the Skylark's tank.

Out here the lights are furious, bright as Maple Leaf Gardens. Thane doesn't stop to enjoy the gasoline smell. He watches the numbers scroll like Las Vegas but is thinking only of Hamilton city limits: fifty-one kilometres, approximately. He makes a mental list of the traffic lights he'll have to manage: one at Highway 6 in Jarvis; two in Hagersville; one at the gypsum plant just south of the Six Nations sign; three in Caledonia, including the one right after the Grand River Bridge; he forgets how many after that. Before the tank's even half full he's coughing from exhaust fumes. He's too nervous to wait any longer when he places the nozzle back in its holster and looks up to see the man in the baseball cap standing up facing the window. His glasses flash. Thane can't see his eyes through their reflection. The man raises both his arms and yawns theatrically; he turns, fussily adjusts the rabbit ears on the TV and settles back down. His boot heels kick back up onto the counter.

Thane puts his hand in his jacket pocket and ambles up to the door: *Pull.* There's a dull ache nibbling at his calf. Under the fluorescent lights, all the oil cans and candy wrappers are immediate, ruthless. He quickly grabs a Pepsi and, as an afterthought, a Tab from the fridge. His upper lip throbs. Black-and-white sports highlights blab from the TV screen. Baseball play-offs: Cardinals vs. Phillies. The man is shaking his head, muttering, "Shouldn't of walked him, they shouldn't of *walked* the bastard." He is all stubble and glasses and nose. Thane takes his father's wallet from his pocket and withdraws the Mastercard, cursing himself for not doing it sooner, before he came in. But right on cue, the man stretches out his hand, smiling without looking at the boy, and takes it. A burnt-down cigarette crackles between his fingers. Thane sees smudged, moist circles where his own fingers held the laminated plastic a second ago. His lip throbs now, a target. Before running the card through, the man puts his smoke between his lips, grimacing. Thane keeps fists clenched tight in his pockets, counting the butts in a glass ashtray. One. Two. Three. Four. Five. Six. Seven. Eight. *Ch-ching!* When he's handed back the card and receipt, his hands are miles away and he finds himself having to use all his weight to scratch "T.F." into the paper. Five small lines, he thinks, and I'm home free.

"Thank you, sir."

The man half nods, takes his copy and settles back on his stool. Two TVs dance on his glasses.

Thane walks briskly to the door, and as he fixes to shoulder it open the man speaks. "Bad idea, son."

Thane's first instinct is to drop the pops and bolt. Instead he turns back, gut skeltering. "Excuse me?"

"Tell your Dad," the man waves the peak of his hat vaguely toward the window, "it's a bad idea to keep that engine running when you're filling up the tank."

Thane watches the man mash his cigarette butt into the ashtray with an oily, dirt-rimmed thumb. It is the slowest, most violent thing he has ever seen. "Okay," he says, pushing the door open against the wind. "I'll tell him."

He peels out of the gas station after slamming the door for the first time ever without being scolded. Yellow and white lines, blood corpuscles, the halo of trees, his hands from the radio light—everything pulses inside and outside his skin. After almost ten miles trapped inside this sensation, he rolls into Jarvis, his first honest-to-goodness town. The grain silos of the local co-op loom over every other shadow in its sky, even the ancient water tower. But Thane smells the town before he sees it: like cat food, like always. When he passes the sign, Population 1,200, a fanfare blast comes over the radio, then a crude splicing of songs alluding to Hollywood, followed by the sharp, nasal voice of the other CKNC deejay once more introducing "Harry! 'HOLL-ywood'! Howard!" The Jarvis streets are well-lit but empty. Hollywood Howard's deep saccharine voice thanks the other voice, insults it, then says, "Now folks, we're going to do a new feature on our show, called 'Go Figure.' It's sort of like *Ripley's Believe It or Not,* but...but it's on the radio and I'm not Jack Palance!"

The two voices laugh and laugh.

There are flashing reds at the only traffic light in town. Thane lays on the brakes, a little hasty, the car bucking forward. He hears the sticks chatter and thunk in the back seat. Glancing back, he notices the huge canvas hockey bag slumped over the seat. A gutted buffalo. Its contents—pads, mask, skates, gloves, tape—spill out of a broken zipper that's long as a tiptoeing Thane with skates on. His father's Koho stick is longer still, teetering on top of everything, set diagonally across the back seat but still touching both doors. The yellow tape wrapped round its handle and blade blushes in the flashing lights. Remembering, Thane flicks down the indicator and waits for the green.

"But why yellow, Dad?"

"Most guys strap the black tape on their blades, right?"

"Right."

"And why is that?"

"'Cos it camouflages the puck. Makes it so the goalie can't see where the shot's coming from, where it leaves your stick."

"Right. And what would you call that tactic?"

"I'd call that an advantage for the shooter."

"Well, sure. But you know what? I call it cheating. See, that's why I put the yellow tape on my blade, so's the goalie knows what he sees is what he gets and that's not going to help him anyway 'cos I'm coming at him with all my guns blazing. Best man wins. It's honest as your hands, Thane. If you got power you don't need any of your advantages. Power is its own advantage. Understand?"

"Yeah, I think so. Sort of like that time during shooting practice you ripped a slapshot at Matt and drove him square in the balls."

"Uh, well, sort of, but—"

"And the puck hit one of those balls so hard it got knocked up into his intestines and they had to take him to emergency! Geez, that was something!"

"Yeah. Well, Thane, that wasn't my point exactly. Tell you what, on your next birthday, you ask me about my yellow tape and I'll tell you all over again, okay?"

"Sure. And you'll sing me the same song?"

"Yessirree."

The mirror's suddenly ablaze with white light, brakes grinding like metal girders. Then a bullhorn rattles the Skylark and Thane looks back to see a Canadian flag filling the entire rear window. He blinks and realizes it's the grille of a SteelCan tractor trailer. He cranks the wheel and steps hard on the gas, peeling onto Highway 6 North. His heart firing like a Gatling gun, he knows he's way over the 50 km/h speed limit and he's just gone through a flashing red but he's not stopping. In the mirror he sees the truck slowly negotiating the intersection, its trailer straining under three massive steel coils. It's those lights, he thinks. You're supposed to go through those lights. Stop and then go. Seen it riding with Dad to early practice.

The Skylark clatters over the tracks at an abandoned CN station. The little grey building recedes into black. As soon as Thane sees the 80 km/h sign, he buries the pedal, hurls himself into the darkness of farms. The SteelCan truck is already lagging a kilometre behind, but Thane looks more at the mirror than at the road the whole ten flat miles to Hagersville.

Hollywood Howard has told two Go Figures—one about a student who set his sleeping roommates on fire with flaming ski poles, and another involving the murder of a circus performer called Lobster Boy—"They should've put him in a steam pot instead! Ha ha ha." Now Hollywood's heading in for a third. "Now last, but by no means least—"

"Ha, you got that right, Hollywood."

"Thanks, Jean. Anyway, here's our third and final Go Figure for today. This comes all the way from Baton Rouge, Louisiana. According to local authorities, a chemical reaction between embalming fluids apparently sparked a fire in the coffin of a dead man in a small church—"

"Hee hee!"

"—just minutes after his wake ended. Workers at the Mount Lillian Baptist Church were horrified to find smoke pouring from the closed coffin after mourners left."

"Spontaneous combustion, Hollywood?"

"Seems so, Jean. But there's more. You see, morticians were called in to work on the dead gentleman, whose name was not released at the family's request—"

"Ha!"

"—because of an *odour* coming from the casket."

"Yikes!"

"You're telling me! Now they believe that whatever chemical was added that second time caused the reaction that started the fire in the body. And—get this—sources say the body was *not badly burned* and the church suffered only minor damage!"

"Heeheeheeheeheeheeheehee!"

"We've only got one thing to say to that...GO FIGURE!"

When Thane looks at the speedometer, the needle is shivering at 130 km/h. He lifts his foot suddenly off the gas, and the hockey gear avalanches into the back of his seat. A sound, almost like a dog whimper, starts squeaking behind him. He shuts off the radio, nearly snapping the knob, and listens. Nothing. A pale blue structure on stilts glows monstrous in his headlights. Capital letters—black and probably ten feet high—are painted across its cylindrical belly: HAGERSVILLE.

If he hadn't stepped off the accelerator, the Skylark would've screamed past the water tower at 80 klicks over the limit. Thane would've been pulled over by the OPP car he now sees up ahead, parked across two spaces in the Tim Hortons Donuts parking lot. From here he can make out two silhouettes in the front seat. And even though he's pretty sure the police officers can't see past the doughnuts and coffee they're holding, he's too afraid to drive past them. At the traffic lights, he stops, looks both ways and turns left. West.

This road he has never seen, even in daylight. No lights here, not even houses. He knows he's moving back toward Nanticoke and that he must take a right soon to get back on course. But after a black mile, fog settles onto the road like sleep. He slows. The glare forces him to turn off the high beams and concentrate on the six feet of tarmac directly in front of him, the white-line curve of the gravel shoulder. Beyond the weeds in his peripheral vision, blurry telegraph poles are chopping past like worn teeth. A break in the pattern means a road. Up ahead he can make out a pair of tail lights. He accelerates, trusting them. Before long the fog lifts and he can even tell the make of the car—a Pontiac Parisienne. But as soon as Thane clicks the brights on, the cloud settles back down with the stubbornness of lead. He's ready to pull over to the side of the road, sit and wait out the fog, when he sees the phantom Parisienne's right indicator flashing yellow a hundred feet ahead.

Tarmac switches gears into gravel. This is a driveway, he thinks. It's a fucking farmhouse driveway. Stones spit and clatter under the car, ricochet around in the wheel wells. Between the fog and the dust kicking up from the Parisienne's tires, he can barely see. Condensation mixes with dirt and forms a thick muddy soup on the windshield. He scrambles around in the darkness, finds and flicks on the wipers. Clean. Without indicating, the Parisienne before him turns, a large red barn looming miraculously in its headlights. Thane's ready to follow the car into the mirage, for good, but he doesn't because the ragged bolt of gravel is still unfurling in front of him. He decides not to decide, only to rumble forward. The whole car shakes and groans around him, its steady percussion slowly lulling him to sleep. Any second now, he thinks, I will fall off the edge of the world. At this moment he sees a stop sign and, beside it, a billboard that says Welcome to Six Nations.

It's small, hand-painted, nothing like the regular sign they see all the time on Highway 6, and for a minute it stops Thane dead in his tracks. He cracks open a pop and sits back. He considers the bubbles fizzing in his mouth. He could turn back now and nothing would change except the odometer and the reading on the gas gauge. He senses a stirring behind him, the carcass of the hockey bag shifting its lifeless weight once more, adjusting to inertia. Thane grinds the Skylark forward, safe again inside the pelting of stones. Electric lights bleat weakly through the fog, every so often illuminating the blurry form of a house identical to that of the last one. The hockey gear hedges again, this time with an animal grunt. Thane ignores it, takes another sip of pop and, frowning to himself, realizes he's been drinking Tab.

"Stop the car, Mommy! You're going the wrong way!"

Thane sprays pop onto the dashboard. "Jesus Christ!" Here's Budder's moon face gaping an inch from his own, twisting from recognition to shock to horror, and now he's wailing, clawing through sticks and pads, trying to bury himself in the hockey bag again. Thane's head is full of sparks. "Bud!" When he finally gets the car pulled over and jammed into P, he sees his father's old guitar is also stuffed into the bag. Budder's tearing at strings, an unbearable noise. Thane clenches his fist and raises it over the seat, bones pushing white through skin. "Bud! Shut up! NOW!"

Whimpering, the little boy slaps at the strings smartly and with finality, as if the guitar's a bad dog's snout. Thane reaches over and grabs the neck of the guitar, silencing it. Catching his breath, Budder snuffles, "Where's—?"

"She got a ride with Aunt Marnie."

"I thought you were—"

"I know, Budder."

"I thought you were Mom driving the car and I thought we were going to Hamilton." Bud lifts his face. His cheeks are two red stones glistening with spider thread.

"I know." Thane lets go of the guitar and lets his hand fall limply into his lap. His pants are soaked with cola. "You scared the shit out of me, goof."

"I didn't mean to scare the shit out of you. I meant to scare the shit out of Mommy and Aunt Marnie."

Thane shakes his head and jabs laughter through his nose. "Is that right?"

"Yessirree."

Thane's stomach buckles. He searches the boy's face for a moment. Turning to face the wheel again, he redundantly checks his mirror. While he's working the automatic stick into Drive, Budder clambers over into the passenger seat, leaving the guitar in the back. Thane ignores him, but it doesn't take long for him to know he's being watched. When he looks over, Budder's face is iron ore. "*You* can't drive. You're not *allowed.*" The little boy folds his arms and glares into the white ahead of them.

"Where are we going?" For the last five minutes, Budder has been yanking at his seat belt, trying to put it on. Fog is layer upon layer of cling-wrap wound around the car. Thane thinking: we could be driving over bones, ground human bones, and we wouldn't even know it. "Where are we *going?!*" Budder has finally lost his cool and is tugging so hard at the seat belt that Thane's afraid he'll let go and slingshot himself into the steering wheel. Thane eases the boy back, reaches across his chest, snaps the seat belt loose like a whip and deftly fastens in Budder himself. Remembering how their father could cover that kid's whole chest with one palm. Pick him up that way, hold him flailing around six feet off the ground. And all Budder would do was giggle and ask for more.

"Thank you," Budder says absently, tapping the seat belt, entranced by the fog. Houses drift past them inconsolably, burnt paper edges of dreams. Sometimes Budder gasps. They pass a car's wall of light and he whispers, "Pretty," the word a mile long and full of nothing but breath. He wipes his face theatrically, first with the back and then the front of his hand. He nudges Thane. "What's that?"

"What's what?"

Budder's thrusts his shiny hand in front of Thane's face, blocking out part of the road, pointing to Christmas lights off to the left. *"That."* A black squatting hulk of a building festooned with multicoloured Christmas lights, only half of them working. Strung along its corrugated roof and down the invisible walls and draped from eaves all the way over to telegraph poles and back onto the roof, they have the look of an abandoned fairground.

Budder coos. "It's Christmas."

Thane shoves his brother's hand out of the way and floors it. "What are you talking about, ya chump? It's the hockey arena. It's far from Christmas."

"But all those lights all—"

"Are you a fuckin' idiot or something? It's Six Nations hockey shed!" He punches Bud's shoulder. "You were just in there last week, remember?"

"Oh," Budder says blankly. "It looks different."

"No shit." Thane punches his arm again for good measure. Waves of fog smash silently against the windshield. For the first time in miles, Thane's aware of his stitched upper lip. He takes a loose thread between his teeth and tugs. An eye gathers water.

"Why are we going so fast?" Budder whines, grabbing onto the door handle. The needle's at 90. Thane presses it down, nudging 100. He feels blood pooling on his dry cracked lips, copper taste lining his gums. Suddenly, from out of the ditch, something small scurries up and across the road. Thane swerves and steps off the gas and sends Budder slumping sideways, exaggerated, as if he's showing off, but his head smacks hard off the passenger window. "Ow!" He crumples back into his seat. Thane, grinding the Skylark to a stop in the middle of the road, grabs Budder and pulls the boy's limp body toward him.

"Jesus, Budder! You all right?" He holds his brother's head to his face, fingers clenched in his hair. "Bud?" He doesn't realize Budder's struggling to let go. Thane only feels skull pressed hard against his lip, and he hugs the boy tighter. "C'mon, stop crying, Bud. I won't hit you again. Promise. We're all we've got."

Finally Budder breaks free and sits bolt upright in his seat, staring at Thane with dry, detached eyes. "Did we kill that critter back there?"

"No," sighs Thane. "I don't think so."

"Good." Budder sits there for some time before he reaches his hand to his older brother's face—him flinching back, then relenting—and runs his finger along the stitches and swollen skin. He brings the finger back close to his own face, regards the black liquid smudge. "Thane?"

His older brother awkwardly turns back to the wheel. Inside, his bones are tired, hollow. "What is it?"

"What happened on the ice at the Six Nations game, after Mom covered my eyes?"

Thane looks in the mirror at the coloured lights fading. He shoots a lethargic stare over; Budder is still sitting facing him. He sighs. "I'm not allowed to tell you, Bud. Mom made me promise."

Budder says nothing at first. Instead, he studies his fingertip some more, rubs it against his thumb, then tastes it.

His face crinkles. He folds his arms and draws up his legs like scissors, tucking them beneath him. His voice is quiet, matter-of-fact. "You're not allowed to drive her car neither."

The Skylark moves north. By Thane's calculations, they are twenty kilometres southwest of Hamilton. They still haven't reached an intersection that could point them east. But the fog is thinning now. White wisps, strands of old women's hair.

"I've *heard* all about the regular game," Budder says, blinking, bored. "I want to know about *after.*"

Less than fifteen klicks away, Thane thinks, it's rush hour. He fidgets with the key chain, flicking it, scratching the price sticker off with his thumbnail. "You're not going to shut your hole till I tell you, are you?"

"Nosirree." Budder smacks his lips shut and puffs air into the space between his nose and upper lip. The effect is such that he looks like a freckled, painted chimp.

Thane stares at him under heavy lids. "You're lucky I said that thing about not hitting you."

"I'm *waiting,*" Budder says. "What happened after Mommy put her hand—"

"Yeah, yeah, yeah." Thane claps his palm over Budder's mouth. Budder slumps back; Thane lets go. Suddenly they are passing over an iron girder bridge, the wheels clattering every other second over concrete fault lines. The Grand River slugs its way beneath them. Remnants of old fog still smother the water's surface, so much so that it appears the Skylark is travelling, not over water, but over some endless black pit. East, in the near distance past Budder's face and the girders slicing by, Thane can see the lights of Caledonia hunkered over invisible banks. He doesn't start talking again until they are halfway across the bridge. "All right. It was about a quarter of the way through the third period, 2-2, remember?"

Budder nods hungrily.

"I'd got both our goals and now the coach was putting me on for a double shift, hoping for a quick goal to put this one away. We're at the end of a power play, four on three. Here I am going down the wing—bareheaded 'cos I lost my helmet back-checking in our end—and I'm waiting on a pass from Buzz who's coming out from behind the net. *Shoom.* I pass our blue line, duck under one of those water pipes and then, *boom,* there's the puck on my stick. Perfect pass. The Six Nations' centre got back there somehow, and he's charging at me now from centre ice, but I see him. I kick the puck off the boards and—*shoom*—I'm back inside him and he slams into the boards. The rest all happens in about two seconds. I'm flying up the right side, no one between me and the net but their goalie. I look up and there's ten seconds left on the penalty clock. I can hear our side booming in my ears, 'Go, Thane! Gooo!' And then, soon as my blade scoops up the puck again, *slam!*

"This big fucker, Evans, jumps out of the penalty box eight seconds before his penalty's over. We had a little tussle back in the first period, see. He just stands there, all six feet of him, on the ice in front of me. It's too late for me to deke him out. He puts his elbows up and just lays me out. Butt of his stick cracks me right in the mouth and I fall like a sack of shit, right on the red line. Puck goes flying into the stands, right into your hands, I guess. Or maybe you fought for it. I don't know; I *hope* so. And I'm bleeding bad. That's when the shit hits the fan…"

"I didn't get to see the shit hit the fan!" Budder's jumping up and down. "Mom's hand went in front of my face!"

"Well, Buzz drops his gloves and he's on Evans like a dirty shirt, just pounds the shit out of him, and Evans is like a *man,* for fuck's sakes. Whistles are blowing like crazy. By the time the linesmen get to Buzz, both benches have cleared, gloves and helmets all over the ice. I see Matt skating down to duke it out with the Six Nations' goalie half way. Even our coach is out there goading on the other coach, but that guy's a pussy. And Evans is taking all this punishment from Buzz, but he just won't go down. Teeth broken and shit. The linesman finally gets his arms hooked around Buzz's, but then Buzz starts kicking, trying to do some damage with his skates. I'm climbing up my stick to get back to my feet, blood all down my sweater. Here's Buzz cycling the air, screaming at him, and there's Evans reefing back and cracking him right in the nose. It just gushes. Buzz has to breathe through his mouth now, and Evans just laughs like *ha ha, look what I did.*"

"What happened then?" Bud says quietly.

Thane's caught up in his story now. "Well, I lose it, Bud. I do a one-eighty and bring my stick over my shoulder like a hatchet. Evans drops, out cold, I don't know how long. He's bleeding from the head, but I'm still not happy. The linesman's busy holding Buzz, but his eyes are on me. And I hear Mom scream something, I don't know what. I look up, and there she's standing up on her seat, holding you in her arms. Her hand's clamped tight over your eyes, and her eyes—*stop right there, mister,* they're saying. So I stop but it's right next to Evans's head. His ear's at the tip of my skate. I remember spraying ice onto his hair and, well, I just remember it, 'cos

I was standing there in the middle of everything all peaceful and everyone was going ape-shit all around me, on the ice, off the ice, and I looked down at Evans and it just wasn't enough, see."

When he looks over at Budder, the boy's face is white, expressionless. "That's why we all had to get out of there so quick, see. It wasn't like there were any cops there to break it up." Thane continues, quietly, stammering, "All I know is I'm suspended till the league says different."

Budder's face is a slice of freckled skin turned away from him before he nods at the road ahead. "Stop. Lights."

Thane pokes his lip gingerly once, twice, wincing. "Shit," he shakes his head. "I shouldn't have told you that."

Flashing reds. The Skylark turns right at the first intersection in twenty-five kilometres. *East.* They are out of Six Nations territory now. Street lights and corrugated tin shacks start materializing out of nothing. Front-end loaders and full-sized Tonka trucks squatting in huge gravel parking lots. The road widens to four lanes. Farms become nostalgia. A gypsum plant pumps an incessant yellow caterpillar of smoke into the night sky. The smell gets in Thane's throat, and when he slides his eyes over, Budder's nostrils are flared, face in a grimace. Thane feels a flame well up in his chest.

"So?" he snaps. "Aren't you going to feed me some shit like, *that's baaad, Thane. That was a very baaad thing to do. Temper, temper?*"

"Don't worry," he says blankly. "I won't tell, but I bet Daddy's gonna—" He perks up and points. "Dinosaurs!"

There, across a wet field riddled with targets, yard markers and hundreds of round white specks in the grass, the dinosaurs shimmer under a blanket of spotlights. Steaming, almost alive. From this new angle the tyrannosaurus is facing the road, teeth bared. Its muscles strain under a thick blue hide, as if it's ready to gallop across the countryside, tearing through farms, industrial sites, towns. The air around it appears scorched. Bud rolls down his window to get a better look. Thane spots the Highway 6 crossroads a hundred yards ahead, the tail end of rush-hour traffic whizzing back and forth. As the car coasts toward the intersection, flecks of water start falling and within seconds rain is pummelling the windshield. Turning on the wipers, Thane says, "Roll your window up, Bud. Don't want to catch a cold."

But beside him Budder is planets away. He lets out a vague sound from his throat, soft but growling. His face, illuminated by the prehistoric lights, is again a wide-eyed and ruddy home and his straight hair lifts off his forehead as if from static electricity. Budder. Brother. Bouncing up and down and pounding the seat, he turns to Thane and gasps, "He's looking at us! He's coming to get us!"

But Thane isn't listening. "Power is its own advantage," he mutters, switching his gaze to the field, not knowing he's spoken out loud. He gently applies the brakes at a waiting green light, then flicks the indicator. He does not turn left—*north*—toward Hamilton.

Thane parks the Skylark on a brambly grass incline, just off the dirt tracks leading up to the Dino Putt's arched sign. The rain is steady now, applauding on the vinyl roof. The dinosaurs and "pro shop," a brown trailer, wait at the end of the laneway, another fifty metres up ahead. Thane decides they will walk. Pocketing the keys when he gets out, he locks and then slams the door, makes sure he enjoys the sound. Budder doesn't budge from behind his seat belt. A small flesh-faced blur through the windshield. "Let's go," Thane says, monotone, barely audible through the rain and car walls.

Budder rolls up the window and stares at him, stubborn. "I'm staying here."

Thane says nothing. He walks around to the passenger door and, before Budder can jam the lock pin down, throws the door open so hard he has to block it with his body to stop it from slamming back. He grabs Budder by his collar and yanks him out roughly through the fastened seat belt. "Don't. *Doooon't!*" But Budder is already plopped down on the slick grass, his legs still flailing so that he slips and falls down on his ass. He starts crying for real.

"Quit it," Thane says, and yanks the boy up once more, his lips firm as a gun barrel. He bats Budder's behind, half brushing off the mud, half spanking.

Budder squeals, but suddenly swallows back the sound and fixes Thane through his tears. "You liar," he hisses.

"You had it coming," Thane says, toneless once more, dragging the boy with him toward the trailer. Halfway there Budder shakes free of Thane's white knuckles, but keeps walking three paces behind.

The parking lot—a clearing of mashed-down grass—is empty, except for a ten-speed leaning against a Pepsi vending machine. Beyond the dinosaurs and trailer a tractor is slowly trundling up and down the length of the driving range, gathering balls in a metal contraption fixed to the back. Thane's arms are aching from the driving, his right calf a big cramp. He stops and, pointing to the back of his leg, says, "Kick me here."

Budder frowns, "No."

"I won't hit you, Bud." Thane says, impatient. "Now, kick me, chump, or I'll—"

Budder's kick cracks hard against Thane's left leg, buckling it, nearly sending him to the ground. The little boy rears back for one more, face determined. But calmly Thane says, "Once is enough," trying not to smile, and Budder uncoils slowly, his chest still heaving. "Good," the older brother says. "Now come on." He strides the rest of the way bow-legged, shoes spitting water. Budder follows for a few feet, then jogs and catches up to his side.

The teenager in the trailer has been watching them. As they march across the grass lot, running shoes and pant cuffs black with wet, he sits chewing gum in the concession-style window, sizing up one brother, then the other. His slow gaze rests finally on the older brother, who has taken out a leather wallet and is now leafing through a thin collection of bills. As he steps up to the counter, the teenager smacks his gum and drawls, "We're closed."

"You don't look closed," Thane says, surveying the baskets of golf balls on the counter, putters hanging between long nails on the wall.

"Yeah, well," the teenager gives a vague tilt of his head, looks over the brothers at the Skylark parked down the laneway. A wiry black bug of a moustache twitches.

"Yeah, well, *what?*" Thane snaps.

"Well, it's raining and I'm getting off at eight and you guys don't have time to finish a round."

"What time is it now?"

The guy yawns. "You got a watch. *You* figure it out."

"I want you to tell me."

Acting bored, but sizing up this mouthy kid in the hockey

jacket, the teenager languidly blinks at his wrist. "Seven fifty-two and counting. Happy?"

"I wanna see the dinosaurs up close." Budder's whining.

"Jesus," Thane mutters to himself. "Two *hours* it took us?" Then, pulling a five from his father's wallet, he smacks it down. "Get me a couple of balls."

"I told you, I'm not renting you any—"

"I'm *buying* the fucking things. Now, give 'em to me. Two balls."

"Yeah. Two balls!" Budder chirps, his chin resting on the counter.

Eyes zoning in on the little boy, the teenager smirks. "What are you gonna do, little Chief Two Balls? *Kick* 'em around the course?"

"Maybe," Budder says, oblivious.

"Yeah, not before I kick your ass around it."

"You talk to him like that again," Thane steps back and speaks quietly, though his fists are clenched, "and I'll break you in half."

The teenager claps the fluttering five-dollar bill down flat on the counter. "Pssh, yeah, *right.*" He leans over and nods at Thane's crotch. "Like I'm scared of a kid who pisses his own pants."

"It's pop," says Budder.

"And I guess you got those stitches shaving," the teenager scoffs, then looks shiftily again at the car.

In spite of themselves, Thane's fingers pass gently over his lip, then he spits, "What if I did? Looks like you could do with some—"

"*Fuck* you," the teenager says in a bored chime, turning away and grabbing a jacket.

"Not until you give me the fucking balls first."

Ignoring Thane, the kid pockets the cash and starts clearing the baskets off the counter, humming, mock happy.

Budder pouts, "Thane, I want to go home before—"

"Sssh, Bud—hey, you fucking asshole!" Thane bangs the wall of the trailer. "I'm not going to tell you again! No bullshit! Either give me the—"

The teenager turns around, two pock-marked, red-striped balls clacking in his hand, and points between the brothers at the car. "Those your folks' wheels?"

"Yeah." Thane turns around and looks at the Skylark, stunned. "So?"

"Where are your folks?"

"In the car," Thane says.

The teenager squints. "I don't see 'em."

"It's *raining* for Chrissakes!" Thane shouts. "*I* can't see 'em from here, even."

"Yeah, but you should be able to see an outline or something."

Thane bites at some stitch thread and mutters, "They're taking a nap."

"That right?" The teenager smirks, his head tilting. "Maybe I should go down there, take a look."

Thane shrugs. "Fuck if I care. You'll just get wet for nothing."

Smiling down at Budder this time, the teenager asks, "Your folks sleeping in the car, little buddy?"

Budder turns around, toe of his running shoe squeaking against the grass, and stares for some time at the Skylark. "Yeah," he looks up at Thane, "they're real tired. Daddy caught a cold 'cos the window was open and now Mommy's looking after him."

"Aw," the teenager says, "isn't that sweet? No wonder they're lying down." Before Thane can think to grab at him, the guy has stepped back and is now threading on his jacket, the golf balls reappearing cheaply out of a denim sleeve. "Well, kid, I hope your dad gets better real soon."

Budder works his toe into the damp earth. "Me too."

"Yeah, thanks for your sympathy," Thane frowns, one hand clapping for the golf balls.

"Jesus," the teenager smiles, fake aghast, "you don't give up, do you, tough guy?"

Thane holds his hand out. After hesitating a moment, the teenager steps up gingerly and, making sure he's at arm's length, drops the balls into Thane's palm. As soon as they've clicked together, he pulls up the counter by its rope handle, claps down the top half of the booth window and locks the two boards together from inside. "Thank you, come again."

"Hey!" Thane smacks the trailer. "What about the change?" He pounds the wood, his open palm now balled into a fist. "I want my fucking change!" Inside, the teenager's laughter is a giddy, embarrassed titter. Budder cries for his brother to stop, pulling at his arm, but Thane shoves him aside. "Go get Dad's stick from the car."

"No."

Thane lunges at him, but quickly checks himself and hands Budder the balls, before storming over the parking lot to the Skylark. His breath steams in front of him. He tries the driver's side door, locked, then fumbles out his keys and swings it open, throwing the seat forward. The stick is pinned under a jumble of gear, including the guitar, which has flopped over face-down on top of the gutted hockey bag. Thane plants his foot on the door jamb and pulls as hard as he can. The stick jostles free, half its yellow tape ripping from the handle, a metallic, naked note twanging so that he's frozen watching the guitar pirouette and fall between the two front seats before it rock-a-byes slowly to rest.

"Thane!" Budder shouts from the trailer. "He's taking off!" Thane looks up and sees the teenager scrambling around the pop machine, grabbing his bike and mounting it from a running start, giggling. Budder chases him for a few yards and kicks at the back tire, but the teenager has gained speed by now and is barrelling toward the laneway. His shrill laugh swarms around their heads, gets tangled in the treetops.

"Two balls plus two losers equals five bucks!"

Slamming the car door, Thane strides back up the laneway, the hockey stick swinging firmly in his hands. The teenager's tires are spraying water in a silver wake behind him. There's only one way for him to go; the laneway is bordered on one side by the brambly bank, on the other side by a chain link fence. When he sees Thane still coming at him, unwavering, the teenager stops pedalling, his face suddenly slack, pale under the lights. A high, shaky whine snakes out from his throat. He stands up and then starts pedalling full force behind bullets of laughter again, his skinny legs a smear of faded denim. Thane slides the stick through his hands so that he's now holding it fully extended. His fingers wrap white around the rain-slicked handle. Little more, he thinks, and that's all she wrote. So close now he can hear the bike's chain clanging, the teenager's breath under the laughter.

"Keep laughing," Thane says, just above breath. "That's it. Ha. Ha." He wields the stick like an axe, winding it up and cutting it forward through the air: hisssss. The teenager tries to swerve too late, his face is wind rain breath smoking out of teeth the hole there hairy blue around the edges frown asking me what are you gonna do kid you gonna kill me kill everybody sirens his pupils dilating furious. On the swing forward the tape unravels, leaving the stick to fly through air alone: a broken one-way boomerang splashing onto the grass some forty feet away, halfway between Thane and Budder. The teenager still barrels without a scratch down the lane, silent until he reaches the highway. Once there, he slams on the brakes, tire arc burned into the gravel, and shouts, "Chickenshit!" Shaky, he pulls away, insults wheeling down the road. Thane still walks straight ahead toward the trailer, with the ribbon of yellow tape still fluttering in his hand. He doesn't look back toward the highway.

"He laughed like a girl," Budder says.

"No, he didn't," says Thane. "He laughed like a coward who knows he's a coward and doesn't care."

"He was lucky! I almost got him, but he was too fast!" Budder shouts. "You coulda got him, Thane. You coulda! He had it coming!"

"Nah." Thane groans as he picks up the stick. "He didn't have it coming, Bud." He wraps the straggling tape around his wrist and musses up Bud's soaked hair. "Nobody else has got it coming." He puts his arm around the smaller boy and leads him past the trailer. "Let's go play with the dinosaurs."

They step under the bank of lights, like football-field lights, the raindrops huge and individually bright, warm stars. A sign at the first hole says: Please Don't Touch the Dinosaurs. The tyrannosaurus waits at the end of the first hole, its eyes not furious and yellow, but black, punched-out holes. From here its body sags more than stands, as if weighed down by rainwater. The blue skin is faded, watery.

"Can't we just go home?"

"No," Thane says, matter-of-fact. But his tone softens afterwards and he acts excited as he points toward a dinosaur at the end of the course. "Look, Bud. A stegosaurus! Look at the plates on its back! We don't see many of those at home, eh? He's waiting for us on the back nine!"

"But why no-*ot?*" Budder stops, folds his hands behind his back. "Why can't you drive me *home?*"

"'Cos." Thane sighs, stepping onto the squelchy AstroTurf of the first hole. "We'll run out of gas before we get as far as Steelford and that's the only place I know I can get it. And stop being a wuss!" He smacks the blade of his stick down, water jumping. "Shoot me a ball."

Bud's chin starts quivering, "Geez, Thane. How're we gonna—"

Thane flashes him a don't-mess-with-me look. Sulking, Bud chucks a ball onto the fake grass. With a flick of his wrist Thane stops it dead. "You gonna play or what?"

"With Daddy's *hockey* stick?"

"No," Thane snaps, sarcastic, "with your fucking head. Come on." Budder steps up mistrustful, but is soon held at arm's length. "Stay back a minute, Bud. Watch me first." Thane slides his hands down so they cover the *K* and first *o* in *Koho,* then hunches over the ball, putting like someone would normally putt, except that the butt end of a hockey stick is tucked tight against the left side of his head. *After I make this shot—and I'm gonna make this shot—I'll lead him through one step at a time, wrap my arms round and show him where to hold the club and that way he won't be so cold for a while, so wet.* He hasn't noticed that the rain's stopped. He takes a couple of practice swings, checks to see if his brother's paying attention: Budder blinks. Thane doesn't feel his stitches stretch when he smiles back down at the ball.

"Thane?"

And one day when he hears that thunder and lightning that makes him shit his pants I'll tell him, Don't let it get to you, Bud. Imagine you're the thunder just like I told you to imagine you're the one who's punching and not being punched when a fight breaks out on the ice.

"Thane."

And I'll tell him to always have respect for his elders but at the same time not to let anybody ever tell him what to do except his—except his mother and me— and to walk with his chest out and to always tell the truth even if it means he pisses folks off.

"Yeah, what is it, Bud?"

And when he gets to be my age I'm going to tell him not to let a girl know you like her unless you're damn sure she likes you. And then I'm going to teach him how to skate for real, and tell him how if he's got power he doesn't need any advantages 'cos that's cheating, and I'll tell him to keep his head up and his stick on the ice, and—

"Thane?"

"*What* already?"

"Thane, is Mommy leaving us?"

When Thane connects, he hits the golf ball square and hard as a slapshot. It skitters over the green surface, hydroplaning until it caroms off a bumper and skips off the course entirely, finally stopped with a hollow *thock* somewhere against the tyrannosaurus. Thane drops the hockey stick and turns around, face bent in disbelief. "Jesus. Where'd you get that idea?"

"Mommy."

"Mom told you that?"

"No," he mutters at his shoes, "she was on the phone with Aunt Marnie and I was in the bathtub and I heard through the door 'cos I don't like it when the door's closed. She—"

"Speak up, for Chrissakes!"

Budder shuts his eyes tight and shouts. "She was saying how the doctors were being nice to her but she could see it in their eyes so she wanted to hit this one doctor 'cos he was always saying the bright side is this and the bright side is that and she didn't see any bright side at all, she was at her wits' end, she said—" he takes a deep breath, and talks normally now— "and then she was saying how she wouldn't want the same doctor because she'd want it straight, no hitting around the bush. So she could make the necess— so she could make arrange—" another breath "—so she could do something. And then she said she was tired and asked Marnie when she'd be able to make it down by to pick her up, and she told her to take care driving."

Thane stands washed out, silent. He doesn't notice how, under the white bank of lights, his clothes have started to steam.

"But she didn't mean it like *that,* Bud," he says finally. "She was just saying *if* she was sick. She's not going anywhere, for Chrissakes." He turns away from Budder and crosses the AstroTurf and steps off onto the thick grass surrounding the tyrannosaurus. Standing beside it, the dinosaur's barely taller than he is. And even here under the bank of lights, he can't locate the ball's red stripe. He turns 360 degrees, still no ball, and on the way round sees Budder pick up the hockey stick and drop his ball, jumping back from the splash. The stick is twice his height; he's wrestling it, its shaft knocking hard against his ear every practice swing he takes. But his face seems placid, immune. He starts singing softly, in a voice that's high and emotionless:

> "Budder, Budder, he's got a putter
> Now what's Budder aiming to do with that putter?
> Is he gonna steal it, no…"

He's singing it right this time, Thane thinks, *for the first time. Words, tune, everything. Except* putter *is* butter. *Clever boy. Clever, like Dad on that birthday when he threw in different words for all the guys there, and they were all blown away 'cos it was like he'd thought so much about all of them, even though he'd never even seen some of those guys till he came in home from work that night.*

> "Is he gonna pet it? No.
> He gonna kiss it? Ha ha, no.
> He gonna kill it? Hell, no…"

There, a few inches above the ground, is a hole in the tyrannosaurus's leg. A round, black inverse mole on its blue skin, but tufts of white making it ragged around the edges. Thane bends down and prods at it with his finger, feeling it give. He taps the skin. Hollow. He works his fist into the hole, enlarging it. Then he forces the length of his arm into the dinosaur's leg. *And my song no different. Couldn't help it. Only had so many notes. The chorus always coming at the same time, always telling him here's what's going to happen.*

"Is he gonna throw it? No!
Gonna lose it? No!
Gonna shoot it? No!"

Both of them poured into us. Fifty-fifty. Mom's eyes passed to me, sort of to Bud too, except when it's sunny. I got her hair. Budder got Dad's. Straight, brown. Dark brown by the time we're older, they say. The teeth Mom's, definitely. My hands thick, wrists and fingers. Shoulders courtesy of Dad. Budder scrawny now, but give him time they say. They say they say. Say we're the spitting image, but they can't say who from who.

"Look out, 'cos Budder's got a putter,
Budder's got a putter."

All he hears after Bud's done the chorus is a thin hiss from the highway. He kneels down in the long grass beside the tyrannosaurus now, reaching into its darkness. He shuts his eyes, thinking this will help, and scrambles around in there. He doesn't see Budder behind him, tensing up. He doesn't know Bud will purse his lips and swing hard, nearly falling. How the putt will dribble a few lonesome feet, then kick off a bumper and somehow gain its second wind, running downhill through a tunnel, straight toward the hole. Budder will gasp, but Thane will only hear his own breath and the scraping of his vinyl jacket against the dinosaur's wound as he leans against it, grasping at the dead dry grass inside, cheek pressed hard to its skin. Clammy, pliant, ready to give. Bud will start stutter-stepping behind the ball. Stick held high above his head, like a gun carried over a river. He'll be panting "Go go go," and Thane will hear this without listening. He'll open his eyes and see, an inch from his face, printed letters under the blue paint's gloss. *Hamilton Spectator Sports,* November 26, 1981. "Ti-Cats Finish off Argos with Roar, Not Whimper." He won't see his brother's mud-stained behind wagging happy down the mini fairway, chasing after the white-and-red blur. He won't hear the sound of a golf ball rattling around in hollow plastic. He'll feel something hard in the blackness. *There.*

"Yoo-*hoooo!* I got it!"

"Huh?" Thane wrenches his arm back out, ball included, ripping the dinosaur flesh but the skin is paper. A whole page of newsprint tears out from the inside, and it won't let go of his arm. He waves at it, but it won't let go. Why, he asks himself, would anyone make a dinosaur out of paper?

Budder screams, "I got it in, Thane! I got one in a hole!"

Thane shakes off the newspaper and swivels around on his haunches to see Budder jumping up and down with the stick swinging above his head. Against the bank of lights his face is ecstatic. "I got it in and you didn't! I'm a big boy! I got it in a hole!" When Thane steps onto the AstroTurf and starts running toward him, Budder opens his arms and walks forward, beaming, but he slips and Thane is there to catch him in a bear hug. "Way to go, Bud," he whispers. "Way to go." They stay holding each other for a long time before Thane finally lets go and steps back and calmly says, "My turn now." He takes the stick gently from his brother's hand and splashes away.

Bud shouts, "Hey! No fair! You got a turn already!" Thane doesn't hear. He walks straight to the tyrannosaurus, then stops short before it, face to face. Its eyes are ugly lidless holes, clumsy and accidental as the hole he drove in there himself. On its snout he can make out a jigsaw of old news items, advertisements, while up close its teeth are triangular chunks of cardboard cut ragged and pointy, painted white. An upside-down Pizza Delight logo on this tooth here. He steps back two paces, winds the ball up. "Don't hurt it!" Budder covers his face, peeking through finger cracks.

At the last second, Thane hurls the ball as hard as he can into the field beside them. They both watch as the tiny white comet's trail is sucked into darkness. Beyond the field, Thane sees the dull yellow glow of Hamilton to the north, its sulphur clouds hanging low, the clouds packing the light down tight to the earth so there is barely a sliver of brightness. Somewhere out on the highway, between the city and where he stands, a siren begins a low wail. Red and blue lights on the highway. Thane slings the stick over his shoulder, looks back at the papier mâché dinosaur. Then he turns to Bud, his eyes flat.

"No! No!" Budder runs at him, but Thane has already spun around and brought the stick down across the dinosaur's chest; it crumples forward, lunging at him, its tiny forearms snapping. He takes another swing and this time its head is cracked open through the mouth, splitting in half and spraying white powder, slumping onto the ground with a tired creak. Before Budder can push him away, kicking at him, screaming for it all to stop, Thane stamps on the half of the skull housing the eyes. It puffs open like a snapdragon, white stuff hitting their clothes.

The siren is clearer now, higher in pitch. Red and blue light flutters against the near sky. The tyrannosaurus is a dusty blue mash of rainwater and paper and Budder is lying down on the ground beside it, spent and heaving and muddy. Thane stands over him, watching a pair of police cars emerge from behind a row of trees, lights flashing. "Hey, little man," he says quietly. "If you're smart, you'll learn how to take it and pretty soon you won't feel a thing."

Budder scrambles to his feet and tugs at Thane's sleeve—"Hide! We gotta hide!"—but when he doesn't budge, Budder runs alone toward the Skylark, slipping and falling over and over again. He wrenches the door open and dives into the back seat just as the first police car pulls into the laneway, spitting gravel and mud. Thane turns away and walks unhurried through the miniature golf course, red and blue swirling in the air around him. He lands a single blow to the neck of a diplodocus. The head, which was made to look like it was chewing at a tree's leaves, stays lodged in the branches, the top half of the neck left hanging there, snowing down white powder. He lances the stick through a stegosaurus's chest, then pulls back and the whole front of the thing blossoms open before a man's deep voice says, "That's enough, son," and the stick is plucked effortlessly from his hands. The sirens swoop into silence.

Thane whirls around, fists flying weakly, but there's only light. Floodlights, headlights and alleylights of the two cruisers, flashing reds and blues. He fans fingers in front of his eyes and squints. He can make out only the large silhouette of a man walking away from him, the hockey stick swinging easy at his side, its blade skimming inches above the ground, until the figure's swallowed up by white. And out of the same bright hush, the shape of a woman. She bustles forward, her high heels uncertain on the wet grass, the halo of her hair curly and tight. Her shadow is some twenty feet long and it stabs at the whitewashed ground between them, yet when she draws near the boy finds himself thinking they are the same height. He stands up straight before her, his arms hanging at his sides, his lips held firm. Close up her face is heavy and beautiful, a moon pulverized into white. Her eyes blurs of mascara. "Hi, honey."

"Hi," he says, barely above a whisper. "So. How'd you figure I was here?"

"Mr. Elias," she says. "He had me paged at the hospital. He said you waved. His voice was breaking, he was so concerned. Such a decent thing for him to do. Most people would've just called the police, you know." She brings her hand up gently, hesitantly, to his face. Accepting it, he doesn't move, yet she draws back from his cheek, her rings slow in receding.

"Car needs gas."

"Okay," she nods. "Where's your brother?"

Thane glances over her shoulder at the Skylark. He swallows and turns back to her face. She makes a motion with her lips but they don't obey her. Her eyes buckle and Thane's legs tremble and then give out and before he knows it he's crumpled on the white wet grass, staring into nothing, rolling his head against the warmth of his mother's legs, the tears full and rivered down his face. Her hand combs his hair, nails scratching at his scalp. Her rings are cold, perfect.

"I'm just four grades higher than him."

"Hmm?"

"Budder. I'm just a kid like he is. I can't—"

"Don't worry, hon. It'll be all right."

"Mom?"

"Yes."

"He was scared…he thought that you—"

"Where is he, Thane?"

"He's in the hockey bag."

"In the *hockey* bag?"

"Yeah. In the car. He brought Dad's guitar."

"Well," she sighs. "Let's go see the little man."

His mother will extend her hand and he'll take it, hoisting himself to his feet. Strong, he'll think, still. But after they give the officers the necessary information, as they pass between the police cruisers and the tall, dark shapes of men, it'll be she who takes his arm. She'll hold on gingerly as they walk along the strip of grass beside the mud laneway. The grass will be slippery under their feet. Halfway to the car she'll catch her breath—"Oh, shoot!"—and her one heel will give, so that Thane must clutch her hand. He won't let go, but instead he'll pull his body taut, so that if she slips again he'll keep her steady, or else they'll go tumbling down together. "You're a star," she'll whisper. Their breath will plume up and gather into one column, then, almost immediately, unravel itself and be forgotten into the sky. Before them there'll be only the blue car beaded with rain and beyond it the highway hissing through the trees. And somewhere inside that high, empty sound Thane will hear the faintest stirring of music, coming perhaps from the car's interior, stopping him in his tracks as he reaches for the passenger door.

"Mom?"

"What is it, hon?"

"I remember where the pain is."

"You've got a pain? Where?"

"In Dad's song. My birthday song. He said I had a pain somewhere and we had to get all the way through the song till we found out where it was. Now I know."

"Oh. So where was it, honey?"

"Well, it wasn't in one little spot like I thought it was. It was all over. Not just me. Everywhere. There's pain all over everything in the world."

She'll let go of his arm, finally, and circle the Skylark, stopping across from him at the driver's side door. "That's not how the song went."

"How do you know?"

"I was *there,* honey, singing too. Don't you remember?"

"I don't know. I guess."

"Even still," she'll say, "your father would've never sung you a song, on your birthday or any other day, where that happens. Ever."

"He would now. If we gave him his guitar now, I bet he'd sing it so the whole world—"

"But he *wouldn't* sing it that way, honey. You'd just lost the Six Nations Tournament the day before. You scored a hat-trick but you lost 4-3. Don't you remember? It wasn't the whole world that was in pain," she'll say, smiling. "No fancy stuff. It was your heart."

"Same thing," the boy will say, climbing into the passenger seat. "It's the same thing."

"Not if you let one or two people in there, hon." Settling herself in behind the wheel, adjusting the mirror, she'll sigh. There will be a murmur from the back seat. "Now where's my little man?" She'll peer back there and Budder, curled up in the hockey bag, his wet, shocked-up hair poking out of it, will stop humming. "Bud?"

"I'm not telling nothing," he'll mumble.

"Don't even try," Thane will say quietly. When his mother turns, ready to scold him, he'll be looking at her. "Don't believe a word he says. It was all me. He had nothing to do with it. I was the one who took Dad's keys and his credit card and I—"

"Okay, *okay.*"

Thane will stare at her mutely for some time before looking down at his hands. "I'm, you know, for the dinosaurs and the car and for being hard on Budder and, you know, how I hit him and stuff—"

"Are you saying you're sorry, Thane?"

"Yeah." Thane will nod. "That's right. Sorry."

"He forgives you, honey." His mother will turn the key over in the ignition, smile in the rear-view mirror as she puts the Skylark in D. "Right, Bud?"

"Yeah," Budder will say, surfacing behind them. "He forgives you."

Lessons from the Sputnik Diner

I LEARNED ABOUT DEATH in the kitchen. From the flies that kamikazed into the hot plate: *tss!* From the cockroaches that scuttled under the sacks of rice when I opened the walk-in cupboard door. The rotten vegetables sitting out back in the dumpster, sucking in the flies. The shrimp curled up in the freezer like embryos. Most of all I learned about death from Marcel. One night, about closing time, a bat got in through the window and flapped about under the fluorescent lights. I hit the floor, wrapped my hair in a used napkin. I could hear Grace scream-laughing from the other side of the door. Marcel came running in with a baking sheet and spiked the bat into the deep fat fryer: imagine Ethel Merman trying to sing "Whole Lotta Love" in a vat of boiling oil. I remember Marcel smiling, like he'd won a prize. Death.

Whenever I broke a dish he'd kick the swinging door open and scream, "Jack, I'm going to *keel* you!"

"My name's Buzz."

"My name's Buzz. What the fuck it matter to me. I'm still going to *keel* you, Jack!"

After a while I'd break stuff just to see him freak. One time he burst in blistered in sweat, shaking a spatula over his head. Red face. White hair shooting sparks out his hairnet.

"Don't look him in the eye," Paul the Dishwasher said.

"Shut up that mouth, Jack." The spatula now pointed at Paul's back. I snuck a look over at him. Pimply kid. Dungeons and Dragons type. He was leaning over the big stainless steel sink, facing the wall, and his shoulders were shaking. I bit my lip, started shredding the lettuce. But when I saw Marcel still glaring at us, chin up like Marlon Brando, I couldn't help snorting. Bad habit. Paul's shoulders were shaking lots now; he was laughing donkey-style. Marcel jumped for him, snatched a dirty plate out of his hand and smashed it against the floor. "Now you clean up *two* plates, dishpig! *You!*" He pointed at me. "Turn that radio down and why no hairnet on that mess?"

I put the tape deck on pause, turning it down being sacrilege. "Funk #49" by the James Gang. Joe Walsh when he could still play guitar half sober. I turned back and stared at the fishnet on Marcel's sweaty head. Him nodding slow, waiting for an answer.

"Hey, Marcel."

"What?"

"Two minutes for looking so good."

He ignored Paul donkey-laughing into the sink. Gave me a tap on the head with his spatula instead and then smiled mean. "You funny guy, eh? Yeah, pretty soon you be funny dead guy." He kicked the door open again, whispering through his teeth, "I *keel* you, Jack. Oh, yes…"

When the door swung back, Grace walked in with a too-tight blouse and a half-eaten Reuben. "You shouldn't talk to him like that. He's upset."

"No shit," I said.

"Vivien's threatening to chop off her ring finger. Says she's sick of waiting for Marcel to put something shiny round it."

"If she does," Paul said, "ask her if I can have it for science class."

Me and Grace raised our eyebrows at each other. Hers were thicker than mine. She shoved the plate of Reuben down on the counter and put her hands on her hips. "Too much sauerkraut."

"It's a Reuben sandwich."

"The woman's a bitch. I'm not going to go back out there and tell her it's a Reuben sandwich."

"Tell her she's a bitch then."

Grace's eyebrows kinked up like black squirrels. Her arms dropped and she laughed, kid-style, teeth biting her bottom lip while her face blushed over. I always felt embarrassed when she did this. It didn't go with the rest of her, the short black hair curled tight around her head. She gave me a soft hip-check and said, "Ham and eggs, a Western, and Marcel says if you don't wear a net at least put your hair in a ponytail."

"Yes'm."

She swept up a couple of new orders and waltzed out again. I watched the zipper on her hip jangle. And her legs, they were freshly shaven because each pore was a shallow brown moon just darker than the skin around it. When the door swung back and forth I could hear strains of "Blue Bayou" on the juke box, Marcel saying, "Not bad for a blind guy," and someone laughing after it.

"I got one thing to say," Paul said.

"Huh?"

"Hospital."

Paul said some pretty weird things. Half the time I just nodded. This time I laughed dumb like I knew what the fuck he was talking about, and tried to wipe the bacon grease from my hair. I felt something else, sticky, on my hand and fore-head. When I looked down the lettuce was soaked with red-black blood. There was the lettuce shredder still whirring around and here was my picking finger, hanging open by the tendons.

"Hospital," I said.

Marcel opened the Sputnik Diner during the Hagersville tire fire of 1990. Said it was an act of God that started the restaurant and a bunch of *steenk*ing kids that started the fire. His grand opening sign said: Why Go to a Pile of Burning Tires in Hagersville When You Can Go to the Moon? Eat at the Sputnik Diner. It covered both windows and the door; customers had to crawl under it to get inside. I think most people only read as far as *Moon* anyway, because the Sputnik never was Grand Central Station. When Marcel bought the place, a family was squatting in what was supposed to be his upstairs apartment—a woman called Vivien, her little boy and girl. Marcel didn't have the heart to kick them out, so for the first couple of weeks he slept on the black and white diamonds of the diner floor. Suitcase for a pillow, old menus for a blanket. One night Vivien felt so sorry for him she let him come up and share her fold-out couch. The next morning he woke up to a fingernail tracing the edges of his pubic hair. Four years later and he was still waking up with her beside him, though he'd bought a Craftmatic bed during the Gulf War.

Nowadays he only went upstairs if he was drunk. Most afternoons he hung the Closed sign up in the window, sat behind the counter with his gin and lemonade, and jawed with George and George, a couple of old pisspots grinning across from him. The first George ran the concession stand at the arena; the second was on pogey. They both laughed at everything Marcel said, as long as the booze kept coming. When Vivien came down the laughing always stopped. Shaky hands running through greasy hair, glasses of gin and lemonade shoved under the counter. One night, when Grace was working close, Vivien stormed downstairs, walked straight for the cutlery drawers, pulled out a Ginsu knife and held it at arm's length. "Here."

"What?" said Marcel.

"Here. Why don't you get it over with?"

"Aw, Vivvy, not again…"

"Just drive it in right here," she pounded her bony chest, "right between these tits you used to rub your fucking frog face in!"

"Vivvy, Vivvy, why you say these things? In front of my guests."

"Your guests, my ass! Look at them, they're starting to shake *now,* they've had to hide their drinks from me for thirty seconds."

"Aw, no, Vivvy. You're wrong."

"Fucking right I'm wrong! Been wrong ever since you walked in with that suitcase and that stupid white hair on your head. Wrong waiting for four years—*four fucking years!*—for you to come around and at least call the kids by their real names, just once. Sean was waiting for you to come up and play Super Mario with him ever since he got home from school, and here you are pissed with these losers and he's asleep on the floor with the joystick in his hand."

Marcel shook his head. "Good kid, that Sean."

"How would *you* know? You're too busy pissing money down the drain with one hand and hiring curvy slut waitresses with the other. And besides," she said, "his name is Lance."

"Ouch," said George.

Marcel sighed, turned an it's-the-gin-talking smile on Vivien. But all he saw was the cash register and soft drink fountain. The thud of footsteps and then a door slamming upstairs.

"Marcel."

"Yes, George."

"That woman's got a mouth on her."

"You're right there."

"Yeah," said George. "And she's got a face for chopping wood on."

"You say that again, my very best friend, and I will *keel* you."

That night Marcel clambered up the stairs, his hands fumbling for the walls in the darkness. The apartment door was locked. When his eyes adjusted he saw the Ginsu knife stuck in the wood just above the peephole. He pressed his back against the door and slid down to his knees, tears lapping over his face.

"Fucking knife," he said.

At least, that's what Grace told me. "Marcel tells me everything," she said. "I mean everything."

It was a slow morning at the Sputnik. We sat at a window booth, nursing coffees and praying no customers came in. I listened as she filled me in, staring at the circuit between her neckline and her face: happy and freckled. But her eyelashes were monsters. Small birds could have used them as springboards, dove right in her coffee cup. I got tangled up in those lashes, had to shake my head hard, tell her start over again.

"I said Marcel came down here from Quebec—"

"Surprise, surprise. Don't you hear him dinging the bell every four seconds so he can shout out he's the former Québécois arm wrestling champion?"

"Yeah, yeah," she said. "Thing is, I think he's wanted." She was bent over the table now, whispering. When she blinked I felt the slightest draft. "His name isn't really Marcel," she said. "It's something La-something."

"Guy Lafleur?"

She slapped my arm. Spilt coffee. "Smartass. That's a baseball player or something, isn't it?"

"Sure."

Grace had those eyelashes and a white blouse that strained full when she bent over the tables, but she had an imagination on her too. "He doesn't have a driver's licence, for one," she said, "and notice how he always pays for stuff in cash? He's got a wife back there too."

I shook my head and looked out the window. Her reflection was spread out against the parking meters, staring wide-eyed at me, nodding. We both looked over at the counter, where Marcel was talking, confidential, over a cigarette with George and George, waving the smoke in their faces. Them laughing, hands fidgety.

"You think he *keeled* someone?" I said.

She ignored that. "This one time, before you started here," she whispered, "I saw him out back by the dumpster with these two guys in suits—never seen them before—and he opened up this briefcase. Full of money. When one of those guys zipped it up and shook his hand, Marcel saw me, just for a second, in the window. Man, was I shitting bricks. He never said nothing about it though."

"So," I said, and smiled. "He doesn't tell you everything."

She shrugged, a little self-conscious, and smiled back at me. "Just about."

Marcel had stopped jawing with George and George. He was giving us the evil eye now. I nodded at him, watched his face get a bit pinker.

"Get your ass out of gears, Jack. I don't pay you for the chatting up of girls."

I learned about carrots by the juke box.

Except for the Georges and a big Dutchman called Noel, every guy who walked into the Sputnik had the same name:

Greyhound Jack from the bus station. Ninety-something years old, also known as That Old Bastard. Ordered the lunch special number one every day of the week, never failing to bitch that his ice water was too cold. Walked with two canes. If you went to the Greyhound office at noon, you'd have to spend a good two hours on the ripped red Naugahyde couch in the "lobby" before That Old Bastard walked the single block back from his Sputnik lunch.

Black Jack. Swaggered into the door every morning with long, dyed-black hair, a black fringed leather jacket and snakeskin boots, black. Also a perfect blond little boy holding tight to his hand. Only thing the boy said was "Daddy Daddy

Daddy can I have juice?" Black Jack would poke a stub of white bread into a sunny-side-up and read *The Toronto Sun* in silence. Export "A" cigarette always lit in the bread-mopping hand. "Crazy Little Thing Called Love" always on the juke box. I used to play minor hockey with Black Jack. He's experienced some changes since then. Alias Thane.

Call-the-Cops Jack. A middle-aged Harley-Davidson guy with hair so thin and blond he'd pass for the grandfather of Black Jack's kid. Taught his own son to box from an early age. Kept him locked in the garage for the whole of August '76, opening the door every four hours to "pound the living shit out of the boy." This little story he told with his chin up and his paw curled round a bottle of Coors Light. "Turned the little crud into a man." I think his son was serving a third term in Millhaven Penitentiary.

Heart Attack Jack. This name covered several regulars.

It didn't take long before I saw that on busy mornings, whenever Marcel dinged the bell and called out, "Jack! Continental breakfast!" ten or more men would rush to the counter with their receipt. Sometimes fights would break out, blood and HP Sauce all over the floor's black and white diamonds. Big Noel would have to step in then, laughing and choking back carrots. Noel was kind of a freelance bouncer. A dumptruck driver by trade, he spent his nights at the Melbourne Hotel, mornings at the Sputnik, afternoons at the welfare office. He had the body of a bear, but was giddy as a cheerleader. If anybody made a wisecrack or even looked at him goofy, Noel started giggling. Problem was, he always ate raw carrots alongside his bacon and eggs. At least once a week someone would notice him get out of his chair quietly and walk to the washroom, his hands round his throat.

"S'matter, Noel? You choking?"

Nod nod, yes yes.

"It's those carrots, Noel."

Nod nod.

Once I caught him all purple in the face, leaning on the juke box. I hurdled the counter and dove right into the Heimlich, but he was too huge: my hands couldn't reach round the other side. Two other men tried before an off-duty cop gave it a good heave and the chunk of carrot shot out and splatted the Wurlitzer logo. "You've Got a Friend" by James Taylor was playing. Noel started to giggle.

It got so whenever Noel sat down with his bacon and eggs and raw carrots, Marcel stood back and surveyed the room for the man with the longest arms.

"Hey, Jack!"

I learned to play guitar in Grace's bedroom, between the butterflies and ice.

On Sunday I got off early because Marcel was sick of seeing my *heepy* face. I hung around the place just to bug him, pouring quarters in the juke box, whipping my hair around to the Talking Heads, shouting out the kick-ass staccato part about it being 365 degrees. Finally Marcel threw down his spatula and said, "Okay, I make you a deal, Jack. You play that song one more time, I get to punch you in the face."

I made like I didn't hear him, just danced and watched Grace flirting with the customers. "I thought you had a heart attack last week, Charlie! ... Is that right? ... Well, no sex for you for a while, eh?" Charlie must've been at least seventy-five. I watched Grace lean over the empty tables, looking up at me every few seconds, her tongue sticking out the side of her mouth as she wiped. Half an hour later my tongue was doing the same. Me tugging at the zipper on her skirt, she breathing into my mouth, her hand a spider inside my jeans. When she saw my bikini briefs she laughed kid-style. Shut up shut up. Thick black hairs jabbed out from her underwear like calligraphy. For a second I had this image of Marcel naked on his Craftmatic. It went away when I fell on top of her and the bed, our ankles tangled up in denim and black cotton.

She was sighing somebody else's name when I heard the noise under the bed. Hollow, like a boat. Then a spring popped out of the mattress, dragged across strings. An open chord. I slipped out of her and leaned over the side, dragged out the hunk of wood and metal. It was a real old no-name beater with scratches all over and a bent tuning peg, and the pickguard was attached to the body with metal screws.

"It was my father's," she said, and rolled over, scooping an ice cube from the glass on the floor. She placed the ice in between her legs and closed her eyes. Her breasts, in the light, looked pockmarked, like fallen dough. On the wall behind her was a glass case: butterflies pinned to a white background. One had fallen and lay crumpled on the bottom, the pin still sticking through its dry black shell, its wings busted like tiny shards of glass all around it.

"What's with you and butterflies?"

"I don't know," she said softly. "They change without thinking about it. Grow up to be what they dreamed about and everybody loves them."

Seeing them up there, either impaled or fallen, I couldn't help saying, "Not everybody." I kneeled down on the carpet, strummed the open strings until my penis was caked dry and only a few beads of water glistened on her wiry hair. "It was your father's."

"Hmm?" she said, opening her eyes.

"I said, the guitar, it *was* your father's."

In two weeks I'd learned the chords G, D, C, and A major and minor. I played "Tequila Sunrise" till my fingertips turned green from the rusted copper-bound strings. One night I was halfway through the second verse, getting to the "hollow feeling" line, when Grace jumped off the bed, saying she hated the Eagles and was going out for ice.

I learned about *Ben Hur* by the window. Grace's white blouse was in my face, she filling up my coffee. "Marcel said he'd marry me if he wasn't so old." I told her not to say stuff like that while I was eating. When she was done with another order, she slid into the booth and smiled across from me. "I got him into bed once."

"What?"

Vivien and the kids were away one weekend. Marcel was giddy as Noel the Dutchman, shuffling along to "Blue Bayou," twirling Grace around whenever she came by with a menu or a plate of steaming stuff. Him singing along with the Wurlitzer in a French-Canadian accent. Then he'd turn to a George, smoke dangling. "Not bad for a blind guy, that Roy Orb*ee*son."

Marcel closed the place at eleven o'clock that morning, broke out the gin and lemonade, and let the jukebox play till nobody wanted to go back to Blue Bayou ever. Around midnight Grace came back to the Sputnik to check up on him. He was blinking slow at the TV, George and George slumped unconscious over the counter across from him. His face looked thin, naked. "They got this machine," he said, never taking his eyes off the screen, "it's a vacuum cleaner and it cuts your hair."

Grace helped him up the stairs, his body surprisingly light. At the door Marcel checked for the Ginsu knife and then nodded, frowning, "It's okay, we go in." Grace laughed too loud and stood in the doorway, watching him trying to take his shoes off. When he started using his teeth, she got down on her knees and pushed his face out of the way.

"Grace, my waitress."

"Hmm?"

"Ben Hur."

"Ben who?"

"No no no no no. *Ben Hur.* Greatest movie of all times. Romans and horses and Jesus and that guy who was Moses. Carlton Weston. You got to watch this man, people of your gen'ration. If I was a woman…"

"Gross," Grace said. "Now let's getcha to bed."

"Nope. You watch it with me tonight. On VHS."

She looked around, sighed, "Okay. Where's the machine?"

"Bedroom." He shrugged and closed his eyes, smiling.

Grace slid the tape in, waited for it to rewind. "Marcel," she said, gazing at the static screen. "Why'd you call it the Sputnik Diner?"

"Because this country. I am proud for being Canadian."

"But Sputnik was a Russian spaceship or something."

"Tell me lies. It's the proper name for that arm in space with CANADA on it. I'm from east of Gatineau. Proud for this country. I know… about the science."

Grace fixed her eyes on the TV till the letterbox screen

flickered up and the credits started to roll in yellow and red Technicolor. "Okay, you happy now, spaceman?"

When she turned around Marcel was sprawled out on the Craftmatic, completely naked. Little white sparks of hair shot out from between his thighs. His cock looked malnourished. He was rocking side to side, and he was crying. "The woman I live with, I don't love her."

"I know, Marcel."

"I pack my suitcase twelve times. Had it waiting under the counter, ready for going. But when I go to pick it up, my hand it reaches for the gin instead."

Grace put her hand on his knee. He took it and held it like money.

"Her face," he said, opening wet, serious eyes. "You can chop wood on it."

He fell asleep mumbling the number ten and something about hamburgers. Grace spread a blanket over him, tucked it under his feet and turned the volume way up on the TV.

"So?" I said, leaning back in the booth. "What happened then?"

She leaned over and plucked a French fry from my plate. "I don't know," she said, chewing thoughtfully. "Maybe he dreamt about Romans that night."

"Marcel. Hire a new waitress. A skinny one."

Vivien's first words after she dumped her kids and weekend baggage onto the floor. Marcel obliged, no questions asked. He took on the first girl who walked in the Sputnik's door. You could hear Anna before you saw her. Bracelets jangled from her wrists and ankles, long dangly earrings made from metal and bone whistled by her shoulders when she moved. She was a porch full of wind chimes. But the rest of her was quiet. If Grace's voice didn't know what to do with itself, Anna's was fenced in with barbed wire, her laugh a squeak with a hand in front of it. Grace's body an extrovert, Anna's thin-wristed and brown, attracted to the outskirts of rooms. And the new girl's hair was long, brown and dangerous. On a hot day there was always the chance it would get tangled up in one of the metal fans dotted round the diner.

Grace and Anna. Anna and Grace. Too opposite for real life. From my window booth I watched the differences happen as Anna moved over the black and white diamonds, her slender hips jackknifing past chairs and elbows. Me making a list of these things.

"Whatcha writing?"

"Nothing."

Tsss! Marcel was watching the differences too, flipping bacon behind the counter. Peameal. I could smell it clear across the room. I could see his teeth, yellowed from cigarettes, smiling at his girls through the grease and smoke. *Done good,* he was thinking. *Hired a new waitress, just like Vivvy said.* Problem was he kept Grace on the payroll, slating her on the same shift as Anna most days. Now Vivien stood at the kitchen door with an electrical storm crackling over her head and stared through Marcel's back, past the two Georges, to the Jekyll and Hyde waitresses pirouetting on the diner floor.

I learned about strawberries from Amburger. I was left in charge on a Sunday morning, frying up paprika hash browns and sausage on Marcel's personalized flat-top behind the counter. The Stones pouting out "Emotional Rescue" from the Wurlitzer, me doing my best Mick Jagger impression. No

Georges around to make fun of me. Vivien sleeping in upstairs. Grace wiping tables in the corner. I'd just twirled round to slap the bell when in walks six feet of fake fur, shocking pink, and hips.

Ding! She had black leather boots that funnelled up her thighs. After that it was pink spandex clammed tight round her pelvis, gold ring in her navel and a furry vest sort of thing that left the sides of her breasts bare. Her hair was dying to stay blonde. And she was carrying a little green carton of strawberries.

"Hi, handsome. Marcel around?"

"Hi."

"Hi. Is Marcel around?"

"No. Hi."

She laughed and I was twelve years old again.

"He still living with Mother Teresa?" she said, pointing at the ceiling.

I pictured a Ginsu knife in Marcel's chest. "Yes."

She laughed again, a low throat laugh. Tongue against teeth. Behind her Grace was wiping the same table she'd been doing five minutes ago. Eyebrows on fire, scowling at me. I made to push my hair out of my face, forgot it was in a hairnet.

The woman set the strawberries down and leaned over the counter. She smelled of menthol cigarettes and Grand Marnier. "Tell him Amber's at the Pump tonight." She plucked a strawberry from the pile, worked it between her lips, then punished it with her teeth. I nodded, stupid in my hairnet: *Okay.* I smelled burning. When she walked out the door I could see daylight through the gap at the top of her thighs.

Not ten minutes later Marcel straggled in with his arm

draped round Noel the Dutchman's shoulder. I was still Brillo-padding the black chunks of hash brown from the flat-top, erection fading. All Noel said was, "Three whisky doubles on the rocks...he fall down...three whisky doubles on the rocks...he fall down again." He eased Marcel into a window booth while Grace got coffee. Marcel slumped over, arm-wrestling the air. When Grace came back to the table, he grabbed for her waist, grinning, but she slapped his arm away and he flopped back in the booth with a low grunt.

"Hey, Marce," I said, carrying the strawberries waiter-style to the table. "Some chick called Amber came by and brought you these."

I felt a sharp stab in my ribs. Grace's elbow. Marcel slapped his arm down on the table and sat up straight. He ignored the coffee Grace shoved in front of him, grabbed the box of strawberries in his massive hands and stared, milky, at me. "Amburger?"

I nodded. Close enough.

A smile spread across his face like jam. "*Am*burger."

"You shouldn't have told him," Grace said, scooping another ice cube out of her glass and running it up the inside of her thigh. I watched a silver trail trickle down around the back of her leg. "He shouldn't be led on again by that...trash. She'll ruin him. And poor Vivien..." I leaned over the bed, my knees sore on the carpet, and lapped the cold up slow with the tip of my tongue. Liquid. Grace started wrapping my hair around her fist, her own hair black and rough against my cheek.

"What do *you* care about Vivien?"

"Don't know what you're saying."

"Okay," I said. "I'll rephrase. Why should you of all people feel sorry for Vivien when she calls you a slut and a—"

"Your mouth's too full. Ask me later."

Later her fingertips were drumming her pillow absently; mine were green and busy with the guitar. I had a few more chords under my belt now: E major and minor, F, B minor. Problem was I'd lost all feeling in my picking finger. The stitches from the lettuce shredder were still buried in there. My skin had grown thick over the nylon thread. Now I had to watch my strumming hand the whole time I played, otherwise I'd be fumbling at air. (Grace noticed this in bed too.) I still managed "Play with Fire," and would've got through "Comfortably Numb" too if she hadn't thrown the icewater in my face.

She sat up, her breasts slouching over her belly. "Ever since you picked up that thing our fucking's gotten, I don't know, *efficient*."

I wiped water off the strings and hit the last chord of the song. Closure. I shook the ice out of the guitar, then laid it careful across the foot of the bed and walked to the door. "Look."

Expressionless, Grace stared at me, wet and hairy by the light switch.

"Bet you five bucks my fingertips glow in the dark."

By the time I flicked the switch back on, the guitar had gone *brummm!* against the floor. Grace was bundled under the covers, facing the wall. I looked in the butterfly case for her reflection, but I couldn't see past the dead insects.

I learned about flukes from Anna. My hands were rich with liver and onions and she was dusting another broken plate into the garbage. Her body sighed. Out the corner of my eye I saw a long dark leg slip out of her skirt, scar visible above the knee. At lunchtime, after Anna brushed off a bowl of minestrone soup, I gave her the Sputnik questionnaire: a) so where you from, and b) what the hell are you doing *here:*

a) *Newfoundland.*

b) *My grandmother. She's dying.*

She stirred her coffee counter-clockwise and stared out the window. Eyes like blue granite. A car floated by in her pupils. I felt my hand, damp, tighten around my cup. Wanted to say something like *my coffee's cold,* but my eyes got caught up in a chain dangling shiny in the V of her blouse, a silver whale's tail threaded onto it.

"It's my fluke," she said, pulling it away from her skin. I nodded, cleared my throat a bit loud. Her watching me watching her. She plucked a strand of hair from her tongue, let it fall slow-motion into the tin ashtray, then stared down at her coffee. Me surprised when she kept talking, twirling the fluke between her long, shellacked fingernails. "I used to go to this little fishing village about a half hour south of St. John's. The wind off the coast there always smelled of pine trees. Always. And there was this cove where maybe twenty humpbacks used to come and...umm...play. We'd sit at the front of the boat and dangle our feet over the edge. You could see them swim under the boat and then surface right beside you. Perfect. Then: *pssh!* They'd bring their flukes up out of the water and it was like they were waving at you. Showoffs, I was thinking. I read in *National Geographic* that that's how they tell each other apart. Individuals. No two flukes are the same. Sort of a whale fingerprint."

She looked back out the window and, nodding quietly to

herself, placed the fluke flat on her chest. I swallowed a mouthful of cold coffee.

"A Chevy Impala just cruised straight through your left eye," I said.

I learned about rodents in Marcel's apartment. Marce was taking Vivvy and the kids to a trailer park just north of Canada's Wonderland; he asked Grace to mind the place for the weekend. Vivien wasn't too comfortable with the idea. Her exact words were: "I'd rather drink Tabasco in hell than have her sleep in my bed."

Marcel, making sure he stood between her and the cutlery drawers, said, "It's okay, Vivvy. We'll drop you off at the CN Tower with some *buy*noculars so you can stand up there and watch all the goings-on down here."

On Saturday night I closed the Sputnik early and went upstairs, guitar slung over my shoulder. (Almost had the 6/4 timing to "Sweet Thing" figured out, dead finger and all.) When I opened the door, Grace and Anna were running around the apartment, screaming. I thought they were pissed until a bat swooped down, ears and teeth an inch from my face. I swung the guitar around, missed, then dropped to the floor. "Coward," Anna said. While Grace was busy jumping on and off the bed, Anna caught the bat in a patchwork quilt and then swung the bundle into the corner. When our breathing died down we could hear the noise, *crick-crick-crick* like a Geiger counter, moving along the baseboards. I said "shit." Grace laughed like a kid. Anna kicked a chair out of the way and came out of the corner a minute later with the bat cricking in her hands. "Open the window."

I was still flat on the carpet, too impressed to move.

Anna nudged the window open herself, but when she threw the bat out over Singer Street she knocked a plant from the sill. A second later we heard it crash on the sidewalk. Anna shrugged, closed the window and dusted off her hands. "No casualties." I pictured a Ginsu knife in her chest.

Three more bats flew in Marcel's apartment that night. After the second one we just left the windows open, trusting they could find their own way out. Later we rummaged through Marcel's movie collection, bypassing *Ben Hur* and settling on *The Good, the Bad, and the Ugly.* Even before the Good saved the Ugly from his first hanging, Anna fell asleep on the floor in front of me. Her hair spilled across the rug like soft coral. In the flickering dark I worked it, silky, between my toes. Grace, bored with the movie, went to the freezer for a glass of ice. She came back from the kitchen with her T-shirt off, balled up in her hand. Curly hairs were visible outside the V of her underwear. Her tits looked disappointed. She said, "I think I'd like to go to Mexico."

"Actually," I said, "they made these films in Italy. Hence the term spaghetti Western."

"I don't give a shit where they were made."

We spent the rest of the night on the Craftmatic. Clint Eastwood squinting on the TV, bats making casual flights around the apartment, my cock dreaming in Grace's cold mouth, and Anna's hair swimming between my toes.

Home from the trailer park Monday morning, Vivien could only find two faults with the place: 1) a missing African violet, and 2) a stale glass of water beside the bed.

I learned about chemical reactions from Paul the Dishwasher. Tuesday morning Marcel came in the kitchen nursing a hangover. Wasn't in there two seconds before he snapped at Paul, "Turn down that racket and after you done them plates, clean out the sink, and *good!*" The big steel basin was corroded, a ring of brown rust sleeping there for what must've been years now. Paul plugged it up and dumped in a whole bottle of Windex. I was fixing up a Sputnik omelette, sprinkling cheese, onions and green peppers into the pan. Humming along to "Chuck E.'s in Love" on the classic hits station. Before the first chorus hit, Paul poured something else into the sink, and then donkey-laughed.

"'S'up, Paul?"

"Check this out," he said, waving me over. I was halfway across the kitchen floor when a blue mushroom cloud plumed out of the sink. Went up my nostrils like razorblades. I saw Paul's legs buckle, then the back of his skull go smack against the tiles. Next thing I knew I was dragging him from the basin, trying to slap him back to life, and Marcel was already peeling me away from the kid like I was papier mâché.

"Don't hit him when he is out like that, Jack."

I nodded. Okay.

"Let the little guy's body handle it. It'll know when to wake up. You don't hit nobody when they're sleeping."

I looked dumb at Marcel. Never heard him talk so quiet and sensical.

"It'll know," he said, tapping me soft on the shoulder, nodding.

For the next few minutes we said nothing, just stared down at the zonked-out teenager. Me kneeling on the tiles, Marcel standing behind me, spatula folded in his arms. Under the fluorescent lights, the walls began to hum lime green.

Objects in the room started losing their names, got naked. Pretty soon I was wiping my hands on my jeans. Behind me the former arm-wrestling champion of Quebec was slapping a cooking utensil against his chest in hypnotic rhythm. The Sputnik omelette was burnt black as cancer. Rickie Lee Jones was whining about Chuck E. being in love with her. And there was something about Paul's face under the lights too. Flaky, almost green. I half expected his pimples to start sprouting flowers. His eyelids flickered. Marcel dropped the spatula and knelt down beside me, propping up Paul's head, his big red fingers in the boy's greasy hair. Me guilty from seeing this intimate gesture. He tapped Paul lightly on the cheek. When the kid's eyes rolled open, squinting against the lights, Marcel slapped him a couple more times then punched him square on the nose. "You *lee*ttle *ee*diot! What the fuck you think you doing?! Trying to *keel* us all!!"

Before he could throw another punch I got him in a headlock, connected with a right and then—*kunggg!*—an accidental knee to the balls. Marcel's face blanched. I struggled on top of him, trying to pin him down, but he squirmed loose, grabbed a fistful of my hair, then went for the throat, shaking me like a bottle of World Series champagne till I snapped up the spatula, held it over my head guillotine-style. By now sinews were electrical cables popping out Marcel's arms. His hairnet had slipped sideways off his head and his face was glaring red back at me. "I will *keel* you, Jack... this time... *keeeell* you!"

For a moment, wind chimes. They danced in and out of the room, just above our breathing and swearing. Froze me long enough for another hand to grab my hair and something cold to touch my neck. Ginsu pressed flat against my skin.

Out the corner of my eye I saw Anna over by the steam table, hand over her mouth. Vivien burst in the door with Noel lumbering in behind her. "Stop it!" she shouted. "That's enough! Stop!" Grace let go of my hair and wordlessly handed the knife to Vivien. I heard giggling, and next thing big Noel grabbed me under the arms, plucked me off Marcel and sat me up on the counter like I was a three-year-old. I looked around the room and everyone else was crying. (Except for Paul; he was pinned under Marcel, out cold again. When he came to he only had one thing to say and I've never seen him since.) Before I knew it I was spilling tears too, saying, "What was that about, Grace? Eh? What was all *that?*" She didn't answer. She was wiping her face, staring at Marcel. When she finally blinked I realized our eyes were watering from Paul's sink cocktail.

I learned about inefficient sex on the stairs. On a Tuesday afternoon I went to the Sputnik to pick up my last cheque. Marcel wasn't around. Vivien, hot and flustered behind the counter, told me, "There's some guy looking for you." She threw me an envelope and said, "Hang on. Got something else for you upstairs."

I waited at the counter, the Georges sitting a few stools down. They both grinned over their morning bottles of Budweiser. "Ya leaving us, young guy?" George asked.

"Yes, George."

"He's going to be a rock 'n' roller," George said. "Be the next Paul Anka."

"That right?" George laughed, his head bobbing between his shoulders.

"Fuck off, George," I said, but I was laughing too.

Ding! Someone came striding in across the black and white tiles. At first he was just a shadow against the sunny window, but when he stepped right up next to me at the counter, his fists clenched, I could tell it was him. Limey, alias Luke Elias. Sad dog face of his. He was thinning on top too, even though he was about my age. One of them who got out after high school, went away to university, kidded himself he was a smart fucker, left one institution just to get trapped in another. "Hello, Buzz," he said.

"So." I grinned. "Lost a few hairs on top, eh, Limey?"

"I'd like to say you've lost a few brain cells, Buzz, but that would be impossible." While I was busy scratching my head and acting dumb as a stump, he said, "Where's my guitar?"

"Don't follow."

"Grace said you borrowed my guitar. I'd appreciate it if you could give it back." He was so serious and polite, and shaking a bit, I couldn't help laughing.

"You must be out of your tree," I said. "She gave me her old man's guitar."

"She doesn't have a father."

"How would *you* know?"

"She and I are close."

"Oh." The ceiling fans whirred. "Really."

"Yes," he said. "She's my... Sorry, um, she *was*..."

"He's gotcha by the short and curlies there, eh, young guy?"

"Shut up, George," I said. Limey was smiling at me in a major pissed-off way now. "Look, man. I don't have your guitar," I lied. "I just borrowed it for a few days, then gave it back. I don't know, maybe she gave it to someone else." Over Luke's shoulder the Georges were nudging each other, biting laughter from their lips.

"Why would she do that?" he whispered. I could tell from his face, all slack and lost, that the Limey wasn't testing me. He just stared down at his feet and asked them the same question. I was so embarrassed for him I almost swallowed my tongue.

That's when Vivien came back out the swinging door with a white T-shirt inside out and bungled up in her hand. "Found it under the couch cushions. Yours, I expect." Before she let go of it, she searched my face for a second. "Seen Marcel today?"

"Nope." I smiled. "Thanks, Vivvy."

"Bye." She didn't bat an eye.

"See ya, Luke." I patted him on the shoulder, a bit too enthusiastic, but he was miles away.

As I walked out across the black and white tiles, "Sea of Love" wobbled from the Wurlitzer. I swore I could feel Vivien's eyes dissecting my back. I stopped outside the window and, cranking up a smile, waved through the sign. But she was looking away, talking snarky to one of the Georges. Her greying hair was stuck flat to her forehead, almost black with sweat. The Limey was still at the counter, staring down at his shoes.

Click. The light was blown out in the entrance to Grace's apartment. This meant blackness, even in daytime. At the foot of the stairs I heard Grace sighing out my name. I ran up a couple of steps, stumbling over a bundle of old newspapers, then heard her voice again. I stood outside the door, listening. Knock. Knock. Squeak. Knock squeak. My name being called again. Knock. Quiet tinkle of glass. After that all I heard was a fan whirring in the darkness above me, a car horn outside. I draped the T-shirt neatly over the doorknob and walked slow down the blackened stairs.

I learned about death by long distance. *The Ten Commandments* was the CBC late night movie and I was splayed out on my parents' couch, Grace's voice crackling in my ear. She was in Albuquerque, New Mexico. Said she'd found this AT&T calling card on the bus station floor. "So here I am calling *you!*" She asked if I'd gotten any of the postcards she'd sent. I said no. Then she told me about Marcel.

"It was awful, Buzz. He was in the back of a cab, had his suitcase with him and a bottle of gin and he was spilling it all over the place. Crying. And he kept saying how he didn't want to be hurting anyone, but Amburger was waiting for him at the Zanzibar in Toronto. I couldn't stop from crying. I don't know, his hair was so white. I could see clear through it, see his scalp. You know the last thing he said?" A shaky laugh. "Drive, Jack."

I heard her voice catching on the fibre-optic line, then she said, "I went back the next day and there was this guy in a three-piece suit asking where Marcel was. He told me how much money Marce owed some people—*some people,* what the fuck does that mean? It's like he walked out of a fucking movie—I said I didn't know anything about it. And first thing Vivien does when I walk in the door is fire me. Canned Anna too. Bitch. D'you ever see her after you quit?"

"Who?"

"Vivien."

"No."

"Well, she took off too, after nobody but the Georges kept coming to the place. Just packed up the kids and left,

God knows where. Gave all Marcel's movies and shit to the Salvation Army. So after a month or so, when the dust settled, I went back and worked at the Sputnik for the new owners. Germans. Nice enough. Stayed out of sight most of the time. No matter how business was, they always said, *Things are coming along very nicely.* Sounded kinda creepy. I can't do the accent justice. I stayed there for a while longer till, you know, some shit hit the fan and they, well, I…" She laughed. "I won't bore you. That's another story."

She gave me time to say something. In the silence I could hear the ghost of another conversation, a pair of southern voices. Something about a fire.

"Oh, and Noel the Dutchman died."

"What?"

"Yeah. Few days after Marcel skipped town. Choked to death halfway to the bathroom. The Georges couldn't get their arms round the poor guy."

"The carrots."

"No," she said. "Diamond ring. It must've fallen into the scrambled eggs or something. When the coroner brought it back, no one claimed it. Then, get this, Vivien tries it on and it's a perfect fit."

"No."

"Uh-huh. Perfect."

Awkward silence. She told me about the food in the hostel, some ("get this") Mexican guy she'd met, and a fat lady who kept picking her up and dancing with her "like I was a friggin' rag doll!"

Switching the phone to the other ear, I said, "Look, I'd better go. This thing must be costing you a mint."

"No, it's all right. It's on the calling card, remember?"

"Yeah, but I really should go. Kinda busy."

"Guitar, right?"

"Huh?"

"Still playing that damn guitar?"

"Oh. Sure."

"You know, Buzz," she said quietly. "It wasn't my father's guitar. I never even—"

"I know."

"No, see, it was another guy's—you don't know him, just some guy. Story of my life. Truth is I never even knew my father. I only met him when everyone was gone and I went back to work at the Sputnik again. Well, one morning shift someone put 'Blue Bayou' on the juke box and I got the shivers. There was just this funny-looking guy sitting by the window..." She laughed. "I don't know why I'm telling you this, Buzz. I don't even like you much. It's just, I'm not the person you always figured I was, I mean, not to say that I knew or cared what you were thinking, but..."

After that her voice got far away and I started saying "yeah" in all the wrong places. When I hung up she was still saying goodbye. I switched the telephone off and set it down on the coffee table. A small pile of postcards smattered to the floor. Charlton Heston was standing before me, six inches tall and gawking at a Technicolor burning bush. Click. I stretched back out on the couch. In the darkness I saw Marcel, white hair luminous as lightning, standing alone at his personalized flat-top on the moon, still waiting for the bacon to come down. A box of strawberries levitating, half full, over the counter. *Ding!* I closed my eyes and rolled over.

"Don't put my fluke in your mouth," Anna said, shifting beside me. "It'll rust."

Painter

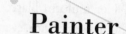

For I must say how much the gifts of Nature and my own striving for knowledge, combined with God's grace and a favourable opportunity, have done for me—I wish in this work to record the deeds of my father, which do not deserve to sink into silent oblivion…

—Anna Comnene, Byzantium, twelfth century

She wasn't even supposed to be in the Sputnik Diner that morning. It was the last April Fool's Day before the Sputnik closed for good, and she'd still been in bed when the phone rang. The first time, she said, "Ha," and rolled over and smacked the receiver down. Joke. But on the second call they shouted before she could hang up that the new girl had called in sick again. So here she was half an hour later with greasy plates slick in her hands and bags the size of sugar packets under her eyes. Her zipper wasn't jangling the staccato way it was supposed to when she jackknifed around the tables and chairs. Her uniform blared bright blue. She had a loose filling, could feel it with every step. It all got worse when some old guy threw "Blue Bayou" on the Wurlitzer. Roy Orbison, plaintive and otherworldly. She'd probably heard the song a thousand times. She held her temples, blew an invisible hair from her forehead.

Now the Wurlitzer man wanted ketchup. He was sitting at a window booth. A skinny out-of-towner with glasses and a moustache. She took the bottle of ketchup over to him, waving it through the air like a tennis racquet. The man's meal was on the table, but his hands were tucked away and he was still grimacing at his laminated menu through thick, black-rimmed glasses. Grease gelled around his untouched eggs. When he looked up, his eyes were far away behind the lenses.

"Here's your ketchup," she said. "Is everything else okay today, sir?"

"Rachel," he said.

"No," she said, raising her brows. She stuck her name tag in his face, then thought better of it and just said, "Grace."

"Oh." He blinked slow-motion behind the glasses, then snapped the menu to attention. "Get me the pancakes with blueberry jam."

"Umm, you've already got your order. Sir." She pointed with her yellow pencil, drummed it between her teeth.

He sat there blank for a second, then dropped the menu and slid the plate in front of him, hash browns spilling over the edges. "Salt," he said.

She pointed to the shaker next to the napkin canister. "Salt."

"Pepper. I meant pepper." His legs were jogging up and down under the table. He was frowning.

She snapped the pepper shaker off the next empty table and plonked it down beside the man's arm. She showed a friendly sliver of teeth. "Enjoy your meal."

"Hey!" She was halfway back to the kitchen when he shouted this. Knives and forks stopped chinking, movie-style. She rolled her eyes and twirled on one foot, ready to crank up the smile again. But when she turned around he was staring out the window, the blue blur red blur of cars zipping past his face. His skin was swarthy, his sideburns an anachronism. She stood over the table now, notepad held to her chest. She had to clear her throat to get him to look at her. He turned, blinked. "You've got sizeable hands."

She blushed. "What?"

"Your hands. They're big for a woman."

She stuffed them in her pockets, notepad and all. "If that'll be all…"

"Your mother, she has small hands, like a bird. But you," he nodded at the wrists sticking out her pockets. "Portuguese hands."

She stepped back. "Gene?"

He shrugged.

"But I'm not supposed to know you yet!" she shouted, slapping the table. "Not till 2:45 next Wednesday! This is all wrong!"

Gene unscrewed the top of the ketchup bottle. He smacked at the bottom till a gob of red splattered a dried husk of bacon on his plate.

⁂

She was supposed to meet him at the Children's Aid next week, in her counsellor's green office, where the social-work diplomas hung in gilt frames behind the wood veneer desk. She was supposed to sense him before she walked in the door, and vice versa. A ripple of white light up both their spines. He'd be clutching a bunch of dandelions, the earth still clinging to the roots, and he'd hold them out to her, soil falling all over Diane Lett's shampooed carpet. And after she took the flowers, laughing in a way that bubbled and jumped like water rolling to a boil, he'd hold her face in his solid hands. "Twenty-one years," he'd say in a vague, inscrutable accent, "they wouldn't let me see my daughter. And finally, I see her. And she has good teeth, like mine." Grace would pull away at first, then seeing his eyes sink, she'd clasp the strong, thoughtful hands and press them back to her cheeks. "You picked these off the lawn out there, didn't you?" she'd say. He'd nod, mock-ashamed. He'd be wearing baggy jeans with paint splotches on them. Fashion wouldn't matter to someone like him. His lips would arc in a solid, exaggerated way, like stone. One of those faces that no one could deny was handsome. Too handsome, some women would even say. And Grace would want to say how it's funny, it was always her mother's face she was hoping to behold at this moment and that, when she found out it was he who'd found her, at first she didn't want to meet, but now that she sees him, sees how opposite he is to her fake father—who was blond and pale, yet somehow blurred—now it was right. Diane Lett would try to get a word in edgewise, but they'd be already out the door, daylight swarming around them.

But when she walked into the office on Wednesday, there was just Diane Lett and a blue file folder. Grace sat down in a fake leather armchair at the corner of Diane's desk and crossed her legs. The other armchair was empty. She snapped her gum, banged her A&P bag against a leg of the chair. She spotted on the desk blotter the perfect imprint of her signature, how hard her pen had pressed through paper when she'd heard the words *wheels set in motion* and *irrevocable*, almost a year ago.

Now Diane sat across from her, pretty white fingers laced together, clear nail polish. She glanced at Grace's work clothes. "Had to rush out from work?"

"No, I took my time. Where is he?"

Diane leaned forward over her folded hands. "He's in the next room."

"Well, then," Grace dropped her bag. "Send in the clowns."

Diane pushed her chair back, got up, then sat back down and frowned at Grace with soft eyes. Counsellor's eyes, Grace thought. Brown as molasses. Bet she went to school to get eyes like that. They pay two thousand dollars a year to get those eyes, to sit behind a big cardboard desk till the invented sob stories inject themselves into their ears, down into their hearts and then through the bloodstream till they come quivering out their eyes. She paid extra tuition to get the black spots in them: with honours. And her kids think when she looks at them, those brown circles are all lovery and real. She studied to get those eyes.

"Any word on her?"

"You mean your mother?"

"Sure. Yes."

"No, Grace. I'm sorry. Now..." Diane picked up the file folder and held it in the air. "Since we last talked I got some more info on Gene's history." She slid the folder toward the corner of the desk, her silk blouse shifting, satisfied, against her skin.

Grace ignored the folder.

"Sure?"

Grace nodded, said a silent yes.

Diane's smile was serious. "Okay." She walked to an adjacent office door and closed it slowly behind her. Grace heard her talking, then the low, warm hum of a male voice. She bit her nails, peeling them back, one by one, across from the corner she'd bitten. *Could be it isn't him at all, could be that guy in the Sputnik was just pushing my buttons. Some people have radar for that kind of thing.* Pretty soon it got hard to figure whether she was chewing gum at all, or just the nails. A small flock of geese was beating about her ribcage. She glanced down at her dress clothes scrunched up in the bag beside her chair, then at the front of her work blouse, the name tag above her right breast. There were yellow-brown grease stains down the front of her uniform that she'd made worse by wiping all over the hips of her skirt. She looked up and saw blurred shapes shifting behind the frosted glass, their hushed voices. *Portuguese hands, my ass.* She didn't want to be Portuguese. She wasn't supposed to be Portuguese. And he wasn't her father.

The frosted door swung open and Diane said, "Grace... Gene."

He strode into the room with a magazine rolled up in one hand. Another hand shoved into a pocket of his baggy black jeans. Grace shook her head. He nodded in her direction, said, "Hey," but he was more interested in the chair at the other corner of the desk. He dumped himself into it, clapping the magazine against his knee.

"Gene… Grace."

His eyes shifted from the carpet to the diplomas to the window. He unrolled his magazine and opened it. *Low Rider.* A tanned blonde girl was on the cover, caressing a red funny car in the middle of the desert. She had black leather shorts and a bodice that laced up at the front, part way. She couldn't see the girl's eyes. Gene blinked long-distance behind his glasses. His hair was brown and poofy, it came up in short wisps at the back of his neck. He grimaced as he read, and Grace remembered him doing so with the Sputnik menu. He had good teeth and thick eyebrows too, like hers.

Diane was still standing at the door, leaning on the doorknob, looking back and forth at them with a sad half-smile on her face. She wants me to say something, Grace thought, those fucking overeducated eyes of hers want me to say something stupid. Okay, I will.

"You left me a shitty tip."

"Eh?" Gene turned a crumpled page of the magazine, then spoke to the next page. "Service was no good. Food was cold. Got what you deserved."

"The food was cold because it was on the table fifteen minutes before I had to *tell* you it was there!"

"Aah!" He waved her voice away, chucked the magazine onto the desk and folded his arms, glaring down at his running shoes.

Diane cleared her throat. "Um, you guys know each other?"

"He comes into the restaurant last Sunday and orders

the breakfast special, then embarrasses me in front of the whole place."

"Is that right, Gene?"

"She's got an active imagination."

"Okay," Diane said. "So you *weren't* there."

"Yeah, I was there for a little while. Just by chance, stopped in for some blueberry pancakes."

Grace shook her head, hand over her eyes. "Lives a hundred and fifty clicks away and he says he just dropped by. I felt about yay big."

"They got Roy Orbison on the juke box there," Gene said. "'Blue Bayou.'"

Diane came and knelt down beside Grace's chair, resting her hand on the buttoned armrest. "Why didn't you tell me?"

"About Roy Orbison?"

"No," Diane breathed hard through her nose, "about seeing Gene."

"I don't know. I don't want to . . . I don't feel like talking today. It wasn't supposed to be so jumbly." She pointed at him. "And you didn't even *have* blueberry pancakes, Gene."

"Hey, call me Papa."

She stared at him through wet eyelashes. He just sat there, not even looking her way. He was folded, stamped and sealed: an envelope with foreign handwriting on it. *Return to sender,* she thought. *There's something wrong with him. There's a lot wrong with him. He's all wrong.*

Half an hour of monosyllables. On her way out of the building, Grace kicked the door open, the fake glass shuddering. Gene didn't see this; he was already jangling his keys out on the wet sidewalk. His baggy jeans were turned up at the bottom, with big thick cuffs. Grace hated those cuffs. He coughed, turned back to face her. For a moment she thought he looked very small. His running shoes were chunky and dumb. He grimaced under the rain, his shoulders hunched, collar up on his leather jacket. "Let's go for a coffee."

"No thanks," Grace said. "I've got to get home."

"I'll give you a ride."

"No," she said. "I'll walk. Thanks."

"Fuck that," Gene said. "It's raining. I'll drive you to this place you call home."

She stood facing her father on the sidewalk. "Geez, I don't know."

"Car's over here," he said.

A bead of water hung from Gene's nose. He fumbled with the key in the ignition, black hairs clinging wet to his wrist and hand. Grace squeaked around on the vinyl seat and watched him in profile: his glasses all steamed up, his eyes muddy and grey behind them, more rain beading on his black curly hair and moustache. And still the grimace, always the grimace. The car wouldn't start. He was jamming the key back and forth, muttering something about the rain. "Too wet. Flooded. Glaciers moving south."

"Excuse me?"

"Eh?" Gene turned to her, his glasses two discs of silver steam. He looked like a house fly with teeth.

"You were talking to yourself."

"Don't talk stupid," Gene said. "It's the reception here," he fumbled for the radio knob. "You can't pick anything up down here."

"Helps if the radio's on," she said, tuning in to the local

AM station. "Free Fallin'" by Tom Petty. The engine turned over then and the car cleared its throat, rumbled to life.

Gene said, "Put your seat belt on." She glared at him for a block. Finally, she reached behind her but the seat belt was hanging slack between her seat and the door. Gene saw her tugging and said, "It's not working. Forget it."

"Yeah," Grace said. "Right. Forget it."

"Here's fine."

Gene pulled over across the street from Fernleigh Flowers. Fake roses buzzed red and yellow and intertwining plastic vines ascended toward the fluorescent lights in the window display. Grace pointed vaguely to the rooms above. "That's my place." A sign that read Weddings Funerals hung below the upstairs windows.

Gene ratcheted back the emergency brake and gazed, unimpressed, across the shiny street. "So where do you live?" he said. "Above the weddings or above the funerals?"

"Ha ha," she said flatly. "Both."

He nodded, wiped the water off his moustache with the web of skin between thumb and index finger. "Getting dark," he said.

"Yup."

"I don't like driving at night."

Grace said nothing.

"Maybe I should stay here tonight," he said, his fingers tapping on the wheel. "Start fresh in the morning."

"Maybe you should go now before it gets too dark," she said. "Nanticoke motels are expensive."

"What? You've got such things as motels down here?"

Grace opened her mouth to speak, but nothing came, and

she knew by the time she stepped into her apartment the comebacks would be knocking around her head like fists. Gene was staring at the pine tree air freshener hanging from the mirror. He flicked at it once, twice. "There's a kind of pine tree," he said, "it releases its seeds only when its cones are touched by fire."

"That's nice." Grace caught her ankle on the seat belt as she got out. "Goodbye, Gene."

"See you next Sunday."

"I can't, Gene."

"What are you talking about? I'll meet you in Toronto next Sunday. See your grandmother, and Christopher."

"Sorry." She swung back the door, ready to slam it. "It was nice meeting you." Before she shut it, she said, "Not that it matters, but who's this Christopher?"

"*Menino santo?*" he said. "He's your little cousin."

"Oh. I... I can't afford the bus fare."

"Ah!" he swatted at the air. "I'll drop by and get you. Meet you at this funeral place after school."

She laughed in spite of herself. "I don't go to school any more, Gene. It's too far for you to drive anyway, down and back."

He waved her off again. "Ah! You have to meet your family! They want to see my daughter!" The steam had evaporated from his thick glasses and his rain puddle eyes were now clear, immediate. "Come on, Rachel," he said.

"My name isn't Rachel," she said. "It's Grace."

"What kind of name is that?" he said, blinking. "It's like something out of—"

"You know my fucking name, Gene!" She slammed the door. The first time it bounced back open.

Gene said, "You've got to hold the handle up."

Slam. This time he said something through the glass. It sounded like *your hair's too short.* Grace stepped into a puddle. "Fuckfuckfuck!" She couldn't see Gene past the rain and the windshield wipers. She stormed around the front of the car, slammed her fist down on the hood and ran across the street into the stairwell of her apartment. She stood breathless, her back pressed against the door, until she thought she heard his Colt pull away. Her breath steamed up into the light till white enveloped her so that she could see nothing and hear only the Colt's muffler grow thin, lower in pitch, turn enough corners to be silent. She willed the small black car down Singer Street, past the main lights, willed it out across ribbons of wet tarmac north through Waterford and Hagersville and smaller towns until it reached regions where there was no longer rain, where it hurtled, infinitesimal, through space, a black meteor hissing through black fields, still moving into more blackness hours later that night when, curled up but still awake in bed, she would watch rain shadows ribboning down the walls like translucent worms and listen to the dumpster in the alley clattering hollow with water.

Two hours into a Sunday morning shift, and still the new girl hadn't turned up. Grace's blood was heavy, sluggish. *So I've got to take the new girl's tables again this morning. Fine,* she told herself, *my mind full of work, not him.* Halfway through her shift Grace found out she was slated to work a double. So when Marie the new waitress sauntered in two hours late, sullen and baggy-eyed, Grace stormed across the black and white diamond floor and shakily thrust two plates into her hands before Marie could take off her coat. "Nice of you to make an appearance."

"Whatever." Marie was all beads and leather bracelets and patchouli oil, but her mouth could be a sewer and in the span of minutes her mood roller-coastered from chrome in sunlight to black clouds. Grace was, if she was honest with herself, afraid of the girl, and for this she hated herself. She was scared to even talk to Marie, let alone touch her or look her in the eye. Today the eyes in question, rimmed with mascara, were two cigarette burns. Her breath hummed stale vodka. She ignored beckoning customers and lingered instead at the Wurlitzer, where she randomly punched in songs. "This thing's like life, eh?" she said. "You don't know what you're getting, all you know is half the time it's the most godawful piece of shit you ever heard." Grace paid her no mind; she was convinced Marie's every action was designed to annoy her. But when "Blue Bayou" came crackling out of the Wurlitzer, Grace stopped in the middle of the diamond floor, felt an electric shudder through her bones. Turning slowly, she scanned the diner, relieved that the only new faces belonged to a young couple who'd just walked in with a little girl in tow. Like clockwork, Marie turned to her and mumbled, "You wanna take that window booth? I think I gotta go out back."

"Oh, I don't think so."

"Come on," Marie said, already halfway to the kitchen. She eyed the booth with a dull, hungover look of contempt. "I'm going for a smoke."

Grace stared after Marie—"Hey!"—but when the kitchen door swung back at her, she kicked it, fuming, and stormed back toward the booth. The man and woman were already deep in conversation. The woman didn't acknowledge Grace when she set down their glasses of water, merely squeaked back in the booth and kept talking. They were arguing but Grace didn't attach herself to what was said. The little girl had curly blonde locks, still baby-fine, and when she smiled at Grace her face crinkled up tough as a potato doll, so tough that Grace realized she was no girl at all, but a pretty little boy. Then the woman cleared her throat. "Excuse me," she said. "Can we have two coffees here, *please?*"

"Sorry," Grace bit her lip. "I—" but the woman's eyes were concrete. "Sure," Grace whispered and spun away. They ordered nothing for the boy. Spoon in the woman's coffee still going pang-a-pang when Grace left them again and hurried through the kitchen's tink and clatter and, out the back door, gulped back cold air, her heart drumming. Across a cinder alley pocked with rain puddles and shards of broken glass, two young boys were throwing stones at bottles they'd set up on a low wall. Shiny jackets with sports logos hissing obnoxious yellow and black. Marie, meanwhile, was sitting on an overturned pop crate, her head slumped between her knees, a thin puddle of vomit on the cinder ground. Her face, streaked with tears and strings of blonde hair, swung around to face her, then settled down again, relieved.

"Oh," she groaned. "It's you."

"Look," Grace stammered. "I'm sorry, but I'm not doing your job for you any more. I don't care if you're sick, it's your own fault. If you can't handle it here—"

"That's my kid."

"What are you talking about?" Grace said, peering at the boys across the alley.

"That's my fucking kid in there. In the booth, with that couple you served." Grace said nothing, silenced by a flutter beneath her ribs. Marie wiped quickly at her cheeks. "Forget them anyways," she sniffed. "I'm leaving all this shit. I'm heading out west. Got a friend out there. Save my tip money and"—she snapped her fingers weakly—"I'm history." She drew a cigarette out of her pack and put it in her mouth and then, after sliding the pack back in her blouse pocket, patted her other pockets anxiously. "Got a light?" Grace, hesitating, handed her a book of matches. "What about you?" Marie asked, in the absent, habitual way smokers make idle conversation, lips pursed. "You've got to do something else than this shit."

"You're holding it."

"Huh?"

Grace nodded at the matchbook. There were designs pasted on the flap, paper cut from magazines. Ad fragments. Plants, a bark-like pattern, tiny shimmers of colour, a horse. Marie turned it over in her surprisingly dainty fingers. "That's it? That's what you . . . that's your . . . ?"

"Art?" Grace snickered, nervous.

"Yeah. You don't do anything bigger?"

Grace apologetically took back the matches. "I used to paint once."

"What made you stop?"

"A sign."

"Hmm." Marie inhaled deeply, her eyes following the matchbook into Grace's pocket. "Well, it's something, I guess. Me, I'm learning the guitar." A bottle shattered and that set one of the boys hooting. Marie regarded them and then her cigarette with distaste and, smacking her lips, butted the smoke out in the cinder dust at her feet. "You know what you are though," she said. "You're selfish."

"Oh, great. I'll add it to the list."

"No offence. I know selfish, believe me. Tell yourself it's because you're shy or you don't want to show off," Marie squinted at the brightening sky. "But you end up keeping it all for yourself. You don't share."

Grace nodded to herself. "He that withholdeth corn, the people shall curse him, but…" she struggled with the words, "blessing shall be upon the head of him that selleth it."

Marie stared at her blankly for some time till she exploded into laughter and then immediately slumped her head and tears poured out again, along with a pale yellow pish of liquid. "I'm not really like this, you know," she managed to say, hunched over, before her whole body heaved again. Grace found herself leaning over the girl and watching her distant hand, as if of its own accord, pat and stroke the trembling, blue-uniformed back. And now she's back in public school, second desk window row, when the old religion teacher Mrs. Beard asks her, and in a monotone, Grace lists all the books in the Bible. And the kids in class stop talking, look at her as she's bent over her desk, staring at the back of the seat in front of her: so-and-so loves so-and-so, what's-his-face sucks the big hog. Her face burning, mottled red, as she recites the names from the list scrolling in her head. What are they all thinking behind that communal silence? Only she and Paul de Konning know more than five books of the Bible. And there's a boy outside the door whose name she won't remember who doesn't have to go to religion class because his father came down to school to talk to the principal. And he presses his mouth to the wire glass and blows, exposing all his teeth and gums, a monkey. The kids laugh. Mrs. Beard, nodding and smiling regardless, like she's already in a higher, cottoncloud place, says, "Go on, Grace, dear." And Grace will carry on through Proverbs and Isaiah through Luke and John and all Paul's letters and on through to Revelation. Mrs. Beard giving her and Paul de Konning straight A's at the end of term, while the rest of the class get B's right across the board because Mrs. Beard can't remember any of their names and there are never any tests anyway.

"Was it your father?"

"What?" Grace said harshly looking down at Marie's face resurfacing, blonde hair hanging limp over eyes now blurred but serious.

"Did your father make you learn all that Bible-thumping stuff? 'Cos, you know, dads tend to—"

"I don't have a father."

"Oh? Last week, you know, when you took my shift, they said he showed—"

"No," Grace said. "I told you. I don't have a father."

"Are you sure?"

"Of course I'm fucking sure."

"Sorry," Marie said softly. "I guess I heard wrong." Across the alley a bottle smashed. "Hey!" she shouted. "Quit it, why don'tcha! You're fucking killing us!"

"Screw off, pisstank!" one of the boys shouted.

"Ah, fuck you," she said, bored, though for a moment the hurt registered on her face.

"Yeah, I'll fuck you!" the boy barked. "Right in the cunt!" They ran away down the alley, hooting and laughing, kicking up water and wet ashes, a hiss of jackets.

"Bastards," Marie mumbled. "All of them."

Grace laughed full and glad and chucked Marie the matchbook. "For your smoke breaks. I got hundreds more at home." Marie, surprised, said thanks just as the new cook stuck his head out the door and told them to get the hell back inside. The two women ignored him; they gazed silently at each other until they became self-conscious and their eyes drifted to the ground before them. Grace had often wondered how the ash got there. It seemed to be coal dust, the crunch underfoot. But now she and Marie were lost in this black ground of broken glass and puddles reflecting roofs and hydro wires and cloud breaking open into blue sky as the opening bars of "Crazy Little Thing Called Love" jangled from the Wurlitzer inside and neither of them thought about coal or its origins.

⁎

Street lights clicked on, buzzing, pink. Grace folded her goose-pimpled arms and bustled down the sidewalk. The April air was cold and sudden but she was oblivious, her mind still back at the Sputnik. During the shift, all the shadow blurs passing by the window wore moustaches and glasses. Grace's back pricked up every time the door opened: duh-*ding!* She expected to find Gene standing on the tiles with something absurd and sparkly in his hands. Silver foil flowers. Mirrorball. But he never did show, and she told herself that was just as well and yet she was, no, that wasn't it, she didn't know what she was.

She walked alone under deciduous trees that were still naked save for a few buds. The rough immediacy of bark, rattle of branches. Brown ghosts of leaves, long hidden under snow, were burned into the pavement, and small worms writhed along the gutters in the muck of a late thaw.

Grace hurried by wind-chime porches and warm yellow squares of light. She passed a child's glove stuck in a frozen wave on a picket fence and didn't think to wonder at the story behind it because she is six years old walking home where, in her bedroom, she'll shape her perfect parents out of Play-Doh. She'll bite off the half moon off her thumbnail and press that into their faces, a smile. She'll cut off snippets of her own long hair and stick them to the Play-Doh heads. She'll cut out pictures from magazines, small ones, fragments, and paste them onto the figures: these will be the clothes. Her father will wear Marlboro ads, cars and football players, pants made from boats and rivers and fishing rods. Mom's dress will be covered in Kool cigarette women, Cheryl Tiegs and Chanel ads, pictures of vegetables and copper pots. Horses. Grace will tear the buttons off her blouses for the eyes. Her fake mother will give her a talking-to at laundry time.

Her Play-Doh parents live in her doll's house. Not really a doll's house; a Fisher-Price service station with plastic, cylindrical smiley people and cars and ramps and bells that go ding. Her fake parents bought this for the boy they believed they were adopting. When they got the call they'd be getting a girl instead, they were crestfallen but took it as the grace of God. "So naturally we called you Grace," her fake mother tells her, quite often. When Grace starts school and the kids get hold of her name, she wishes she'd been called Danielle or something totally different, like Rita or Racquel. She runs home to her perfect parents. She stows them away in the office of the service station. She won't show her fake parents their enemies. She sits in the window of her room and talks in a voice above her real voice, so no one but dogs and her clay parents can hear. But the paper clothes will peel off after a couple of hours. Mom and Dad will be bald and naked by suppertime.

In the window of Fernleigh Flowers the flower display was missing, carnations and azaleas and chrysanthemums packed away into refrigerators for the night, even the fake roses gone, leaving only fake vines to ascend toward the fluorescent lights. Grace climbed up the stairs to her apartment. The light was blown out. When she bent to retrieve her key from under the mat, she found it was sitting openly in the wedge of light under the door. "Idiot," she muttered. She heeled the door shut behind her and kicked off her shoes on her way to the bathroom, where she stopped up the tub and turned on the water. Undressed, she sat on the toilet seat and watched the water roll out of the tap. She looked down at her nakedness, the pale breasts slouching over her belly, thick black murmur of hair between her legs.

She left the tub to fill while she put on her kimono robe from behind the door and then padded across the hardwood floor to the kitchen. Cup and tea bag out of the cupboard, brown sugar spooned from a pot. She watched the sugar squirm and separate after it hit the bottom of her cup. She absently filled the electric kettle, set it on the stove. As she did so, something, a flash of colour, caught her eye. She spun around and there, through the doorway, alone on the couch and meticulously slicing an orange into quarters with a Swiss Army knife, sat Gene. Grace laughed stupidly for a moment, then mindlessly flicked the burner on under the kettle and stormed into the living room. "What the hell are—Jesus Christ! How the fuck did you get in here, Gene?"

He set the knife down on his knee and said, "You shouldn't use His name in vain."

"Don't tell me about—Jesus Christ!" She looked down, her hands fumbling to cinch up her kimono.

"Pah!" Gene waved her off. "Nothing I haven't seen before."

"Shut up! Who the hell do you think you are anyway, breaking into my home?"

"I'm your father," he said through a mouthful of orange. "And I didn't break in. I used the key. You should be more careful. You don't know what kind of crazies could get in here."

Grace silently stormed to the front door and opened it, waiting. Almost a minute went by before Gene shrugged, said, "Bathtub," then stuffed a fresh orange wedge into his mouth. Grace slammed the door shut and strode into the bathroom, where the water was ready to spill out the sides of the tub. She cranked off the hot water, rolled up her sleeve and reached into the bath, pulling the plug. She marched back to him. "What the fuck do you want from me?" Gene, his eyes glazed over, only groaned in response. "You're sick," Grace said. She found herself suddenly dizzy. The air in the apartment was thick, cloudy. Gene's eyes were bugging out now and staring at something before him. "Gene?" she said, quiet. "Are you okay?"

His eyes were full of tears. He was thrashing at the couch with one arm, the wedge of orange a gag in his mouth.

"Gene? Are you having a stroke or something?"

Finally he pointed at the kitchen and spat out the orange. "Fire!"

"Jesus!" The kitchen was all fireworks, big blue flames spitting and licking up over the plastic kettle. "Shitshitshityoudumbfuckingbitchshit!" She ran onto the linoleum, danced around in front of the stove. She tried turning down the burner but the plastic was dripping over the knob. She picked up the kettle instead, globs of burning plastic falling onto the linoleum. Next thing she was running to the window, smacking it open with her elbow and letting the hunk of flame arc over the alley.

She stood trembling at the window. Thick plastic smoke poured black all around her shoulders. The kettle flared on the black ground like a torch, lighting up the alley and the windows of the building across the way. She saw her reflection, illuminated from behind, but the fire below was bright enough to show her in her stupid kimono. The kettle started whistling below her. She stepped away from the window and fell back into the chair. Behind her Gene began, slowly, to clap. She turned to him, her eyes black. "Get out."

"Not without you." He was standing now, hands clasped together like a maître d'. "We're going home."

She shook her head in disbelief. "You must be off your rocker."

"Hey," he said. "That's no way to talk to—"

She slapped her hand down hard on the back of the chair. "You're not my father!"

His eyes scanned the apartment, as if searching for something, but when his eyes met hers once more, Grace realized it was a look of disgust. "Get yourself out of that thing," he said. "We're going."

Grace got up and walked briskly past him and swung open the door. "You're going."

Gene lingered in the doorway. "I'll wait in the car."

"Sure," she laughed bitterly. "Whatever."

He nodded and fished some loose change out of his pocket,

then thrust it into her hand. "For the orange," he said. She shook her head dumbly, watching him walk down the blackened stairs. She heard him mumble something, "... no idea how disappointed your mother will ..." but his voice trailed away outside as Grace slammed the door shut with her back and slid trembling and exhausted to the floor. The smoke had faded from the room now. Outside the window there was only black. She rolled her head back against the door, skull hard against wood. She looked down at the coins in her hand then threw them to the floor with such force that they bounced and skittered, one of them rolling away over the floorboards and in its quiet roily sound she's chasing down another coin, a dime perhaps, that rolls down the linoleum floor of a hallway long ago and her bare feet go slapping after it until the dime slows and totters and is clapped down under a boot, a man's boot, and she's looking up into a yellow wash of light, and other than a dark halo of curly hair, she remembers nothing of what the man's face holds. And she's lifted up, perhaps across days or months, and she's set down in the back seat of a noisy car where glass towers and red-brick buildings fall away on all sides and there are feathers or cottonwood parachutes floating thick in air, blue sky skittering of clouds and smell of apples, people standing on ladders in an orchard, their heads lost in trees, the black tree trunks gnarled and tumorous against the long grass flowers and now the burning smell alongside the highway, swaths of grass burned black in the ditches all along the roadside and this smell is creosote, she will realize much later, that's what it is because the window is rolled down and a woman, it must be her, is in the front seat and all she knows of this woman is long reddish hair whipping about, licking around the headrest and her laughter lilting and forever and the gentle upturn of her nose as she turns to the driver, his wave of curls and his gruff laughter warm underneath too and past him there's the woman's voice again and she's happy with the sun flapping in her face that she can't see, but she loves it when it turns to her and she always wants more warm and laughing and sits back waiting for it to come around to show itself again like the sun because this little girl can never see enough of it.

Grace awoke curled up in the Colt's passenger seat. A gas station, McDonald's and Baskin Robbins glared white outside the car window. She squinted against the fluorescent lights, her face rumpled. Gene was sitting behind the wheel, muttering under his breath at the expressway shining stark and sleek beneath the night sky. When Grace stirred he turned to her and said quietly, with the utmost seriousness, "The earth's a genius."

"Huh?"

"It works of its own accord, and then you got us with our fingers and our Styrofoam and our electrical wires jumping on its hide. We're empty glasses," he said, "waiting to be filled with plastic beads."

"What are you *talking* about?"

"The tree's rotten," he nodded to himself. "Time to chop it down."

She ignored this. "Where are we, anyway?"

"Nowhere," Gene said. "Oakville." He jingled his keys and pointed to the strip of shiny new structures. "Know what they call one of these in the States?" Grace stared blankly at him. "An oasis," he said. He laughed then, loud and brash, the first one Grace remembered him offering. "C'mon," he said. "You're hungry."

"No, I'm not."

"Yeah, you are." He opened the door and got out. "Your stomach was singing opera."

Feeling violated, Grace walked three paces behind him into McDonald's. "You go ahead," he said shiftily, turning and handing her a twenty-dollar bill.

"I'll pay for it myself, thanks."

"Ah!" he dismissed her. "Get me a coffee. Two creamers on the side."

He was seated at a table by the front window, tapping the yellow and green laminated plastic, when she came with her order, plus two extra creamers. "Here," she clapped down his change, a bit carelessly, so that some of the coins skittered onto the floor. "Sorry," she said, insincere, but Gene paid the money no mind. His eyes scanned the bright room. She noticed his hands fluttering, still tapping away. His left hand was missing a finger. She couldn't believe she hadn't noticed before. When he blinked up at her quick, Grace grabbed a bunch of fries and dabbed them in ketchup.

"So," she said. "You sell cars, eh?"

"No, we don't *sell* cars. We work on them. We got a body shop, not a dealership. Body work, tune-ups, lube jobs. Shit like that." He looked at the fries quivering at Grace's mouth. "You care about cars, or do you just wanna look at my hand?" Before she could say anything, he'd slapped his left hand down on the table. It was dark and naked against the lime green plastic. Three fingers and a thumb pointing out, with thick black hair on the knuckles, and a half-inch stump where the ring finger was supposed to go. A mutilated starfish. “I lost it somewhere out west in the seventies,” he said, nudging up his glasses and rubbing his eyes. “Maybe Alberta. I don’t know. Lots of yellows and greens.”

“It’s a big country,” Grace said. “Anybody could lose a finger out there.” She smiled across at him, but he didn’t catch it.

“Maybe,” he said, turning his palm up and nodding serious. “Maybe.” They sat in silence for some time.

“I was out west once,” she said. “With my fake parents. We went to see dinosaur bones.”

Grace’s mouth was wrapped around her burger when he spoke again. “Where’d you get those?”

“Those what?”

He nodded quickly at her breasts.

“Fuck, Gene,” she swallowed. “They just grew there, okay?”

“You’re mother never had ones like that. They were more like, I don’t know, pimples that needed popping.”

“That’s nice.”

“So they’re not fake, eh?”

“Not that I know of.”

“Hmm.” He pondered this for a moment. “These Hollywood women, they’ve all got fake ones, with fibreglass in them. They die, they get buried, they rot. Dig them up in a thousand years and all you’ll get in their coffins is these two little bags of fibreglass.”

“They’re silicone.”

“That right? I thought you said they were real.”

“We’re supposed to be talking about something else besides tits, Gene.”

“Okay. Fine with me.” He tapped at the tabletop for a spell. “So,” he grimaced. “What do you do?”

“You know what I do.”

"Yeah yeah yeah," he waved her words away. "Really though. What do you want to do with your life? You want to be a nurse, a lawyer, start up a business? Don't you got any training?"

"I *was* going to art school, but they—"

"Art?" Gene sat back violently, studying her through his bifocals, chin up.

"Yes," Grace continued. "But then I ran out of cash. So I quit."

"What about loans?"

"Don't believe in them," she said. "I don't owe anybody anything. I guess you wouldn't understand that, would you?"

"Hey," he said, oblivious. "You left-handed?"

"Yes." Grace automatically hid her hands under the table. "So?"

"That means you're smart." Gene looked down at his mutilated hand. "I'd gnaw off my right arm to be left-handed."

"Please, Gene," she sighed. "We're supposed to talk about other stuff. Real stuff. Like what the hell's happened to the three of us the last twenty or so years, why you left me on someone's doorstep—"

"Pah!" he said. "Doorstep nothing. You were put in a home. Besides, your mother was the one gave you up."

"Okay. Who the hell is my mother and—"

"Your mother's left-handed."

"Yeah?" Grace leaned forward. "And?"

He closed his eyes, nodding. "You look like your mother. Except her hair's longer."

"My hair used to be long."

"No shit, Dick Tracy," Gene said. "I saw you when you were real little."

"You got rid of me when I was *three.* No kid's hair is long at three."

"Wanna bet? Your hair was down to your ass when you were six months old. And Rachel didn't *get rid of you* neither. She just couldn't give you the life she thought you deserved."

"Jesus, you sound like a freaking foster home ad! What did this chick with long hair and small tits know about what I deserved? And where were you all this time?"

"Hey," he said. "Don't talk about her like that. First she said you weren't mine…"

"One can dream."

"And after the tests came in she didn't want me anyway. Said she could handle you by herself. I kept coming round to see you both, but she just acted like I was a piece of dust in the corner." He took a gulp of coffee.

"Did you hurt her?"

He froze and glared at her, steam in his face. "I loved her, right up there with my mother. Your grandmother. She wants you to come to Toronto too."

Grace rolled her eyes. "Puh-*lease,*" she said, and peeled back the lid of a creamer and drank just as Gene was about to do the same. They paused, eyes grazing.

"Yup," he said. "Left-handed." He was serene now, drinking back his second creamer then gazing alternately at her and the rest of the room, his usual grimace airbrushed away, wiped clean. "I used to take you to McDonald's," he said. "And I remember one time—you'd just started stringing words together good—you said, 'Daddy? Eat drink eat drink. Life. Eat drink eat drink?'"

"And what did you say?"

"I don't know," he said. "I probably made something up. You called me Daddy then. You were a smart cookie."

Grace laughed into her hands, loud and bitter.

"What's so funny?"

"Nothing," she sighed. She shook her head, fake happy, and sucked on an ice cube from her pop and then crunched it. She thrust the wax paper cup at Gene, offering it to him, but he slunk back in his seat, pale, folded in on himself. He watched the highway, binary pricks of light streaming across his glasses. Then he turned to her, his glasses flashing, a motion she suddenly felt she had seen a million times before, and it scared her, a white flash of light through her breastbone. "Let's go," he said quietly. Grace laughed once more but it was empty. She picked up her tray and walked to the garbage and by the time she opened the swinging *Thank you* gate and let the contents fall into the bin Gene was already outside.

⁕

Back in school, Grace is the serious one. She carries a hand mirror in the pocket of her shirt. When a painting she's working on hesitates, starts to doubt itself, she looks at it in her mirror, to see it new. She holds her face up to the canvas, her nose stained orange or blue or whatever, she so loves the smell of paint, and has known its taste. But in the company of the other students, whose confidence and carelessness she hates and envies, she's a shadow of herself. Silent, giving away nothing, she moves from class to class in a fog, considers dropping out before Christmas. And one afternoon, in first-year painting class, the instructor sticks three prints of old paintings up on the wall. "Perspective: before and after Giotto." A stifled groan somewhere across the room, a yawn. "Giotto was a prism," says the instructor, pointing to the *during* picture, "a window through which the human could see itself anew, alive for the first time. A note of profound feeling didn't appear in painting until Giotto and, in turn, his visionary work led to the pinnacle of Renaissance art in Michelangelo." His pointer then taps at the *after* painting, one that Grace will soon forget, all heroic muscles and sentiment, but the *before* painting hits her hard and sudden, a bright thump of recognition that opens her ribs like petals.

Duccio's *Rucellai Madonna.* The instructor's voice doubles back only to pass over it in a grey blur of negatives, "woodenprimitiveunnaturalcolourslackofrealism," but Grace is already inside it. Virgin and Child against a gold-leaf ground, a gilt-encrusted throne held up by six angels suspended in air, with shimmering, iridescent wings. Swaying figures all of them, with long necks and tall shoulders. Except for the Christ Child, his balding head old and wise already, and that pudgy right foot of His that pushes against His mother's leg. The Virgin's blue robe is the centre, the calm. Its gold edging frames her face, and then ripples downward, fluid as coloured water, all its swiftnesses and hesitations. It curls across her lap, passing beneath the body of Christ, down and forward over her knee and down again into soft folds, ripples of light, that cover her feet until the hem once again circles back up and around her, serene, eternal. Her face knows, in all its innocence, it knows all. If Grace could dissolve into the light of this face, corona of quiet gold around this inclined head, these lowered, slightly drooping eyes.

Afternoon light spills in through the classroom's frosted windows, touching Duccio's painting, the other two prints pale under the weak fluorescents. Grace scans the classroom only to see bored, closed faces, and she thinks, *Cows.* She wants to shout: *Don't you see?* Soon she'll read how certain Byzantine wall painters added shadows to the figures of Christ and the Virgin to match the angle at which sunlight moved through apse windows. While other students will leave class talking perhaps of Koons, or of the ancient Rothko, Grace will steal away and leaf through books on Cimabue, Theofan Grek, and her Duccio. She'll share them with no one, ashamed of herself, her betrayal. Long after she stops painting she'll be content to journey through a steady procession of library books filled with ikons and mosaics, some books never before signed out despite their age. They'll feel familiar and strange to touch, smell. And all this time, incomplete but insistent, like directions given by a man with no fingers, they will gesture toward Byzantium.

The day she stops painting she's sitting at a bus stop, and sees, on the sidewalk before her, an arrow fashioned from red electrical tape. "Sinner," scrawled in fading chalk, pointing to where she sits. There are three such arrows, but she's alone on the bench. In class she suffers a cramp in her brush hand. Her wash is spotty, her strokes stiff and self-conscious. She knows she'll never attempt such works as Duccio's with her own hands, not only because she's stranded here in the present tense, but for all the profane things her hands have done. She tears off a sheet and starts over, but her hand can hardly hold the brush. She tries something with her right hand instead, simple bold lines, a crude seated figure, vermilion and black. Rinsing off her brush, she spills her can on the floor; cruddy black water spreads over the speckled whitewash. Numb, she looks about the room but no one pays any attention, all the vacant faces, beautiful in their momentary innocence, lost in their work. The model yawns without opening her mouth, her jaw muscles tensing. *I won't need paint any more,* Grace thinks. *I've needed it all this time. Other people don't need such things, they have families and dinners and love. To be happy. If I'm happy I won't need such things either.* She packs up her things slowly and carefully and leaves without a word to anyone, which is how she always leaves. The next day she takes a Greyhound south, back to Nanticoke, to the Children's Aid office, and when she signs the form blood beats into her hand, so much so that she thinks it will seep through her skin and onto the paper where she's pressing down so hard.

The Colt sat clicking in the driveway of a small, scarlet brick house in the suburbs somewhere north of Toronto, one of many colourful houses lining a quiet, well-kept street. If this was summer, Grace thought, the street lights would be casting their aureole through the trees, as if the trees themselves glowed, their leaf veins immediate, translucent. But now in the spring thaw the wind blew unhindered through the bare, skeletal branches. Through the curtain of the house she saw a television screen's blue flicker. Gene ratcheted back the emergency brake. When Grace shoved the car door shut, the slam echoed in the night air, shuddering through her and suddenly her hands were slick with sweat, her legs hollow. She followed Gene close up the driveway. When they rounded the side of the house past a red sports car, under a kitchen window busy with food smell and clink of china and glass, an automatic sensor light clicked on and Grace tripped on the path. A dog barked through a chain link fence. "Shaddap!" Gene gnarled and the dog stopped instantly, its paws shushing away through the wet grass. At the back steps there were vines spreading and networking across the bricks up to the roof, covering the wall, clematis thin and fragile and leafless, and it was then Gene turned and said quietly, "It's okay." And Grace, nodding, said okay dumbly back at him with her hand on the rail at the bottom of the steps and this she had seen and heard and acted out a million times before too.

The door opened to a jumbly chorus of voices and water rasping in a sink. *"Chega!"* Gene shouted. A small boy came running out of the kitchen laughing and ran in a circle around Gene's legs then hugged them tight and looked up with a devilish grin. His blond hair waved thick on his head, as if painted with oils. Gene patted it and laughed low and dumb, as some men are prone to do in the ruthless energy of children. *"Menino santo,"* he said softly, like a prayer.

"Christopher!" a woman's voice shrilled. "Get back in here already!"

The boy ran again, giggling, circling Gene once more until he ran into Grace's legs and jumped back, startled for an instant. His eyes were bright blue. He stuck a finger in his mouth, looked up at her shy, mistrustful. Grace kneeled down and said gently, "Hello, Christopher, I'm—" but he was gone again, back into the kitchen. Gene, watching him go, grinning.

And next the water in the kitchen was shut off and

moments later an old woman came around the corner wiping her hands. She wore a sky-blue dress with clouds all over it, and below it her legs were panty-hosed and bowed. She wizened her face. "Gino?"

"Ma."

She lifted her face to his kiss, and then kissed him herself with a strained, wavering pucker, her hands fluttering on his arms. She squinted past him. "Eh?" She peered into the shadows where Grace stood, said something Portuguese to Gene, then waved Grace closer. "Light," she said, waving Grace closer still. "Light." Grace edged nearer and the woman's face broadened, her eyes shining. She crossed herself and kissed her fingers and looked up at the ceiling, muttering. She took Grace's face in her hands and that same pucker, sharp with hair, met Grace's lips. *"Chega."*

The woman was shaking with tears by now. And from behind her an elderly man appeared and stood already crying, unashamed, above his smile. He looked younger than the woman, a paunchy red face and bulbous nose and thin white strands of hair slicked straight back over a shiny head. "Rachel," he said, nodding at Gene. "Rachel." He took her roughly in his arms and swayed. He smelled of mediciney aftershave and onions and this made Grace want to break free but her arms were folded inside his hug.

"No," she said patiently. "Not Rachel. Grace."

"Eh?" The man spoke roughly like she'd heard before, but his face was kind and he laughed. "Grace, yes. Grace." He took off her coat, eager and thus a little rough as well, and gave it to Gene to hang up while he led her into the kitchen, patting, encouraging. The table, clothed in white, was covered with bowls of bread and sauces and olives.

"*Lulas.*" The old woman took Grace firmly by the arm and led her to the counter where three squid were lying dead on a chopping block. She pointed to them and smiled. "*Lulas.*" Grace nodded politely. There were bits of purple skin covering the body sac. The woman grasped one by the tail and head and pulled the squid apart, effortless, as if it were designed solely for such a thing. She then, with two fingers, carefully lifted the silvery grey ink sac from inside the tail and set it down in a sieve. Her hands, dark and complicated by wrinkles, worked quickly, unconscious of themselves. Grace watched them pop out a small cartilage from the base of the tentacles and pull out a clear tail skeleton, like an icicle or a plastic imitation of one, and throw that away too. Done, the old woman smiled at Grace, and the thought occurred to Grace that this demonstration was perhaps the only reason she was brought to this place and now that she'd beheld it in all its glory she could go home.

"That's how Ma talks to Canadians," Gene said.

"How long's she been here?"

Gene shrugged. "Thirty-something years," he said. "Ever since the volcano."

Grace nodded—*Of course*—and mutely followed Gene into the living room. Christopher peered around the doorway at her, then ran into the room and behind a big screen TV blabbing CFMT, the multicultural channel. A man sat on a chesterfield along one wall, beneath a luminous airbrushed painting of a snow-capped mountain and crystal lake. He wore blue jeans turned up at the cuffs and a white T-shirt with splashes of neon and a Ferrari logo across the front. His peaked eyebrows moved alert and black on his ruddy face, and he was balding, already at the stage of the old man, though the few hairs still rooted to his head were wiry and black. He was engrossed in the television, muttering foreign abuse at it.

"Hey," Gene said. He kicked the man's foot. "Hey!"

"Whaat?!" The man lunged, kicked back at Gene.

"Tony. Say hello to your niece."

The man looked Grace up and down, languidly, enough for her to redden. "Hey." Grace said hi, and bit her lip over her nervous laugh. She looked self-consciously around the room. It was quite threadbare, aged, save for the big TV in the corner. In the armchair adjacent to the brother sat a tall, thin blonde woman, her stilt-like legs bruised here and there along her pale shins. She kicked them absently. She wore a garish yet expensive-looking emerald dress. And she was smoking a cigarette, her hand cocked in a funny way. She blew smoke in a sharp stream and said, "Christopher! Getouttathere!" The boy peeked around the big screen, his cherubic face, then giggled at Grace and disappeared once more. The woman rolled her eyes and smiled, perky. Everything about her reminded Grace of a bird, a crane perhaps. "So you're Gino's little girl, eh?" Grace, for want of something better to do, nodded silently. The woman nodded back incredibly fast, so fast Grace thought she must've often suffered from headaches. "I'm Kelly," the woman said, and butted the smoke out anxiously.

"Gino! Everybody! Eat!"

The television was shut off, talk ended, Christopher was picked up by Gene and whisked away, and everybody else followed the mother to the kitchen table. Tulips, bowed limp and heavy from heat, were removed so a bowl of seafood soup could sit steaming in a casserole in the middle of the table, amid bottles of home-made red wine and bowls of yellow-fleshed potatoes. The old woman stood and motioned Grace to the chair across the table from her, then pointed at the vacant place beside Grace. "Papa," she said, smiling, and Gene sat down in the designated seat. Grace offered a weak smile back as the woman doled out the fish soup. "Eh," she nodded at the dripping ladle. "Eh." And finally Grace held out her bowl.

The old man said something in Portuguese and everybody laughed. Then Kelly leaned toward Grace. "He says you look like you eat pretty good, so he wondered why you acted like you don't."

"Oh."

The old man spoke again, concerned. "No offence," Kelly said, touching Grace's arm so she flinched. "You know Portuguese, they—"

"I don't know Portuguese," Grace said.

"Hey!" The clean-shaven brother pointed at his wife. "Don't talk about us like that, at our table."

"Take a pill," Kelly said.

Gene, who had up until now been shovelling soup back without stopping for breath, looked up sharply. "*Basta!* On my daughter's homecoming. I've heard enough."

"You don't hear jack," said Tony. "You got too much interference upstairs."

A silence. Grace watched Gene stuff his massive napkin into his collar, his chin jutted out in caricature. The old man leaned over the table—"Eh?"—and shakily poured wine into Grace's glass. Some dribbled down the side and Grace said, "Sorry." The man looked up at her, his bright red eyes. Save for Gene and Tony, everyone else at the table smiled.

Dinner passed in Portuguese, closed and sibilant to her ears, with smatterings of English and the sound of mouths chomping and swallowing and cutlery grinding across dishes, bread being broken, glasses of wine being supped from and spilled, oblivious, so that the whole tablecloth was soon spattered with blobs of crimson blushed into pink. They cared about Gene enormously, Grace could tell. How, with the exception of Tony, they'd lean his way and speak more softly to him. Gene, meanwhile, paid Christopher endless attention, seemed entranced by the boy's big eyes and blond locks. Grace was spooned out bowl after bowl of soup by the mother, and despite her protests, she ate most of it and was left eating long after everyone else was done. Out of nowhere, Gene withdrew his napkin, threw it down on the table, and pronounced, "Childless women. They remind me of street trees. Good for decoration maybe, but being without fruit, what are they good for? They're good for nothing."

"Hear, hear," applauded Tony. "Sometimes you actually make sense, brother."

"Oh, puh-*lease!*" said Grace, laughing. Everyone stopped to look up at her, save Gene. He grimaced at his plate, muttering something. Grace felt her face mottle red.

Clearing his throat, the old man reached over and clinked her glass, his nose redder now, more bulbous. "Grace," he said. "Grace." He laughed and took another drink. Grace, smiling, raised her glass in return.

In the fridge hum silence that followed, Kelly began fussing with the old woman's dress. "Don't you love your dress, Ma?" The woman smiled, stiff, impatient, under the hands blindly pawing her blue sky and cotton clouds, until she could stand it no longer and roughly gathered up Kelly's bird hands and shoved them back into her own emerald lap. But Kelly was unfazed. "Isn't it a nice dress, Grace?" she said. "I made it for her myself."

"Oh, really?" Grace said. "It's lovely. Did you make your own too?"

"No," Kelly said abruptly, brushing invisible crumbs from her lap. "Tony bought it yesterday. After we…you always buy me things after we have a misunderstanding, don't you, baby?"

"Don't start," Tony grunted.

"Should have a whole store's worth by now," muttered Gene.

"Hey," Tony got up clumsily, swaying. "Who asked you, you sorry sack of… "

The parents moved to hold back his arms, sit him down, while Kelly sat far back, her hands still nervous on her dress. In the ruckus, Christopher slid down from his chair and started running around the table. After one lap he was shouting at the top of his lungs. "MEMEMEMEMEMEMEMEME!!" Gene watched him, grinning. *He can't stop staring at the boy,* Grace thought. But just then his eyes flashed up into her own, and she glanced quickly away, focusing on the ruined tablecloth. The boy came barrelling behind his chair and around the table—"MEMEMEME!!"—and then, sliding between Grace and Gene, knocked her glass so it spilled down her front. Grace jumped back in her chair and wiped at her sweater but it was soaked. The table froze. Christopher hid behind Gene and sulked his red face back at Grace. Gene laughed low, his face nuzzled in the little boy's hair. When Grace took off her sweater even her T-shirt was soaked in pink. Gene offered her his napkin. She ignored him, imagined herself far away and sealed off from this bright room. Tony gave a low whistle. "That's *Rachel's* kid?"

Gene stood up slowly. He set down his glass and stared at it until the red liquid lapping up to the rim gradually subsided and came to rest. Then, swooping up Christopher in his arms, he sighed, "Time for bed, *menino santo,*" and they were gone.

A plaid shirt, one of Gene's, was found for Grace. She sat at the table, humiliated, silent, more naked than if she was nude, while her clothes swirled downstairs in the washing machine.

Gene sat beside the boy's bed, his voice measured and gentle. "…And then the cowboys climbed out of their Lamborghinis and stopped in a saloon for pops and chocolate bars, because they'd been chasing those Ferrari bandits for many a long day and now, finally, their work done, the bandits in jail, the Lamborghini cowboys could kick back and live happily ever after…till the next time! The end."

Christopher clapped, his nose crinkled up, satisfied. "Tell me another one, Uncle Gino."

"Eh?" Gene gruffed, soft. "Aren't you sleepy?"

The boy shook his head emphatically.

"Ah, all right," he sat back and gazed at the wall before him. "Once, in times now long ago, there was a man who lived alone in a blue field. Now this—"

"But I don't want *that* story." Christopher pouted, sitting up from his pillow. "You said last time was the last time, you promised."

"Well? Which one you want?"

"More cowboys!"

"Hmm. Cowboys, he says." Gene scratched his head and suddenly sprang up and tickled the boy, who kicked and squealed in delight. "Too bad," Gene said, his voice once again in rough clothes. "Hush your mouth and I'll tell you what I started anyways." From where Grace stood, through the crack of open door she could see the boy pout and Gene sit back down and take off his glasses and lay them lightly on the bedside table, his eyes naked and blurred strange. In spite of himself, Christopher theatrically bundled and readied his pillow, his curls spilling over it, and waited for Gene to begin his story again.

"Once, in times now long ago, there was a man who lived alone in a blue field. Now this man had neither house nor home, only his field of blue flowers, which he considered home enough. Of course, he was thought to be a strange man by folks for many miles around. No one knew who he was or from where he came, least of all him. Sometimes his own shadow would surprise him for its shape and size, sometimes for not being there at all, though he was not, as they say nowadays, scared of his own shadow.

"Now there was a path that ran along the edge of the man's blue field, and every Sunday along this path there came a young woman. Of all the people who walked by his blue field this woman was the only one he fevered to see. There was no end to her loveliness. She moved with beauty and ease, her long brown hair shone gold when the sun caught it just so, her skin was smooth and her bare arms were darkened by summer, her eyes were a kind of green you've never—"

"Tell me the story," Christopher punched his pillow. "Come on, Uncle Gino, get back to the story."

Gene laughed a low laugh and said he was sorry, and then continued, "So…ah, yes…well, she was a beauty, she was. So finally, on this particular Sunday, he plucked up enough courage and called to her from his blue field, 'Excuse me, miss, but would you ever consider…'

"'Sorry,' she said, 'but I'm afraid I can't hear you.'

"So he came closer and his flowers, all blue and crooked and tall, leaned against him as he asked her. 'Would you ever consider, perhaps, if I were to ask you to give me a sign betraying your feelings…?'

"'Sorry,' she said. 'Though yours is the bluest field, today you are too timid a man. You must ask me next Sunday.' And as she walked away his flowers closed like tiny blue fists.

"So the next Sunday she passed by his blue field again, and she was *so* lovely, and *so* fair, that the man could not help himself from running up to the path and shouting at her, 'Please be mine!'

"'Sorry,' she said, 'but not now. Though yours is the bluest field, today you are too rough a man. You must try again next Sunday.'"

"But why?" said Grace, and clapped her mouth shut.

Gene, his eyes closed and dreaming, didn't register her voice. "Well, that's what *he* said. But the woman gave him no response. She only turned and walked away down the path, her hair shining in the sun. And so the next Sunday, which was grey and filled with rain, the man sat in his field all morning and brooded. *What did she mean each time before? And who does she think she is, making me act so, like a fool? And who am I, to let a woman make my head so fevered? What am I doing here in this, the bluest field?* So deep and troubled were his thoughts that on this occasion, when the young woman passed by his field, the man resolved not to pay her any mind. He even turned his back on her and sat among the flowers, acting like he hadn't seen her at all, though he secretly wanted there to be great joy and love between them for many a long night. Beholding his actions, the young woman, in the warmest voice, called to him, 'Sorry, but though yours is the brightest, bluest field, acting deaf, dumb and blind will get you nowhere. You must ask me again next Sunday.' And so she walked on and the man hung his head as the flower petals closed like fists all around him.

"So the next Sunday the man told himself he would be ready. He stood tall in his field and watched her come all the way down the path. She kicked up a fine dust and her dress swirled all about her like clouds. As the man walked toward the edge of his field, the flowers rippled around his waist like water. He stopped beside the path and there he asked the young woman quietly but clearly, 'When will you marry me?'

"And, lo and behold, a funny thing happened. For the first time the young woman stopped walking. She paused to pull away a few stray hairs that the breeze had blown between her lips, and as she did so the man noticed how her top lip was just a bit thinner than the bottom one. She held her locks of shimmering hair in her hand and gazed at them for a time. Then she looked past him at his blue flowers and smiled and said, 'When your blue field turns to gold.'

"The man looked back at his field, but when he turned to speak to her again the woman had already flashed her green eyes and tossed her gold-tinged hair and was gone. Once again the man's blue flowers closed like fists. Now for the rest of that day the poor man could do nothing but think of her and the condition she had set. He sat in his blue field and thought all the livelong day. *Perhaps it is merely a riddle,* he thought, *or perhaps she means she will marry me when the sun is low enough to turn all fields, whether they be blue or white or red, into gold.* Yet try as he might, the man could do nothing to ease his worrying; less still could he think of anything that would truly turn his field to gold. If hope was a bird, it was losing all its feathers. And so the man went on thinking by daylight and by moonlight, through rain and shine, and when sunlight finally began to dawn on the next Sunday…"

Opening his eyes, Gene checked to see Christopher fast asleep, finger wet in his mouth. He put on his glasses, ruffled the boy's hair and reached to flick off the lamp.

"So what happens?"

"Eh?" Gene looked up, startled.

"How's the field turn to gold?"

"I don't know," Gene said. "Can't see how it could."

"But that's not a happy ending."

"Never promised one. Didn't figure I'd get that far."

Grace gazed upon the boy sleeping. "What if he didn't fall asleep?"

"He always falls asleep, always at that same part, when the guy's left alone in the field, thinking. Never fails."

"Well, it's half a beautiful story, anyway."

"Who says I was halfway done?"

"Still," she said, reddening. "It's beautiful. Where'd you hear it?"

"Nowhere," he said. "In my head." He flicked off the bedside lamp and sat there in darkness. "Anyone can come up with a story," he said. "You just need a few lies and a few loose wires upstairs and enough time alone to tie them all together."

"Maybe you could tell me the whole thing sometime."

"You'd fall asleep."

"Oh yeah?" She leaned against the door jamb, her arms folded.

"Yeah," he said. "I'd just keep telling it day and night, make it so long you'd have to fall asleep."

"I have trouble sleeping. Maybe I'll catch you at the end of the story one day when you're not looking."

"Nah," he said, his knees cracking as he stood up. "I could tell that story forever, 'cos you wouldn't want to get to the end. Trust me."

She laughed, a hollow reed. Not because of what he'd said about the story, but because he had told her to trust him. "Where is she, Gene?"

"Eh?"

"Come on," she said. "You pretty much told me she was waiting for me here."

"Did I?"

Grace's voice, below her breath, was a scream. "You don't even know where she is, do you?"

"Yeah, I know."

"Well?"

"I know but I can't go there."

"What kind of shit are you trying to pull?"

"Basta!" he hissed and pressed his finger to his lips, looking back at the still slumbering Christopher. Closing the bedroom door behind him, he said, calmly, "My head hurts. I'm tired. I'll tell you tomorrow, after church. You're in the guest bedroom. Downstairs. Your grandfather'll show you."

"Gene."

"*What* already?"

"Did you ever tell her that story?"

"Sure," he said. He stepped back against the wall, an animal suddenly cornered in the narrow hallway. "So?"

"So"—she looked at him shyly—"she ever hear the ending?"

"No." He shook his head. "She said yes before I could ever get there."

⁂

The old man showed her downstairs to the guest bedroom, where he made a point of displaying the sepia photographs of himself and his wife arranged on the dresser. He pointed to one of a uniformed young man on a motorcycle, and prodded his chest with a meaty finger and said, "Carlos." She nodded and smiled. He picked up another, less aged, photograph of a sandy-haired little boy in a man's arms. The boy, himself holding a monkey in his arms, was scowling off to the left of the camera, sad at the prospect of being alive. Both boy and monkey were wearing striped T-shirts, though this was surely coincidence. "Gino," the old man smiled, and Grace felt a shock run through her, though of course it was Gene. The old man grinned and pointed at her. "Grace," he said. His glassy eyes twinkled before he closed the door.

She was soon sleeping deeply, her face drunk and warm. On the left side of her face the sunflowers are leaning over into the dry light of the road. And men are coming up the hill toward her, hammers swinging from belts, their faces blackened from coal, pink of their mouths. And though they brush by her on both sides she's invisible and her dress still sparkles white. Afterwards it's only her and her mindless shadow stapled to her feet and when she walks it flaps black along with her. At the end of the path the sunflowers lean away and they are not sunflowers at all and now there's a woman's voice, pure as water, and Grace stops. Her shadow is very small now. It comes undone from her heels and she kicks at it, carbon paper, till it rustles and flaps away, a jagged black puddle left in the middle of the path. Through a broken window of a burnt-out house she sees a man draped over a table naked and scratched all over. He's flipping through the pages of a photo album. But as she floats through the window the pictures inside the book are not photographs but Fra Angelico, Cimabue, Rublev, Giotto. The colours running. "I remember that," the man says. "Those were the days. That one, I don't know, think maybe they left something out. Too bad." *Close it,* she says. *They're running.* He looks up at her and says, "They'll come back." But she can't make out the rest since water's falling from the roof and outside the window and everywhere is the sound of water, but there's the woman singing in sunlight through another window. Her hair is wet and falls in slick black columns over her skin and when the man turns her way she is gone and she is back again threading her arms into the sleeves of a man's shirt, her face cascaded over with hair and her voice fades and Grace sees he has no fingers and Gene looks up from his book and says, "Without your own home, you're a nobody." And he turns back to pages bled white, as a bull comes charging down the road.

Grace awoke to the sound of skateboard wheels hitting the cracks in the sidewalk. Wedge of light and she felt someone shadow into the room, heard the chair beside the bed creak. She felt a hand on her head. She tensed herself but did not move. The hand softly, gingerly pressed at her skull. "You fell from a bed once," he whispered. "I turned away for a second and there you were on the floor. Landed square on your head. Boy, did you kick up a noise." Grace stared mutely at the wall, the whorls and grooves of the panelling coming into focus as grey dawn light filtered into the room. "Told myself I wouldn't tell her, but what if you turned out not right in the head?" His voice caught. Grace was still lying there, stone. She let him stroke her hair, till his breath steadied and calmed, till he got up and closed the door behind him so there was only the clicking of the baseboard heater. Outside the window she could see the backyard come into clarity above her, bare grapevines clinging to lattice work, sunlight singing through.

⋇

Breakfast was a quiet, almost sullen affair with fruits and leftovers. Christopher and his parents had left first thing. Grace sat silent, as the grandmother, in a black dress with black stockings, muttered about the table, and in the crisp morning light Grace for the first time saw how tired and used-up the woman looked, though nobody else seemed to notice. The old man, red-eyed, grunted foreign responses from his chair, barely acknowledging Grace's existence. He was a stranger. But regardless of what had happened just two hours before, Gene was still Gene, especially when he came into the kitchen holding up Grace's still-stained sweater and said, "Guess you're wearing your pyjamas today." The old woman took it out of his hands and, after a brief slamming of cupboard doors, was scrubbing furiously at it with a salted teatowel. Grace agreed she'd pick it up next time, though in her mind she'd already said goodbye to it.

The last thing she remembers from Gene's house. How the old woman, before they left, wordlessly handed her a photograph. The child in the picture was Grace, standing in front of a white house with what appeared to be aluminum siding and the vines sprawling across, reaching for something out of the picture. She is so little she has to climb up the stone steps one at a time and there at the top she turns and looks back at the house and her shadow's cut perfectly by the sun, her hair her fingers her one sock rolled down, and she jumps and she sees her shadow stay up there for a long time, floating in the air. There are other houses all around; she takes the time to take in the neighbourhood around her before she hits stone, hard and cold and crying, the blood on the leg, dirty. They swoop her up, them all warm with laugh and sigh. Her alone by the front door with sticks of Plasticine bunched together with dandelions in her hand, that sock still down, a Band-Aid on her shin, her curly blonde hair licking around her face. They want her to smile for the camera. She cries because she wants to blow the dandelion fluffs but there aren't any, there are only the flowers. The day they come to get her with their station wagon and their starched clothes.

Later she saw, on the back of the photograph, in a sure hand that seemed accustomed to English, "Leave him alone."

After breakfast Gene drove her downtown. On the way he hummed along to the radio, flicking at his pine tree air freshener every few minutes for good measure. Grace, hung-over, mumbled any necessary responses. She didn't want to set foot out of the car, her excuse being the shirt, but she did finally follow him into a small church courtyard, closed off from the city by wrought iron fences and cedars. The courtyard itself was dotted with stone carvings. Grace walked past Saint Teresas and Virgins toward the church's large oak doors. "The carvers come from all over," Gene said, gesturing vaguely.

"Why?"

"Holy Week," he said.

"Forget it," Grace said, sitting on a fountain's wall.

"Wassamatta?"

"I already told you, I'm not going to church."

"We're not *going to church.*" Gene sighed. "We're just going in the church for a minute. I gotta talk to this guy."

"How come you're so damn chipper this morning?"

He shrugged. "It's a new day."

She watched him closely. "Got a good night's sleep, eh?"

"Yeah." He kicked at a stone. "Sure." He left her and was swallowed up in the darkness beyond the church's oak doors. Grace got up and walked around to the back of the church but there was no graveyard, so she came back to the fountain and sat and watched people pack up their carvings, load them onto pick-ups. Most of the courtyard was cleared out already; rough, chalky patches of dust and chaff were left here and there on the ground. Across the square two men were trying to lift a huge stone carving onto a flatbed truck equipped with a hydraulic crane. The figure was hardly finished, though Grace could make out the intricate featherwork of a wing and what appeared to be breasts making a rough breastplate swell. If the thing was supposed to be an angel, its face was monstrous, pocked and blurred, as if melted. A small crowd of people gathered around the truck as the men, after fitting squares of cardboard snug below the shoulder blades and armpits, laced chains over the embryonic wings. An old couple, wandering in off the street with the help of gnarled walking sticks, came and sat beside Grace on the fountain wall. Grace couldn't help noticing the woman's drastically bowed legs. The man perched his chin on his cane and watched the men's progress. It was so slow that some children soon climbed onto the flatbed and one of them, a little girl, imitated the workers' efforts with a bit of string threaded with beads, her necklace perhaps, looping it over the wing. One of the men turned to her and, instead of being stern, chased her jokingly across the flatbed, kicking her behind softly, tickling her ribs, and picking her up and setting her gently down into the arms of a woman standing below. The girl, seven or eight, screamed in delight and Grace is seven years old again sitting with her fake family near the front in the Baptist church out by the Nanticoke Airport and the pastor leads the congregation in a prayer for the skydivers. Grace can hear the parachutes ruffle open and the voices screaming at the top of their lungs hundreds of feet above the primed grey ceiling and church steeple while the pastor drones on about the arrogance of those who don't rest on the Sabbath. Grace draws the pastor in the margin beside Ecclesiastes 2:26. He's skinny with glasses; she makes him skinnier, like a saint. In her drawing he wears a robe like her fake father does after he takes a bath: black and white and full of creases. She turns the robe into a parachute. She catches her fake father staring sideways at her halfway through the sermon. She closes her eyes, almost, and peers at him through her eyelashes. Blue and green stained glass shining behind his pink head. His arms, blond hair on them, are thick as both her legs put together. She shuts the

Bible, but he still makes her go up to the pastor after the sermon and show him what she's drawn. Frowning back tears, she hands the Book to him, eyes fixed on the black-and-white faux-marble floor. The pastor purses his lips, ready to laugh perhaps, but her fake father's standing tall and earnest next to him so he fixes his face. "Take it home and erase the drawings from the margins, Grace," he says. "And bring it back next Sunday, okay?"

"Excuse me, pastor," her fake father says, "but I don't think that's enough. I think she should stay behind until you think she's learned. Look by where she drew it." And he's sure to speak the words humbly, but with measured zeal. "*But to the sinner he giveth travail, to gather and to heap up that he may give to him that is good before God. This is also vanity and vexation of spirit.* Now, if that's not vanity, I don't know what is."

"Well, yes"—the pastor clears his throat—"I suppose I can show her something." After his congregation has left, and he's managed to say his farewells to the second half of them at least, he goes to the adjoining rectory and some moments later returns leafing through a large book with brown pages. "Where's your father?"

Grace says nothing.

"My, my," says the pastor. A cloud of dust kicks up in the parking lot, brown ghost of a car rolling away. He hands her the book and points absently to one of the pages.

"It's a picture," she says. An ikon of a ladder with many rungs, ascending from the darkness of the bottom left corner where tonsured monks climb diagonally up the page against a red desert ground, to where Christ greets them and lifts them through a window into Heaven. Yet some monks are lassoed around their necks and hands and dragged down by winged creatures painted black. They fall into a hairy gaping mouth at the bottom of the painting, while laymen and other monks stand by, looking on. Grace doesn't know why they don't help. She doesn't know why some make it to the top of the ladder and others fall. She has heard about Jacob's Ladder but she knows in her bones this is something other. She knows and she knows.

"Not there," the pastor says, tapping at the facing page. "There."

"Vainglory entwines itself around everything: I am vainglorious when I fast; but when I break my fast in order to hide my abstinence from others, again I am vainglorious, thinking myself wise; I am overcome with vainglory when I dress in fine clothes; but when I put on poor clothes I am vainglorious too; if I start to speak, I am overcome with vainglory; but if I am silent again, it overcomes me once more. However this trident is cast, its points will always be uppermost…"

While Grace reads on, stumbling over syllables like slippery rocks, the pastor's wife comes bearing apple juice and two liquorice sticks and sets them down beside her. "Your father takes the church very seriously," she says, before talking her place at the organ once more, as if she lives on that bench.

"He's not my father," Grace mumbles.

"Excuse me?" says the pastor.

She pats the weathered pages on her lap. "How much farther? Do I read more?"

"Oh. Well," the pastor sighed. "Do you think you understand what vanity is, Grace?" She swallows an inch of chewed liquorice and, pondering for a moment, shakes her head. "Fair enough," he smiles. "I'm not so sure myself, after hearing that again. But why on earth did you draw that picture, do you think?"

"I don't know," she says. "The skydivers. They're so high up. They get closer to God than any of us. You, even."

"Hmm." The pastor sits down beside her, hands drumming his knees lightly. "Well, wouldn't you know." At that Grace claps the book shut. *Philokalia.* Warm dust coughs up in her face and they laugh, the both of them.

For the rest of the time they sit there in the front pew listening to the pastor's wife play the organ. The pastor stretches his legs and Grace is surprised to see his socks are chequered in red and white. When he catches her staring at them, he takes his shoes off and flexes his toes. "Now *those* are parachute colours," he says. Grace bites her lip, giggles. She starts scrubbing her pencil eraser at the margins of the Bible until the pastor stops her hand and, taking the Bible, winks at her and she winks back with both eyes, chomping on red liquorice. She kicks her legs back and forth as the pastor's wife plays the opening notes of "A Whiter Shade of Pale." When her fake father comes to get her she doesn't say a word and she doesn't want to go.

"Let's roll." A key dangled before her dreaming face. "C'mon," Gene said. "Chop-chop." Grace slapped his hand away. "Hey!" He laughed, then followed her eyes to the carving. The men had secured the chains around the statue's wings. One of them now stood up on the flatbed and worked the crane controls while the other man vainly tried to hold the great stone bulk steady. Children, playing in the courtyard, stopped and stared; Grace noticed the little girl's beaded string hanging limp in her hand. When the distorted angel began to rise slowly, the small crowd started to applaud, but the crane couldn't take its weight for long. Flakes of stone fell from its wings. The truck creaked over to one side. The chains slipped, the man jumped back, and the angel thunked down and tottered on the cobblestones, rocked slowly to rest. The crowd sighed. "Well, so much for homely angels," Gene sniffed. "Come on." But Grace kept watching for spite. Bored, Gene threw the key into the air and caught it with a swipe of the same hand. "So we're all little chunks of God," he said. "Big whoop."

Grace folded her arms. "I'm staying here."

Gene held his palms open to the sky, beseeching. He turned to the old man sitting beside Grace and spoke to him in Portuguese. The old man said something back and Gene nodded and filled Grace in. "They need a bigger truck, he says, with a bigger boom. But they'll have trouble getting it through the gate."

Grace's blink didn't give a shit. "I want to go home, Gene."

"What's it gonna be?" Gene said. "Stay with the angels or go home?"

"Home."

"All right then." Gene squeezed her shoulder. "Let's go see our home."

"Don't touch—" She checked herself, but he'd already pulled his hand away and muttered an apology. Slightly ashamed, she followed him out just the same as they had entered, her fingers brushing the rough skin of remaining saints. His pants were coming unrolled again, scuffing the sidewalk. Sometimes he seemed a much older man, Grace thought. Stooped, burdened by a thing beyond his expression. At the gate she looked back. The people stood waiting around their ugly messenger, silent, expectant, and Grace wondered how it would find its way and how it got through the gates in the first place when Gene's words finally registered in her brain, and she shouted after him, "What do you mean, *our home?*"

⁂

They drove west out of the city, past towers of concrete and glass. They passed through Etobicoke and Mississauga until the strip malls grew tired of themselves and fields started to appear. He turned onto a winding gravel road full of buzz and twitter and Grace, finally turning to him, said, "Okay, where are you taking me?"

"Home."

She stared long and hard at his profile but it gave no sign whether he was telling the truth or not. She wound down the window and let the crisp air disturb her hair. Sun flapped through the trees, long grass ditches matted down save for odd pocks of snow here and there, trillium sparking out through the darkness of trees. Braking, the Colt slowly swung into the grass-rutted driveway of a small, dilapidated white house. The kind of house, plonked in the centre of a large, cleared lot, where the foundations still showed two or three feet above the ground and a crooked set of concrete slab steps led up to the front door. A rusted wrought-iron railing, for good measure. A bleached For Sale sign was staked at an angle into the knotty front lawn.

"Charming," Grace said. "Is this where the deal's going down?"

Gene turned off the engine and got out. He made a point

of surveying the ragged countryside and inhaled a theatrical breath. "Hurry *up,*" Grace chided, hoping he'd go round the side of the house but expecting him to whip it out and take a leak right there on the ratty excuse for a front lawn. But instead he told her to hurry up herself and walked up the steps and flicked at the rusted wind-chimes hanging from the eavestrough. She watched him fish a single key out of his pocket and unlock the front door and enter. She sat, stubborn, in the Colt. She started counting to a hundred but gave up after thirty. The heat through the windshield was a bore. She ran a finger along the grey dashboard and studied the linty dust collected on her fingertip. She made herself empty and became the forsythia that flowered, unhindered, along the side of the house. Starlings darted back and forth from the thin branches to the ground. The wind brushing this cheek, then subsiding. A seagull bleating overhead. Here, miles away from Lake Ontario. Grace looked up, squinting, and when the bird passed between her and the sun its variegated wings were translucent, immaculate. Does it matter, she thought, that any of this is beautiful? This syrup light? Does this matter?

He was standing in the middle of what once was a living room when she came in. "They haven't changed the sign yet," he said. "And it's cracked."

"The sign?"

"Nah." He nodded impatiently at the front window, its pane broken and plastic flapping, nailed to the outside of the frame. "Kids, I guess." He himself was framed by wallpaper suffering from both rising damp and a lime-green pattern involving pineapples. And, standing there with his pant cuffs coming unrolled, in a slanted rectangle of sunlight on the floor, he looked small once more, though his shadow trailed long and thin behind him along the hardwood until it dissolved into a shaded stack of old newspapers and magazines and dustballs in the corner. Grace thought she heard a cicada wind up its drone outside, but no, this was still April, it was hydro wires, surely, and soon they too were clouded by a shimmer of wind-chimes. "So?" Gene turned to her, scuff of his shoes resounding. "Whaddya think?"

Her eyes closed and her voice was honest. "I think you'd better get me home."

He laughed that gruff, immediate laugh of his and walked into the next room, the cuffs of his pants pinned beneath his heels. She followed him, but her patience was worn. "Look, Gene, I'm supposed to be at work."

"Remember this?" He ran his mutilated hand along a speckled kitchen countertop.

"Sure," she sighed. "Formica."

"She used to sit you up here," he said. "Make like the spoon was an airplane and you'd open up and go mmmm and your heels would be kicking—"

"No." Grace closed her eyes to the dark veneer cupboards. "It's not true."

"Sure," he said. "She even had you up dancing on here when we had friends over—course, she'd hold your hands the whole time. She'd never let you fall."

"No." Grace shook her head. "This isn't supposed to...you're putting me on. This isn't fair, Gene. It's not funny any more."

"When you were, I don't know, around three, I don't know if it was your birthday or not, she bought you this kaleidoscope and you just loved it. The patterns, how everything was perfect, beautiful, symmetrical. But you were so curious to see how it did that that one day you smashed it to bits against the floor here. And there were just beads, loads of tiny multicoloured beads, scattered all over the linoleum. But she didn't get mad at you. Never raised her voice against you, nuh-uh. You were an angel. You were crying your head off though, you were so sad and guilty." He laughed, a glimpse of perfect teeth. "And I remember she had friends over and you stood in the middle of the room with just these two beads in your hand, a blue one and a yellow one, and, oh, the face you pulled! 'Look!' you said. Well, I don't know what possessed her, but she got you to repeat after her: 'Two beads or not two beads, that is the question.' You were a smart cookie. You walked around the room to everybody, and shoved the beads in their faces, and you had this lisp and your face was so fierce. 'Two beads or not two beads...THAT'S the question!' Everybody bust a gut. You had the biggest grin on your face and you had no idea why. You were thrilled at the idea of being alive. That's what a doctor told me once, when I brought you in one time after you fell. Oh, yes. It was your world all right. If you were angry...look out, we all had to suffer."

"But the beads, that was *her* making me do that," Grace said. "That wasn't me being funny or *cute*. That was all for her own benefit, so *she* looked clever, so *she* was the star. She was just using me so they'd love *her*."

"You're wrong. It was always you. You were the only one she loved."

"No," Grace shook her head at the tiny, myriad blurs of colour in her mind's eye. "It's always been about her."

A child's bedroom. A forest scene unfurled across the walls, painted in shaky freehand, and clumsy approximations of Disney characters posed among the trees and vines and flowers. Their dimensions distorted, so much so that Bambi looked like some malnourished spotted dog, and a hulking grey mass that spilled over from one wall to another was left half-painted, its ears and trunk merely pencilled outlines of what was supposed to be, as were the last leaves, above where Gene sat, huddled in the corner. He pinched at the reddened bridge of his nose, his glasses dangled loosely from the other hand. His lips were moving but Grace could hear nothing of what they said. "Speak up."

"She never finished."

"It's a good thing." Grace laughed, wiping at her eyes. "I would've had nightmares."

"You did."

Their eyes sparked quickly inside each other's and when they stopped laughing the room was emptier. Gene rolled his head to the side. There were ragged scribbles of crayon there by his profile, an infant fist's handiwork. Yellow, green and blue. He stared at them. Motionless, almost catatonic. Grace was just about to speak or shake him, or do something at least, when he came to. He put on his glasses with care, pushing them up his nose. He laid his starfish hand down on the carpet before him. "You know this finger? It's there for nothing but the ring. That's the only reason people need this finger. So when I didn't need it no more, I took it out west."

"I know," she said. "You told me."

"You told me, you told me, you told me—" He bobbed his head from side to side. "I told you nothing! Jack shit!" He glared at her while the colour rose, lingered, and finally subsided from both their faces. "Like I was saying. One night I'm in a motel called Selkirk on the Trans-Canada, somewhere where trains shake the walls. There's a Bible verse hanging over the TV in this old-fashioned lettering with flowers around it, something about Jesus and me. There's this family…"

"There's a town called Selkirk just east of Nanticoke," she said quickly, "on the lake."

"Yeah, so what?"

Grace bit her lip. A fly battled the window pane, making noisy progress up its surface until it skittered back down to where the dead husks of others were curled up on the sill.

"There's this family in the next room. They're talking and laughing and shushing and shit. On the TV a man's pretending to be a woman and he's kissing another man. And this family's trying to keep quiet because of me, because they've been told to feel sorry for me, everybody has my whole life so that's why they act the way they do, even though I see between the cracks sometimes, when they're not watching. But they hate me, this family, see. They want me to die and so does the woman who was a man and so does your mother, and if she does, then so do I. They all tell me to. They sound like a choir, pretty, but I know they want me to hurt everyone. Your mother. You."

"Don't, Gene. Please. Don't do this."

"Don't worry," he said. "I won't let them hurt a mite scuttling over your body. First I try setting the bed on fire, but motels, you know, they use shitty stuff. The covers won't light, polyester or something. So I get out my pen knife. It takes a fair bit of hacking. I hear I should mail it to her, but how the hell can I mail it to her when she's somewhere…when she's at that new place now? And I can't keep the finger in the room, what with Jesus looking at it all bloody in the sink or the waste paper basket. So I carry it out into the snow. It's like…like a mouse or something in my hand, you know? I cross the parking lot and bury it in a field behind the motel. She's cold out there too, what with those prairie winds and my shirt off and the bare feet. When they find me the next morning, I guess I'm sitting in a bathtub full of pink water with my jeans still on. Go figure. The one guy, he says all they had to do was follow the blood. See, that's what *I* was thinking: If I ever want that finger again, I can follow the blood drips right to the spot. But of course," he laughed, "I forgot about snow, didn't I? Snow thaws." He shook his head, then looked up into the ruined eyes of Grace. "I bet you think I'm pretty dumb, eh?"

"No," she whispered. "I don't think you're dumb."

"No?"

She didn't speak. She came across the room and kneeled on the carpet before him and began folding back the ragged cuffs on his jeans.

*

In the window her reflection, outside the window murmurs of rain. The face in the glass was a freckled globe. Shadows for green eyes. Lashes long and curved, the charred bones of fish. Lips full, made firm by real and fake smiles and full laughter and winces from sun and a million moments that glinted gold and were forgotten, like dust motes in a summer room. All of these things she now saw for the first time as the property of somebody else, filled with rain. Her teeth, his. Him behind her at the kitchen table now, silent, save for that spoon singing in his cup of tea.

Earlier, on the way home, he talked of the Azores and of stars. He told her how, in 1959, after the eruption of the Capelhinos Volcano, on Fayal, the Oliveiras were one of a hundred Azorean families who came to Canada by boat. She asked him what the volcano was like and he said he didn't know, he was a boy, sleeping. He spoke of how, arriving in Ontario, the men first got jobs on railroads and tobacco farms, and Grace told him, "Nanticoke is pretty much the tobacco belt," and he said, "Yeah, I know, that's where my father worked. Nanticoke." She found it strange how Gene didn't see this as coincidence or fate or *something*, but he just carried on in a steady voice gnawed at the edges. How the unskilled workers rushed to the cities, to promises of factory and construction work. How English sounded just like noise, and how, once in Toronto, his father was taught this country's language by some cement finishers who'd taken him under their wing but after a few weeks he realized it wasn't English he'd been learning all this time but Italian. Yet no matter what befell their family they couldn't go home, Gene said, for an immigrant will not return a failure. *Imigrar e travar uma grande luta,* he said, and Grace didn't need him to explain it in English. And when he said things that were strange, like how nowadays there are so many millions of teeming eyes able to look out at the world but what do we want to do other than look at ourselves, the bacterial culture, the noise coming off us, Grace steered the conversation another way, toward Mexico where she'd always wanted to go except that really didn't have much to do with Portugal, or else she peered through the dark, melted glass of Gene's recollections. "What about you? What was it like for you as a kid in Canada? School and stuff. I mean, it must've been tough. Kids are mean."

He nodded, but instantly fast-forwarded to her. "When your bones were soft I held you. I'd stick out my finger and let your fist wrap around it. Check out the grip, I'd say, and Rachel would laugh, she had a laugh like you. No rules in that laugh."

And Grace, determined to stay light, finding herself disappointed to hear the same clichés she'd heard in other people's homes, searched until she lit on something else. "Hey. Did she give me a middle name? I got to have a middle name."

"Nothing else, no middle name. Didn't you see those forms?"

"Yeah," she sighed. "Sure."

He reached across her once, for the glove box, his voice straining. "You wanna hand me those cigarettes?"

"You smoke?"

"No. But I bought this pack a while back."

He tried the car lighter then cursed it when it didn't work. Grace handed him the matches in darkness and of course he didn't see the designs on the matchbook. She took a cigarette herself though he said he didn't like her smoking. The cigarettes were stale, awful. Here she was out on the rural concessions at night, bumming cigarettes off her father just so she could light them and throw them out the window, watch the sparks flash and fizzle on the tarmac behind them then disappear into the darkness. "Look!" she said. "Look!"

Him smiling but keeping his eyes on the pale ribbon of road unfurling from his headlights. "It's cold," he said. "Roll up your window." Obeying him, she pointed to the steelworks, lit up brilliant and sterile on the lakeshore, and Gene asked her what it was. When she told him, he said it looked more like hell, and she agreed. She peered up through the windshield at the sky shimmering high above the headlights' acre.

"So many stars."

"Stars nothing," he said. "In the Azores you can see more stars during one night than in Canada during the whole year. You know why?"

She shook her head, smiled.

"This is because in Portugal God stays closer to the people."

This, she thought, is something I would have laughed at yesterday.

And now rain began to fall hard as, in the window's reflection, he drained the last of his tea and got up and walked to the stove. He poured another cup from the cooking pot that acted as her new kettle. The stove ruined, burnt black plastic fused to the burner, dribbled solid down the front of the oven. "You should go back," he said. "You start to ache when you sit in the same place too long."

"I can't." She watched the young woman in the window shake her head slowly. "I've got to work in the morning. Bills to pay. Rent. I've got my own life here—" She stopped and laughed at herself.

"Artists," he said. "They're selfish." They stood there for some time. "But money," he felt for his shirt pocket. "You need money before you can go back to school."

"Who says I'm going back to school?"

"Be an artist, like your mother."

"Artist," she laughed. "Like her. I saw what kind of artist she was. Here ..." She strode over to the table and started leafing through a stack of magazines, calmly at first, flipping them open and showing the cut-out holes from perfume ads—see?—and cigarette ads—see?—and illustrations for articles on depression and seven ways to make better love to a man. She smiled tightly at him and then opened a pot and took out a handful of her matchbooks and chucked them down on the table, their tiny, bright patterns blaring blurs of colour. "There," she said shakily. "That's the kind of *artist* I am, that's what I do. I go into the bars and sell these. Cafés, strip clubs. I even leave them on the tables at the diner. How'd you like that, huh? Is that what you want to send me back to school for? You proud of your daughter?"

"Hold still," Gene said. He sat on the edge of his seat and reached to pull away a wet lash from her cheek, but she flinched. She was shaking. He sat back gruffly in his seat and stared at her for some time. She got up suddenly and gathered the half-empty cups, took them to the sink and dumped them out, ran hot water over them, and walked to the window. Her heart hollow, scraped clean. She wiped her eyes and watched rain rattle the trees, the rusted machinery in the lot across the alley, lush wetness of weeds. She saw Marie, dressed in that blue uniform, turn the corner and walk down the alley from the Sputnik. Her blonde hair clung wet to her head but her face was an empty vessel, as if unaware, not only of the torrent falling, but of the cinder path beneath her and the buildings and hydro poles and weeds all about. Breaking the spell, Marie brought a hand to her forehead and, with the web of her forefinger and thumb, wiped the water from her face. She folded her arms tight and kept walking. Grace waved, hesitant, but Marie didn't look up. She walked on under the window and away down the alley through the rain.

"I'm your father now, aren't I? What game is this we're playing now?"

"I don't know," Grace laughed. "You're not exactly what I expected."

"Chuva."

She turned to him, annoyed. "Now what's *that* supposed to mean?"

He nodded past her at the rain. "One night," he said, "when you're still a baby, you fall off the bed. Rachel's out with friends and I'm in your bedroom, singing. I leave you out of my sight, turn round for just a minute, and there you go, off the edge of the bed. Land right on your head. That's why you get those crazy bumps up there."

"Hmm." She saw herself in the window, absently touching her head. "But I turned out all right," she said brightly, turning around and curtsying. "See?"

"It's pouring rain this night. Just a minute before I'm singing you a song, an old *fado* they used to sing:

Porque os meus olhos se apartam
Dos teus não lhe queiras mal
Que as andorinhas que partem
Voltam ao mesmo beiral
Eu hei-de voltar um dia
Eu sou como as andorinhas.

Because my eyes leave yours
It doesn't mean I wish you harm

Let the swallows that depart
Return to the same nest
One day I shall return
For I am as the swallows are.

And now there you are on the floor. You don't stop crying. I think your head is cracked open. I never forgive myself for this. These twenty-one years, no matter where you are, whenever it rains, I worry about you. But this night all I can do is hold you. There are no cuts on your head. I feel around but there's no damage. You're still crying though. Your face is so red I think it's going to burst. What can I do? There's no ice in the freezer. I open the window and hold you in my hands, out in the rain. *Chuva.* Across the way there's a woman in the window of her apartment, watching me hold this baby out of a second storey window, singing. To see her face. Ten minutes later and there's cops at the door."

In the window's reflection she watched him tell his story. His head bowed toward the table, those blurred, illegible eyes. When he was finished talking, she saw his hands, which were held several inches apart before him, fall away from each other, the damaged hand coming to rest near the ring left by his teacup. She extended her fingers toward the window pane, slow and quivering, and there, touching the cold, wet glass, she covered his reflected hand with her own. Gene didn't see her. He ran his hand along the tabletop, stood up and turned to go.

"Bye," she said, more to herself than to him. He was already out the door and down the stairs. She gazed out at the leaves swelling green under the light at the edge of the vacant lot. A dog wagged its dripping tail through the weeds and slunk over to the water pipe, where its tail licked the underside of it, then it stopped to drink from the calcified tap. All this rain, she thought, and it goes there. She stood at the window until the dog was done drinking and wagged away, until she thought she heard Gene's car start up and hiss down the wet street once more. She imagined the Colt, rank with cigarette smell, hissing tranquilly all the way home to the rest of the family. She pulled a chair up to the window. The rain fell as cool, incessant music and she sat there for what was perhaps hours watching and listening, smelling it, until she nodded into sleep and Gene is standing down there in the lot full of weeds, watching a woman pass under Grace's window and on down the lane to where birds twitter in the bushes that weren't there before. Marie, her hair shimmering in the rain, treading on perfect pebbles of water that break into dust beneath her feet, Marie, her sadness radiant, walking past the lot full of weeds where the weeds aren't weeds at all and the man is left alone.

The darkness slowly dissolved into a warm hum of light above the rooftops, and it woke her. When the condensation had bred its way up the pane she wiped it away and cooled her forehead and neck with the run-off and she opened the window and let the rain spatter and fall on her head down her shoulders her bare arms and down off her nails her fingertips while across the alley the weeds began to open their small fists to the daylight, revealing tiny flowers that had started to bud. Chicory, small flecks of blue here and there. She quietly repeated the word he had spoken, *chuva,* before closing the window, ready again for sleep. And when she turned back to the room he was standing in the doorway, soaked through to his skin, and there was something broken in his face that made her forget to be angry. "What is it?"

"To cause it to rain on the earth, where no man is; on the wilderness, wherein there is no man."

She sighed. "Gene, you got a bad habit of—"

"I was standing out there, in the rain."

"Yes."

He took out the house key and put it down on the counter. "Here."

"No, you don't," she said.

"It's yours now."

"Nuh-uh, Gene."

"I bought it for you."

"I don't want it."

"I'll leave you alone with it for a while, and I'll move in and afterwards we can, you know..."

He took a chequebook out of his pocket and, clicking a pen, began to write in it. His face was a grimace and his glasses were steamed up like she remembered them being the first time he brought her home. "This'll get you started," he said, peering over the rims. "Touch up the place, get it like we used to have it, all nice. And there's clothes," he mumbled, "and school in the fall, but one thing at a time."

"It's not your money I wanted, Gene," she said, yet she found herself moving toward him. "Why are you being such a parody of yourself?" When he was finished, she stood next to him and picked up the cheque—three thousand dollars—then set it quickly back down.

"Ah," he laughed low and dumb. "You're playing a game with me again."

She slid the cheque toward him. "No. I don't want anything from you any more, don't you understand?"

"Ah, you said that before." He turned and swung his arm around her, pressed against her, so she was pinned against the counter. She felt the strength in him, the breath on her cheek. He bent toward her. "Rachel," he said, and he held her face tight in his hands and his mouth came down on her lips her chin her forehead her eyes and his scruff burned her mouth.

"Mmmno!" she cried and pushed him off her. "Fuck!" She spat and wiped violently at her mouth. She stood there shaking. His eyes were full of tears and the fridge hummed inside the sound of rain.

"Please," he held his arms toward her, his head tilted, pleading. "This time, I promise."

"You'd better go, Gene." She added, coldly, "Keep in touch, eh?"

"Rachel."

"I'm not Rachel! And I'm not Christopher either! I'm Grace! You get it, you fucking...ah, Jesus..." She slid down to the floor, her legs splayed, and she wept. "I'm Grace, I'm..." He bent down to touch her, but she slapped his hand away and buried her face in her hands. "Get out of here."

"I'm sorry," he said. He stood over her, leaning on the counter, sunlight streaming cool across the alleyway, slanting into the room, across her legs. "I'm sorry," he said. "This has all happened before."

She sat there long after he had closed the door silently behind him and buttery light filled the room. "I'm *Grace*," she said. "Grace."

⁂

Ultramarine. Orpiment. In all Duccio's paintings of the Virgin, she wears the same blue robe with gold edgings. And at Duccio's invitation, Grace journeys back through brittle gold-leaved pages to Byzantium, where colours were said to embody spirits and their vehicle was light. Ikons were everywhere, carried on poles through the streets, packed on the backs of travellers, hanging on the walls of the humblest dwellings, in the churches and cathedrals. A world of the visible living and the visible dead. People saw more ikons than they ever read books, and an ikon wasn't art so much as a window between this world and the other. Grace can only imagine the brilliant paint before the dirt and layers of varnish, before the surfaces were worn away and darkened by candle grease and smoke, by supplicants who would bring their prayers, some even writing on the ikons, others touching and kissing them. *Aspasmos.*

⁂

"Do you have an appointment?"

"You know I don't."

"Well, I can't do much for you if you don't have an appointment."

"Look, I want to see her, now. It's an emergency."

"She's seeing someone right now, miss."

"I'll wait." Before Grace took a seat, she added, "You know my name."

The walls of the reception area in the Children's Aid office were bright green, the chairs and table wood veneer. She bet if she were to pick one of the books off the shelf it would be sealed shut, plastic. Finally, the receptionist slid back the fake glass. "Grace?" She smiled and raised her brows.

"Thank you so very much," Grace said.

She walked through the doorway and down the hallway to the office, but bumped into a woman on her way out. "Take her easy, why don'tcha," Marie muttered, and kept on her way.

Grace touched her shoulder. "Hey."

Marie, turning and slowly registering who it was before her, said, blankly, "Oh." Her slack face was draggled with wet strands of hair and her eyes were empty. "You were fired," she said.

"Fine," Grace said. "It's not the first time." Smiling, she stared into Marie's face, but the other woman wouldn't look her in the eye. "I dreamt about you last night," Grace said.

"It was a nightmare then."

Grace reached to remove a hair stuck to Marie's cheek but then drew back and they both said *excuse me* at the same time and then carried on as if they'd never seen each other. Grace walked into Diane's office without knocking.

"Hello, Grace." Diane motioned across the desk. "Please, have a seat. Now—what's the matter?"

"What's the matter with him, you mean." Grace sat perched on the edge of her seat. "There's something wrong with him. What's wrong with him?"

"You mean Gene."

Grace sat back stiffly in reply.

"I'm sorry," Diane leaned forward and laced her fingers together. "But I did offer you his latest biographical information. I tried, but I couldn't force it on you, Grace. You just wanted to meet him—"

"No," she said. "I wanted to meet *her.*"

"It's not shopping, Grace," Diane sighed. "You can't get an exchange or a refund just like that."

"Listen, I don't need your metaphors right now."

"All right," Diane said. "Gene's schizophrenic."

Grace covered her face for a long time. "Christ," she whispered. Glaring quickly at Diane, she said, "Don't give me your fucking eyes."

Diane sat back in her chair, her slender fingers still threaded on the edge of the desk, forehead furrowed above the eyes in question. Grace watched the pretty hands separate and retrieve a pale yellow file folder from her in-box. A throat was cleared, professionally. "Well, this may not be the best timing, but I have to tell you…" She paused and Grace could almost hear the numbers being counted in the woman's head. "Your mother, Grace, she's—"

"She's dead," Grace said.

Diane whistled to herself. "Oh, boy." She dropped the file onto the desk blotter. "And what, if you don't mind my asking, leads you to believe that your mother passed away?"

"Things he said. Things he didn't say mostly."

Diane slowly slid the file folder across the desk. She got up and, after levelling what Grace took to be another textbook compassionate look, walked to the adjacent office's door. "I'll leave you alone for a while, okay?" Before disappearing behind the door she nodded at the file folder and said, "I suggest you read what's inside this time."

Grace watched Diane's shape make slow poetry beyond the frosted glass then fade and come to rest in some dark, blurred approximation of a chair. For a moment she thought she discerned another figure, a second voice, but there was silence, nothing more. Outside the window the Russian vines buzzed, their young leaves reddish in the sun, white flowers busy with early spring bugs. The room was close, hot, buzzing in its own silence. The file folder sat on the desk before her, a burnished yellow now, saffron from old sunlight filtering through venetian blinds. A piece of paper was sticking out of the folder before her, spindly writing she didn't recognize. She drew the folder toward her quickly, as if it would burn her fingers. Barely legible words in a nervous, backward-leaning hand. Grace withdrew the page from its file and swallowed and then began reading.

When Diane stepped back inside some minutes later, her face ready and appropriate, the file folder's contents were strewn across the desk but the chair was empty and the door to the hall was left open wide.

When Grace is six years old her fake parents drive out to Alberta. "We're going to see dinosaur bones," her fake father says. The car smells like onions; she wonders if the family has always smelled like this and she's never noticed before. She sits in the back seat of their station wagon, listening to him sing hymns and nursery rhymes all the way from Lake Erie to Medicine Hat. *Momma's little baby love short'nin', short'nin', momma's little baby love short'nin' bread.* He can't sing, there's no joy. Her fake mother does needlework, sometimes singing along and checking the mirror to see if Grace is too. She mouths the words, badly. She's thinking of onion cooties.

They pull into a Husky service station, go in the restaurant for breakfast. The waitress is nice. She wears glasses and tight purple jeans. A ponytail down the back. Grace wants jeans like that when she gets older. The waitress leads them to a table by the window. There's country music on the radio, a bunch of Southern voices singing "Will the Circle be Unbroken" with fiddles and whiny guitars. There are phones beside the tables too. Grace picks one up, dials a couple of numbers before her fake father slaps her hand. "Those are for truckers, not bad little girls." He points at her with a fat pink finger, gives her a purgatory look. She can't remember what it is she did that made her bad. She pouts and goes to hang it up, but he grabs the phone out of her hand and clumsily jams it into the wall. Ding! Fake mother gives her look number two. The waitress comes back, smelling like lemons.

"Ready to order?"

Later they are standing at the cash register, whispering violently. Fake mother doesn't want to leave a tip, says the waitress's bra showed through too much. Fake father says he didn't notice. His wife asks him why he forgot to give thanks at the table then. Grace walks between them, pushes the front door open with her hands on the glass, and steps out into the parking lot. The sun has swung up high enough to hit the sides of the two grain elevators across the highway. The buildings stand on either side of the railway tracks, a freight train crawling between them. The closest elevator is dark green, rusty in parts, with a faded smiling sun on the roof. The far building is bright red with a yellow roof. It says Gull Lake on the side, and the farmer's name, which she can't pronounce. Something foreign. She stands there on the gravel with the wind kicking up dust against her dress and the sky blue and immense above her. Thinking: I could leave them there in the Husky restaurant. I could hop the train, ride slow to the ocean on a bed of straw. Swim in water blue as mouthwash. Could stay with the waitress and wear purple jeans and see-through blouses. We could live in the big strange house that says Gull Lake.

She takes her elastic out of her dress pocket and gathers the hair at the back of her head. She pulls it tight, leaving those wisps at her neck that she likes. But before she can thread the ponytail through, her fake father grabs her high on the arm and swings her up onto the hood of the car. His finger wagging pink and huge. "Don't *ever* leave us like that again! *Never* think that you are so important you can go off and do as you please."

"You're hurting me." All she can see is salt water and the shining hood of the car.

"Yes, I am, aren't I."

They stop for the night at a motel in Swift Current that has orange-flower bed covers and sunset paintings that are screwed to the wall. Her fake mother's in the bathroom, making sandwiches from the Wonder Bread and mock chicken she bought at the IGA on the main drag. Her father undoes his belt buckle and slouches back against the headboard, flipping channels with a remote big as his shoe. His white undershirt sags over his pants. Grace stays away from his sock feet at the foot of the bed. She kneels on the green shag carpet and sings a mumbly tune to herself until her fake father says stop it. She follows his eyes to the TV. There's a car crash with fire. That's us tomorrow, she thinks. Fine with me. I don't want to live to see dinosaur bones.

After her fake mother's done making sandwiches it's time for bed. Back in the motel in Thunder Bay, Grace had slept in her own bed. It smelled of bleach and the stale ghost of smoke. But her fake mother says she doesn't want to sleep in the same bed with the "big lug" tonight. "A double bed feels like a twin with you rolling around in it," she says to her husband. "What if you roll over in the night? I'll be flat as a pancake. Either that or you'll smother me." Fake father immediately rolls off the bed and grabs his wife underneath the arms and swoops her up and drops her onto the next bed. She yelps and Grace laughs because she has never seen them play. "There ya go," her fake father says. "It's decided." There's a spare bedspread in the closet, but no cots are left at the front desk. Grace will sleep on the floor.

She wakes up scratching her leg. She's fully dressed under the blanket, but still she's cold. Her cheek is wet with saliva and so is the carpet. The TV's flashing "O Canada" into the room, across the bed where her fake father snores on top of the covers, his chin resting on his chest, his hand stuffed in his briefs, dormant. Shirt off, his skin looks hairless, ripe. She presses her cheek to the damp carpet again and stares at the maple leaf flag flapping on the screen. A cockroach scuttles across the green shag, a few inches from her face. She jerks her head back. Reflex. But then she ticks her arm out slow and flat across the carpet. The cockroach stops, antennae groping at the darkness, and climbs onto the back of her hand. Grace slowly sits up, gets to her knees. The TV has switched gears into white noise. Her fake father snorts and rolls over, his arm crashing against the mattress like timber. He smacks his lips soft, like in the cartoons. The roach is tickling her wrist now. She stands up and walks, arm outstretched, to the bathroom. Click. She puts the seat down and stands on the toilet, turning around to face the mirror.

The insect is shiny brown under the fluorescent light. It's tapping out Morse Code on her forearm. Friends. She gets down off the toilet and flushes it, the cockroach still balanced there, busy on her skin. She quickly opens the window and sticks her arm out. She leaves it out in the muggy air till there's no more tickling. The fields are full of bullfrogs and mosquitoes and other things, buried underground.

⁎

For these melted and metallic bodies when they are reduced to ashes, being joined to the fire, are again made spirits, the fire giving freely to them its spirit. For as they manifestly take it from the air that makes all things, just as it also makes men and all things, thence is given them a vital spirit and soul—Stephanos, alchemist, Byzantium.

It was midsummer and she was lying on her bed beneath a glass case of butterflies that hung on the wall, one of them fallen from its place, one wing broken off at the thorax. She was leafing through an old notebook, a pen tucked behind her ear. There were many blank pages left in the book. On the last used page she'd scrawled a quote from Pissarro or Picasso, in her writing it was hard to tell. The ink was blotchy, nodes of faded blue streak from the drag of her left hand. *Having found, after many attempts (I speak for myself) that it was impossible to be true to my sensations and consequently to render life and movement, impossible to be faithful to the so random and so admirable effects of nature, impossible to give an individual character to my drawing, I had to give up.* She ran her fingers over the page, until they drifted onto the blank cream page beside it, and then she studied her fingertips closely, searching for any residue they might have collected. It must have been Pissarro. She gazed out of her window at the empty lot, the chicory buds closed in the early evening light. The phone rang, startling her. She leaned down from the bed and when she picked up a man's voice said, "Hey."

"Hey."

"You know who this is?"

"I've got a good idea."

"Did you get those cheques?"

"Yes, I did. A few days ago."

He sniffed. "Good." There was a silence. "You want to know how the story ends?"

"The story," she said. "Oh. You know, Gene, it's okay. We can forget about it. I'd forgotten about it anyway."

"Hmm." His voice was measured and quiet, but had an echo to it. Grace pictured him pinching the bridge of his nose, easing back in a chair. "So the man went on thinking in his blue field. And when Sunday dawned, and the flowers cracked open their knuckles, he watched the line of trees down by the road. He closed his eyes and pictured her hair, rehearsing the words he would say to her: 'I know that once I was but timid, and once I was but rough, and once I acted deaf, dumb and blind…' Yet when he looked about him his field was not gold at all but still filled with blue flowers. Their stalks leaned against him like old friends, and he hated them. The insects that had shared his days buzzed about his head, and he swatted at them. A cloud of dust rose up on the road. He looked for her dress, but it was just the wind. And lo and behold, a long, dark cloud covered the sun and the blue petals began to close their fists. At first the man stood still and waited patiently for the darkness to pass. He soon began to panic and to rush about, trying to pry the flowers open with his big, fumbling hands, but the petals refused to give. Before long his mind grew tired and heavy with grief, and he laid himself down to rest. And when the cloud finally passed on he awoke and looked about him and saw that his field held no flowers at all. It was a field like any other, full of dry and brittle grass."

Grace cleared her throat. "So…that's when she came?"

"Eh? Why are you mocking me?"

"I'm not."

"You're down there, aren't you? Of course you didn't come. I bet you don't remember, but from the field I hear laughter coming from our white house. I walk past the windows flapping plastic, and in the back door. Smoke, music, people I don't know. I'm not good around people. You're on the couch, the old black-and-white blinking. A man with his shirt off is sitting beside you. The hair on his chest looks like a donkey's head, nipples for eyes. His hands are busy knowing you so I sit down in a chair where the light's a magnet over my head. When your dress rides up I can see the bruise on the inside of your leg. His thumb smudges it. The man on the black-and-white is sweaty. He hasn't shaved for days and he falls down in the street. Your eyes are closed but you're the only one who laughs. 'Where's our baby?' I say. You say nothing. 'Where's our girl?' I turn off the TV and the donkey man points down the hall. There's our little girl, sleeping in her crib with food streaked and caked on her face. I shove people out of the way and take her to the bathroom to clean her up. It's just us and the mirror now. But when I'm done scrubbing her face I look at me and there's nothing there. So

I make faces just to be sure, and our girl starts laughing with tears on her cheeks. I grab our things and you don't stop me because you're sleeping again, your head on his chest. 'You want me to go?' I say. Your hair's strung across your face and your laugh embarrasses me. I'm so quiet, you know, so quiet you don't know what's going on up there. I cross the room with our girl in my arms, but it's hard through the smoke. 'You want me to go?' You roll over and your green eyes flash for just a second and you say yes before I can ever get there."

"I'm sorry, Gene."

"Where was I?" he said quietly. "Ah, yes. So I walked down the driveway to where my car was waiting. I took a lighter out of the glove box, a can of gasoline from the trunk. Gas sloshed onto me and the grass, but I dumped most of it over the flowers. Flames caught on my pants; I had to slap them out. The dry stalks caught one by one but the fire went backwards across the lawn, back to the house. The siding caught up one side, shingles spitting like firecrackers. Imagine what fire was before we had a word for it."

"But this just happened, right?" Grace said. "This is new. This is, like, today."

"Smoke damage to half a house, they said, and what wasn't done in by smoke was burnt down. Arson, they called it. I said, 'You wouldn't know arson if it came up and burned you in the arse, son.' When they hit me they said it was never my house. And it doesn't matter if you set a bunch of fucking weeds on fire first, they said, you still burnt someone's house down. Ah," he coughed away from the mouthpiece. "It wasn't supposed to touch the house."

"That's a good thing, Gene. You can say that. Have you told them that?"

"It was wrong what I did. All the little creatures that were burned alive."

"You can't think about that."

"My family never liked you."

"I know."

"You weren't Portuguese. They say it was your fault I got sick. They don't believe in words longer than three syllables. You're not a retard, brother said. When I got put on medicine after going out west, he kept flushing it down the toilet. You went to school, he said. You read Dickens, for Christ's sake. Poor brother had to run the shop that I started up. All I could do was work the counter, till I got put on holidays for poking customers in the eye. See, I was taking medicine on the sly before that," he said. "But when I knew I was seeing our girl again, I figured it's over, I don't need it. When you've got the things that matter, you don't need anything else. Like the ring finger. You think it'll be good for you being with me, so you can be magic again?"

"No. I just want you to get better."

"If I get better, I bet you'll think, 'Here goes all that beauty.' That's what you'll think."

There was an echoing scuffle of feet then, voices.

"Where are you, Gene?"

"In a telephone room."

"Yes, but where?"

"Peel," he said. "That's what it says on their uniforms. The region of Peel. There's a guy watching through the glass. He thinks I'm going to shit myself or something."

Grace couldn't help laughing. "A police station? Come on, Gene. Help me out here."

"Sometimes it gets so narrow in here."

"Listen to me, Gene. You've got to talk to somebody there. You need to tell them you're not well, you need medication."

"Yeah." Static. "That's what you said before, when you couldn't string two words together. So Gino flew our little bird away from home, didn't he. Our little swallow. Borrowed money from the store to help get you dried up and our girl, well, I knew I couldn't look after her much longer. When my head said take her out west I knew if I went far enough we'd reach the glaciers."

"No. You don't know what you're saying."

"You were out of your tree," he sniffed. His voice shook. "What was it, a week before you noticed we were gone? We were on the Trans-Canada. Now that's a highway. At the truck stops they got phones at the tables."

"Yes, I know."

"We got as far as a place where trains shook the walls. The woman at the desk was a big one with Coke-bottle glasses. And in our room, sitting under the Bible verse, I knew you didn't want my ring. I could feel ice rumble underground and when it shone through the floor I got scared. I carried our girl back across the parking lot to the office and I handed her across the desk. "I'm taking a shower," I said. The woman looked at me like I had two heads. I wasn't wearing a shirt, I think, but she nodded without a word and put our girl down in a nice plush green chair. Back inside the family through the wall was trying not to laugh and that shitty polyester wouldn't light. When they found me in the tub our girl was still asleep, bundled up all nice in that chair. They sent her back to you, but I guess when they found you gone they put our baby in a home—don't worry, she was only there for a little while, till a nice family took care of her. My family told me you were dead. I bet you were still wearing that same dress, weren't you. And now here you are again, back from that other place. You packed up the whole shebang, all the past and present tenses, and you did it all left-handed, carried them in that dress of yours and dumped them out at my feet again twenty-one years later."

"Rachel's not dead," Grace said. "She's living in Windsor. She moved there in 1984, after marrying a man in the upholstery business. But you know this, don't you, Gene, after them putting a restraining order on you. She manages a luggage store now, and before that"—Grace laughed—"she worked in a bead store, among other places. She has no other children. She's forty-two years old. She has brown hair and green eyes. She likes swimming, crosswords and, get this, painting. That's my mother, and you're my father, Gene." She could hear a bang, a shuddering. "Hello?!"

"Forget about it," he said. "I'm going to the glaciers as soon as I get the call. The guy who's caretaking the glaciers right now, his contract's running out. My money's no good up there. There's something in the money here that gets passed on from hand to hand; the poison gets in your bloodstream. But you're strong. You can take the money."

"I told you," she said, staring through the hundred-dollar bills fanned out on her floor. "I don't want your money, Gene."

"You spend that money," he whispered. "Hear me? Use it for school and be quick about it. See, I borrowed it from the shop and brother doesn't know. He's coming to bail me out tomorrow, but I'll get him to swing by, pick you up on his way. Mum's the word, okay?"

"I'm really sorry. I'm not going anywhere. It's for the best."

"We're coming down then, all of us. We got so much to talk about before you see me off."

"I can't. I'm working straight through till—" She caught herself and sighed. "Jesus, you're just better off without me. Your family doesn't even want me around."

"Lies," he said. "Yesterday I was getting let out of my room and I was sure I was forgetting something. I looked under the mattress, in the toilet, the sink. I was sure I left something behind."

"Go on," Grace said. "Go back and be with your family."

"There's always tomorrow. I'll see you tomorrow."

"Wait!" She shouted.

It was a while before he grunted, "What?"

"What you've told me. Is it supposed to be the truth?"

A crackle of other voices on the line; Gene snapped a muffled yeah away from the phone. When he returned to the receiver his voice was immediate and gruff once more. "About what?"

"Taking your little girl away. The house. Me. Is any of that supposed to be real?"

"There is no *supposed to,*" he said. He hung up before Grace could say anything. The phone emitted four staccato notes then clicked into dial tone. She put down the receiver and sat there watching her hand's dampness vanish slowly from the white plastic, a backwards time-lapse photograph. Before her a page of her old sketchbook was filled with words he had spoken, and there were drawings along the margins, a roadside motel, a woman reclining on a couch, a baby in a chair, and in the top margin a sketch of an open field with swift, blue-inked strokes of long grass and here and there the small fists of flowers reaching toward a light somewhere high above the page.

⁂

She's been working all morning. Cottonwood and milkweed parachutes fall around her, some landing in her hair, sticking to her stained plaid shirt. There are speckles on her watch face and her hands are rich with colour, viscous as semen between her fingers. Flies buzz about her head, drawn to the smell, but she moves on, oblivious. She steps over a rusted axle and sits down on it, rinses off her brush. Ochre swirls and eddies in water. She squeezes a fresh sliver of colour onto her palette. A white plastic model from the only art-supply store in town, complimentary with any purchase over a hundred dollars. She'd been waiting on the front steps when the store opened. The stock was limited, so she had to gather all the different pigments she could find. Aurora and cobalt, ochre, cadmium. Three brushes, assorted sizes. She had more than enough money. The girl at the cash register, all black lips and gothic skin, was annoyed at the loss of an entire colour. She stopped punching in the numbers long enough to raise an eyebrow. "Let me guess: your favourite colour's red, right?" Grace laughed, no rules in that laugh, as the girl went on punching in numbers.

She walked home past the church where bells pealed in a descending loop as the congregation filed in the doors. She walked by the Fernleigh Flowers storefront, fresh chrysanthemums humming under fluorescent lights, and went around back to the small empty lot overgrown with weeds and chicory. The stalks leaned affectionate against her legs. A tin of water had been set there, ready. She emptied her bag and chose a tube of cobalt yellow. She then picked the most slender brush and put it in her mouth, as once was her habit, running its fine hairs out along her tongue, between her wetted lips. She dabbed at a thick, bright slug of cobalt and painted one petal, then another. She soon realized that with a larger brush she could apply one quick stroke and take care of the whole flower. When she began, the chicory was a torrent of powder blue. Yet as Grace moved outwards from the back of the lot, a touch here, dab there, cobalt giving in to ochre, the blue slowly melted into buttery light. If a bird flew over, she thought, it would mistake this small field for a slice of the sun that had broken off and fallen to earth.

"I don't think I've ever seen anything like this before," she hears a voice say, and at first she tries to ignore it. "Perfect." Grace starts humming a false melody so as not to hear. "You live upstairs, don't you?" Finally, she looks around. A woman stands in the back doorway of Fernleigh Flowers, a tangle of plastic vines over her shoulder. Flecks of grey shine silver in the sun, rings on every finger. "I thought I recognized you." The woman pauses and squints against the unreal brightness of the flowers, nodding. "Beautiful."

"Thanks," Grace laughs nervously.

"But they'll be dead before long. You're killing them, you know that."

"They'll grow back."

"I should hope not!" the woman laughs. She swings the fake vines up and into the dumpster. Then, dusting off her hands, she draws a forearm across her brow, spark of dark hair in her armpit. "Last thing I need out back of my store is a bumper crop of weeds." Her face is pale, wrinkles settling at the corners of eyes and lips, yet her age has worked happily into her skin, leaving a quiet glow beneath. Grace can't help but think of the word *patina.*

"They're not weeds," Grace says cheerfully as she bends back over her work, moving along in silence until the woman clears her throat.

"They're weeds all right. Still, you'd better hurry up if you want to do them all today."

Grace gazes up at a speckless, ultramarine sky, then regards the woman once more. "How do you figure?"

"Those chicory petals," the woman says. "They close up at noon."

"How do you know? You an authority or something?"

The woman, smiling, taps the side of her head, and turns and walks in the back of the florist's. Grace stares at the shuddering glass. She mimics the woman's gesture, leaving a smudge of ochre on her temple.

An hour passes, full of fumes, heat and colour, the odd drink of water. Grace's thoughts have acquired the rhythm of her hands until they're one and the same. A wind kicks up black dust from the path. She has to shield her eyes with her sleeve. Squinting, she can discern the blurred figure of another woman walking down the alley towards her, a blue dress humming in the haze. Only when the woman's quite near does Grace recognize Marie. She looks wide awake for once, freshly made-up, her hair brushed smooth and full. Her dress is immaculate even though Grace knows, by the direction she's coming from, that Marie's on her way home from the Sputnik Diner.

"Just came by to drop off your paycheque. It's been gathering dust for weeks."

"Cheque." Grace shakes her head. "Great. Thanks. You can put it in my bag over there."

Marie doesn't move. "I live just up the block," she says. "The big red brick place, up there on the end."

"Yes." Grace bends over her work once more, another slug of ochre on her palette. "I've seen you walk by."

Marie nods. "So..." she says, gazing around. "You've gone off your rocker, I see."

"It's a long story."

"Oh yeah?" Marie murmurs. After a minute she looks down at the cheque in her hand. "So that's your surname, eh?"

"Yes. That was my foster parents' name," says Grace. "My fake parents." And so she tells it from the beginning: a skinny out-of-town Wurlitzer man, his thick glasses and starfish hand, how it was her mother she'd wanted to see all along. She tells nothing else of her mother but otherwise she leaves out very little, only certain details, like the time she was sleeping in the guest room and he stroked her head and told her another story; this one she will keep for herself. But she tells the rest with patience and clarity, as if speaking of someone else, and all the while she is working, slow but steady, on the flowers. When she's finished talking, the sun is already descending. Marie's silent for a long time.

"I'm sorry."

"You don't have to say that," Grace says.

"Well," Marie says. "It's just...don't expect me to tell you my story."

Grace smiles. "Fine. But I'm a sucker for a good story. Hell, all I am is a few stories cut and pasted together."

"Well, you'll have to wait for someone else," says Marie. "They'll tell you. How I'm the most selfish, horrible person in the world."

"Well, till then I thought we could be friends."

"Friends."

"Yeah." Grace slowly surveys the lot. "You know, buds." And it's now she sees the flowers are closed up like thousands of tiny fists. All except the ones she's painted. "Sorry, Grace, I've got to go," Marie says, but she stands there listlessly. Grace sets right back to work and before long she finds that by squeezing the base of each unpainted flower she can make the petals yawn open. And though it's in the flowers' nature to slowly close back up, by gently working in her thumb, then folding back each petal, she can assure they'll stay open with a quick dab of paint. Watching, Marie bends down beside Grace, and taking up a brush, she begins to follow suit.

"Just dab it once," Grace says. "That'll be enough." Marie nods, engrossed, her face open and serious, like a child's.

So they work as the sun slides slowly down the sky. Bugs natter about their heads, the air settles, grows colder. Grace checks her watch, which she can barely read for the spatters of paint.

"You're expecting him, aren't you?" Marie says.

Grace doesn't answer.

"I've really got to go soon," Marie says, looking up at a blush of red spreading across the rooftops. "I'm meeting someone." She looks at Grace, long enough for the other woman to feel she's being watched. "You won't finish it all in time by yourself, will you?"

"Of course not," Grace says. "Never will."

"Why'd you start at the back then? We always want to be seen. Don't be all fake humble about it. Start at the front. You know, so if you don't finish at least it's like clear-cuts."

"No, I don't know."

"You *know,*" Marie says. "How they keep a thick strip of trees along the highways so it looks like the forests are all full and lush when really there's nothing there."

"Who are you?"

"You should get in touch with your mother."

"What makes you think she's alive?"

"You should." Marie nods. "She'd want that. Believe me."

"No." Grace pauses, dabs another flower, then shakes her head. "No, I don't think we're ready. Not yet."

When their eyes meet, there's a glimmer in Marie's that Grace can't place, something curled up, as if it was bottled in such a way long ago. For a moment Grace knows she's utterly lost. "I don't know if I'm doing the right thing."

"But it's not for you to say."

Grace puts her brush between her teeth and looks about at her day's work. She throws out her arms and gives a garbled shout. "All this colour!" They both laugh. A flurry of feathers suddenly swoops over their heads, little birds alighting on telephone wires. They can hardly see them for the low sun and the fumes that hang over the lot. Grace has to step out of the flowers, if only to catch her breath. From here she can see the birds clearly, their folded wings dark against a crystalline sky, breasts pale save for spills of red at the throat. "Grace." They're gone, startled by the voice, off and away across the gold, rust and leaves, the rooftops. "Grace," Marie calls again, and points toward a car pulling into the alley, crackling over the cinders. In the low sunlight they can tell neither its make nor its driver, only that it's a hatchback and there are two silhouettes in the front seats. The car stops some distance from them. After a minute the driver's side door opens and a man gets out. He has long hair, dark glasses. He opens the back door and effortlessly lifts out a small child, a boy. They walk up the alley, hand in hand, while a lone, unmoving silhouette sits looking on from the passenger seat. "But he's not supposed to be here yet," Marie says. Grace's heart is a hammer in a bell. She says nothing, since she knows and she knows and she knows.

The Blue Line Bus

THE YOUNG WOMAN came in out of the heat. She had to shove at the door a number of times, working up a panicked sweat, before it finally gave. A knapsack weighed her down, along with a hardshell guitar case. And she was overdressed for the weather, a leather jacket hanging over her burgundy tie-dyed dress. She set down the guitar case and looked at the old man behind the counter. Nudging back her cap, she gazed around at the room. There were red Naugahyde seats and plastic plants and the small upper window panes were grimy so they cast a yellow pall over the whole room. Its dark panelling and red shag carpet were thick with the smell of old smoke, humans and must. Two baroque metal ashtrays at either end of the ripped couch held permanent offerings of butts and ash. The laminated pictures of once-gleaming Greyhound buses passing through the greatest hits of North American countryside were now sticky, faded yellow artefacts, as if they had spent long years hanging over stoves, greasy hot plates. *See the U.S. & Canada the Greyhound Way! We'll Take You Where You Want to Go!*

"When's the next Victoria bus?"

The old man had been staring at her since she'd first struggled in the door. He stood silent behind the counter now, motionless save for his muddy grey eyes that blinked back at her once, twice. She noticed how his hands, which were folded lifeless on the counter, were pale, more the colour of driftwood. As if aware of this, he lifted one of them and considered its yellowed fingernails, set it down again slowly, then turned his grey eyes up at her once more. "Eh?"

"Victoria," she said.

"No local buses here, missy, let alone a Victoria Street bus."

"No," she said. "Victoria, B.C."

"British Col*umbia?*" He squinted at her. His was not a gruff voice with the jovial dance behind it. It was gruff and hard, period. "What, can't you fly, girl?"

"Can't afford it," she said.

"Shit. Bus'll cost you more'n flying, you ask me."

"I didn't. How do I get to Victoria?"

The old man supped on his gums, as if he had a mint in there, a habit that perhaps he'd perfected over many years, since his cheeks were now drawn in, puckered, even when he spoke. "Now, what's in Victoria that's so damn special?"

"Stuff," she said. "Trees. Water. Mountains..."

"Oh." He spoke without humour. "There's none of that here, I suppose."

"Not much here at all," she said. "Except tobacco fields."

"Must be something here," he said. "Otherwise you wouldn't be leaving it."

She eyed him, mistrustful. "Listen," she said, "I just—"

"How about Lake Erie? There's your water. And Hamilton Mountain…"

"That's not a mountain," she said. "That's an escarpment." She shook her head quickly. "Look, man, all I need is—"

"Seems to me," he pressed a thinking finger to his nose, "you'll have to take a Toronto bus first. Then…"

Impatient, she peered over the counter, then turned and surveyed the walls, flung her arm out at them, sending a waft of patchouli oil into the close, musty air. "Don't you have charts or something?" she said. "Any cross-Canada maps?"

He brought the finger from his nose to the side of his head and tapped. "Keep it all up here."

"So?" She let her mouth hang. "What do I do after Toronto?"

"Take another bus, I suspect. Ask in Toronto. They think they know everything up there."

"Thanks a *lot*," she muttered as she turned away. "Jesus. Who the hell do you think you are?"

"I'm a sumbitch," he said calmly, almost cheerfully. "Just an old sumbitch. How about you?"

She gathered herself, let out a long, tremoring breath. "Look," she said, the cuffs from her jacket rattling their plastic buttons on the counter. "When's the next Toronto bus?"

"It'll be along shortly."

"When?" Her tongue stayed pressed behind her teeth.

"A quarter to five."

She looked up at the clock; the hands read quarter to five. "That clock slow?"

He turned round awkward, contemplated the time, then blinked back at her. "Nope."

"Shit!" She rifled through her woven purse. "Whyn't you tell me?!"

"Just did."

"Fuck. Forget it. Just get me a one-way ticket."

"Toronto?"

"Yes, Toronto!"

He turned from the counter, not before gathering something from underneath. He moved slow as history and before long she could see he was walking with two canes and that for some reason the canes had been painted red. Such was the slowness of his walk to another counter at the back wall of the room that she stuffed her money back in her purse. She let her knapsack slump heavily onto the Naugahyde couch and paced over to the window, where she tapped at the glass with her purple-painted nails and looked out across the street. The old man paid her tapping no mind. He continued at the same doddering pace as if all his concentration and energy were thrown into the pained movement and the rest of him, for that time at least, was nonexistent. His feet stutter-stepped until he reached the counter, where he hung his canes on a large hook, steadied himself before a machine at the back wall. He threaded a slip of paper into it and typed slowly, deliberately, at the numbered keys on the machine with his index fingers. The paper ratcheted through. The young woman flinched against the noise; she blew at her straw-coloured bangs and studied the street once more. It was Sunday, and so the street was quiet. Shadows careened from parking meters, heat hummed off car hoods. The bus stop was still empty. She shook her head in contempt for all she saw out there. "They got computers that do that, you know," she said. "In other bus stations."

He spoke to the wall. "That right."

She nodded; her eyes blurred as a truck rattled by.

"And I suppose," he paused to punch the last digits through the ink ribbon, "you've seen a good many in your time."

"Sure," she said absently. "Hamilton, Buffalo, Rochester."

"Hmm," he grunted, whipping the receipt out of the machine. "And what's a young thing like you doing gallivanting all over in those places?"

She smiled. "You didn't say pretty."

"Eh?"

"You said *young thing like you,* but you're supposed to say *pretty young thing.*"

"Sorry," he said. "Can't do that."

"Why not?"

"Young ladies like you don't like being called pretty nowadays," he said. "I read it in the paper. Feller in California went to court for calling a lady pretty."

She laughed. "Just because it's in the paper doesn't mean it's true. Specially if it's a shiny paper."

He nodded. "Yup. That's another thing I read about you. You don't believe in nothing neither."

"Is that right," she said.

"It was in the paper," he sniffed. "So basically you unpretty young folks are running all over the place with your not believing in nothing, and doing what else all over Hamilton and Buffalo and wherever, I want to know?"

"Following the Dead," she said.

He took his first cane down from a hook on the counter, propped himself against it, slipped the receipt into his shirt pocket, then grabbed the second cane and started to squeak back across the eternal linoleum. "The dead?"

"The Grateful Dead," she smirked, watching his hard complication of wrinkles work without changing expression.

"Now what on God's green earth," he said, "would possess you young folks to go following any kind of dead, let alone a grateful kind of dead? Seems to me they'd be the worst kind to be associating with."

She smiled. "They're a band."

He didn't do what she expected of an old man. He didn't throw back his head, mock theatrical, and say, *Oh! Why didn't-cha say so in the first place?* and follow it up with a wink or quick, knowing smile or maybe nothing at all, just dead-pan. He merely shifted on his canes, shook his head and looked past her at the sunny street. "Nope. Don't get up to Hamilton much nowadays. Forget the States." And when he finally returned to the front counter he didn't hang up the canes, but instead leaned over and nodded down at the receipt, which furled out of his pocket, quivering just below his chin. His shirt was cream-coloured and might have been white once upón a time, subject to the same yellow weather as the posters. Through the cotton she could see a white vest with sky-blue trim. A cleft sagged there in his loose chin, its folds ungathered, a C-section belly. "Self serve," he said.

She flexed her fingers first, tickled her own palm as if sand was caught there and plucked the receipt from his pocket. A shiver went through her as her fingers brushed his shirt. The ink had stained the receipt and she noticed there was ink smudged on his shirt as well, clear through the pocket. Though from the angle she knew he wouldn't see it till he either looked in the mirror at his implacable face or took the shirt off that night.

She picked up her belongings and left the office without a

word. The door was stuck again, she had to use all her weight to force it open. "You've got to learn to be responsible," the old man said.

She spun around, speechless and furious as he lifted the counter gate and now, taking up his canes again, started toward her across the shag carpet. "Comes a time people like you've got to stop running around and face up to things," he said. "Even a pretty young thing like you." His mouth was pursed and in this perhaps she could have read a smile, a concession of sorts. But she turned away quickly instead and pulled the door shut before he could get any closer.

He locked the door behind her and flipped over the sign and she stood on the sidewalk and watched him make his stubborn way back across the red shag, lift the counter gate and cross the linoleum. She thought she heard the sound of his canes clear above the sparse lazy traffic on the street. She watched until he stopped and picked up a bunch of papers, flicked off the light at the back. "What the hell do you know about anything, anyway?" she muttered. "Old bastard."

She crossed the street. A horn blared at her; she didn't notice the car until it passed, its blue hide glinting in the sun. She would've given it the finger, but her hands were full up. There was no one else at the bus stop. The sidewalk on this side was stifling, the sun still had work to do before it sank down behind the Greyhound office and the other faded, forgettable buildings across the street. Her straw hair could ignite, she thought, flare up like a candle, just like that. She took her jacket off. She lit a cigarette and stood with her hip cocked beneath the baggy dress. The smoke was unbearably dry. After four drags or so she butted it out on a pole. At least the bus would be air-conditioned. She sat down on her knapsack and pulled down her cap against the sun. This not enough, she took her shades out of her purse, the ones with the narrow plastic frames and yellow lenses—she had others—and put them on. But they were for looks more than use.

There was a dog tied to a parking meter across the street, outside the Salvation Army. It was a tawny cross, probably between German shepherd and Lab. Circling the metal post, it got its hind legs tangled in the leash and then finally, dejected, crossed its front paws and laid its head on them, whimpering. The young woman was fixing to cross the street and release the dog, but there was a man approaching, walking crooked down her sidewalk, so she stayed sitting with her belongings. The man, his stride faltering, stopped in front of her. His face was in shadow. "Hey," he said, pointing at the guitar case, then letting his arm drop heavy against his leg. "Play us a tune there, darlin'."

"Sorry," she smiled tightly, as much from sun as discomfort. "Not today."

His figure remained standing there, swaying, apparently comfortable in its shadow. "I know a thing or too 'bout guitars," he slurred. "Got some right around the corner, at my place." He sidled up closer, his zipper inches from the peak of her cap. He stank of beer. "How 'bout you, darlin'? Whatcha got there?" he said, toeing at her dress. "What model you got packed away in there, eh?"

She stood and picked up the guitar case. "Winchester," she hissed. She tried swinging it at the man but she nearly threw herself down on the sidewalk with its weight. "Fuck off!"

He danced away, giggling like a child. He was shorter than her. In sunlight he was pale, with curly hair and a Blue Oyster Cult T-shirt. "Tha's pretty good. Winchester," he scoffed, grabbing his crotch. "Me too. Me too." He rubbed his stubbly chin and staggered away. He looked back at her a couple of times and grabbed himself again, twirled around, then kept on crooked down the sidewalk.

"Asshole." She sat back down, breathless and shaking. "Nothing but fucking assholes here." She fumbled for another cigarette, but her hands weren't obeying her so she cursed the pack and stuffed it back in her purse. When she looked up, the dog was gone. She scanned the sidewalk over there: deserted. There were only the dark windows of the Greyhound office and the Salvation Army, the gutted store between them, its floor piled up with a riddle of oil cans and car parts, a motorcycle chassis, an old *Coke It's the Real Thing* sign faded into pink. And yet there too, behind the store buildings, she saw trees mushroom up into the sky. When traffic lulled she could hear the rustle of leaves above the street, see their pale undersides turn over and shiver in the sunlight. So many trees here. She remembered thinking this back in high school, kicking leaves home on late October afternoons, a crisp sky and her knapsack full of books seldom opened, the dry rustle of yellow brown red underfoot, thick dead smell of them. She remembered the trees down in the gully behind her subdivision when the boy put his hand down there and she soared inside and the trees flew away with the sky and his face and then she held his penis like a lighter, pulling at it with her thumb till he rasped that it hurt but he was laughing and stiff too and a minute later she watched it spray across her jeans, the slow slug shine of it spread across her knuckles. That little scar on his upper lip when they were full and guilty but flying inside as they walked home under the trees.

Half an hour and still the bus hadn't come. The sun baked. She picked up the rank, cutting smell of the Nanticoke Co-Op grain silos slugging across town. "Get. Me. The fuck. Outta here," she muttered to herself. Dry, bleached weeds poked up out of cracks in the sidewalk. Saplings, with candy wrappers and pop cans scattered about them, runted out of the gravel around the planted maples. How's that possible? she thought. Cars and trucks rattled by, belching slow, tired exhaust at her. She could make out a young boy watching her through the tinted window of a slowing family van that was looking for an address maybe. She smiled and the kid frowned back before turning his hard face and saying something into the front seat. She gave the van the finger.

She contemplated going and knocking on the office door again, waiting forever till the old man opened the door, and nodding past him at the big yellowed Greyhound poster on the wall. "Didn't take *me* where *I* want to go!" Instead she picked up her things and lumbered down the block to the old diner. She had worked as a waitress here some time ago. Today the place was empty. Pre-wrapped sandwiches and submarines sat on barred shelves in a refrigerated glass display case where a counter once stood dotted with red leather stools. Along a wall that had been shared by milkshake machines and soda fountains there was now a fridge, with a sliding glass door, full of pop and fruit drinks. Above it, fixed to the wall and ceiling, was a black steel frame that once held a television. She ordered a coffee at the counter—the girl there must've been new; it took forever—then paid, took it and sat at a window table in the corner. In the short time she had been outside, her skin was mottled pink, already giving off a raw sun smell. It was unbearably hot there behind the glass but it was the only spot from where, just in case, she could see the bus coming up the street. The floor's black and white diamonds were cleaner here, untouched by years of grease and sun, and there were rivet holes in the floor where booths had stood once upon a time. Beside her, along the west wall, there was another, smaller clean square on the floor where a juke box once whirred. She sipped on her coffee and thought herself stupid for ordering it in this heat.

She was half done her coffee when—a hard, low swoop inside, up and under her ribs—she saw them walk by the window. A young man and his wife, a little boy swinging his weight back and forth between their hands, singing. The wife was dressed all in black like the man, and like the man also, her hair was dyed black. The boy was blond, almost white blond. He wore a striped T-shirt. Seeing them, the young woman slid down in her seat and lowered the peak of her cap, but it was the cap that signalled it was her in the first place. When they came in the door the boy ran across the tiles to the counter and the young man said get back here, but ended up following the boy, black boots clopping over the tiles. She pretended not to see them, though their progress across the floor pulled on her attention like hooks, marionette strings. It was the wife who noticed her first. A stiffening of the shoulders. Purple lips spread thin across a white face and small teeth said, "Oh. Hello, Marie. Didn't think I'd see you again so soon. Why are you sitting right in the sun?"

She didn't answer.

The wife looked down at her things on the floor. "Going somewhere?"

"Victoria." She sipped her coffee. "Bus is late."

"A bus? To B.C.?" the wife said, already turning around, her cheeks pinched around a cigarette. She blew smoke up at the ceiling. A fan demolished it into the hot air. She called to the man at the counter. "What's he want? Juice?"

"Yep," the young man said shortly. He didn't turn around. He stood akimbo, his black clothes absurd in this heat, and his one foot tapped as he watched the girl behind the counter work the coffee machine. The boy was absently body-checking his legs.

"Juice juice juice." The wife rolled her eyes and smiled at Marie but Marie was watching the street.

"So," the wife said, taking a seat diagonally across from her at the next window table. "What's in Victoria?"

Marie craned her neck to see past the parked cars. "Oh," she shrugged, "I don't know. Stuff."

A minute passed. The wife spent it looking her up and down. "I like your dress." She smiled and ashed her cigarette in the tin tray. Her arms were thin as bamboo. Little blue veins networked at her temples.

Marie nodded. "Thanks."

The young man came to the other table with two cups of coffee and sat beside the wife, across from Marie. The boy followed him carrying a glass of orange juice in both hands. He frowned down at the glass, his feet pacing out steps slow and careful as if on a tightrope, his tongue sticking out the side of his mouth. Juice still managed to lap out the sides. He was concentrating so intensely that he walked past the couple's table and came instead to Marie's. When he set the glass on the laminated tabletop, a thick orange ring puddled instantly around it. He climbed up in the chair next to her.

Looking up, he took in her face and his surprise didn't know itself from joy. His smile was a rat-tat-tat of tiny teeth.

"Over here." The wife eyed the boy gravely. She dragged a chair around the side of the table so he could sit close to her. "Marie's going to Victoria," she said, chipper, her eyes still serious on the boy.

"Oh, yeah." The young man looked at Marie blandly over his coffee. Setting the cup down, he fumbled with a pack of cigarettes and looked out the window. He had pale blue eyes, full of yellow from the sun. His ears were red, transparent when the sun hit them. His black hair was tied back in a ponytail, wisps of it lifting from the fans dotted round the diner so that, except for the hoop earring, he was a burly white samurai. She could see his old, lighter brown hair poking up from his scalp. She remembered how once upon a time his hair had been almost as blond as her own. Her face reddened at the thought of it.

"I think that's great," the wife said. "It'll be good for you. I had a friend, Jody, who was out there. She just loved—"

The man reached across her and slapped at the hand of the boy who was pouring salt into his orange juice. "Quit it right now," he said, his eyes two full stops. He took the salt shaker and clapped it down in the middle of the table.

The boy slumped back in his chair and pouted. "Don't."

The man shook his head. "It doesn't work that way, buddy."

But the boy's mind had already butterflied on to something else, his eyes flitting all over the room. His legs kicked under the table. Marie watched him intently, the happy globe of his face, yellow blue eyes of his father.

The young man gazed over at her gear on the floor. "You never played guitar," he said. "Not far as I can remember."

"Leave it alone," the wife said, snatching the salt shaker from the boy's hand.

"What are you gonna do this time?" the man said. "You gonna *busk* out in B.C? On the street?" She didn't answer. "No, I know," he said. "You're going to be a star, right? Make it big and all that." Marie sat back silently and folded her arms under her loose breasts. The wife regarded her cleavage out of the corner of her eye. "You know what you need that you don't got?" the man said.

Her head bobbed side to side as she spoke. "No, *please* tell me. What do I need?"

He leaned forward and spoke slowly, patronizing, and cupped his palm as if holding the word. "Talent."

She, a child under his gaze, sullenly fingered her coffee cup. But unable to sit back any longer, she waved her arm—another waft of patchouli oil—in a vague motion over the faded, obsolete menus pressed below the laminated tabletop, across the window with its streaks and ghosts of hand-painted signs, taking in the sidewalk and parked cars and traffic, the Salvation Army. "What's here for me any more? Shit, what's been here for me the last couple of *years?*"

"Nothing far as I can see," said the wife.

"It's been three years," the man said, idly plucking a vinegar bottle from the boy's hands and setting it down again in the middle of the table. "Three years, almost to the day."

Marie settled back in her chair once more and punched back her cap. "I know how old he is," she said quietly.

The man's eyes lazed from the boy to Marie. Smoke scrolled from his cigarette. "Okay," he said. "So tell me this: what's out there for you in the land of milk and—" He paused, and made a bitter, disgusted face. "Take those stupid fucking things off, would you?"

After sitting stubborn for a moment, Marie whipped off her yellow sunglasses and glared, not at him, but down at the shades, the orange puddle on the tabletop beside them.

"Do you got any jobs lined up out there?" he said.

"Well," she pulled a stray hair from her tongue, her eyes still not meeting his. "My friend Ange, I met her at the Rochester show, she's an amazing person. She's going out there too, we're meeting in Regina. Friend of hers works at this big fancy hotel right by the parliament buildings in Victoria, can get us jobs, she says. And the first week I get there there's a show down in Seattle and then—"

"What kind of show?"

She started, frowned quizzically at him. "Dead show." Ignoring his rolled eyes, she resumed. "And afterwards we're coming back up and hitching across to the west side of the Island. Clayoquot Sound. They're clearcutting there, these trees that are hundreds, *hundreds* of years old, and there's all these people protesting. It's old growth," she said, excited now. "They're these huge, fucking beautiful—"

"So you're gonna be a tree hugger," he said, studying her over his canoeing cigarette.

"Yeah, right," she said, cold. "Sure."

"Pfff." He looked away. "Flavour of the month."

"I think it'll be good for you," the wife said, her mouth pursed as she butted out her smoke. When it didn't go out, she ground it into the ashtray with her thumb. "Good for you to get out of this town. I envy you."

"Yeah," Marie smiled, insincere. "So you said."

"Look!" The man pointed his cigarette at her, his face

shook. "There's certain responsibilities here still," he said. "Loyalties. Unlike you, I can't afford—"

He checked himself just as the bell clanged above the door and two teenage girls breezed in and crossed the floor's black and white diamonds. All tanned, smooth legs and short shorts and hair up in ponytails wisping at their necks. Their voices rang sharp and confident in the air, owning it. They grabbed two Cokes out of the fridge and teased the counter girl about a boy and she told them to fuck off. Laughing, they waltzed back out across the diamonds and out the dinging door without paying for the pops. Marie watched them walk by the window; the one girl was talking and the other grinned and pressed a sweating Coke can to her forehead and in a vague, empty moment her eyes caught Marie's then sparked away. When Marie turned her eyes back to the man he was still pointing his burnt-down cigarette at her, as if the whole time he'd been frozen in that position. "Unlike you," he said slowly, "no, *because* of you, I can't afford to be a kid any more. I can't be flying by the seat of my pants out into the wild blue yonder whenever shit doesn't work out the way I want it."

"Kid, you call me," she said. "Ha! After what we...shit, we're the same age, and *she's—*" She waved her hand dismissively at the wife, then leaned forward and addressed him as if he were the only one in the room. "You told me, remember? How it didn't matter...you'd take care, you know, till I got my shit together..." She trailed off, her eyes wet.

"That was then," he shook his head. "That's history."

"No, it was always, you said, you know...remember, how we—"

"No!" The wife slapped the kid's hand. Salt sprayed over the table. She pointed at his glass of juice. "Drink it."

The boy scowled. "Nooo."

"Drink it." The wife grabbed the boy's hands and clasped them tight round the glass. The juice shook. She poured in pepper. She snapped up a vinegar bottle and shook it until her knuckles were white, the veins at her temples swelled a little. "Drink it now." She tried to push the glass to the boy's lips and said to the man, "Tell your kid to drink it."

"Leave him alone," Marie said.

"You mind your own business, you," the wife whispered. "I wasn't talking to you. I'm his mother. He doesn't even know who the hell you are. You're some lady in whacked-out hats who comes breezing by every few months, or whenever she feels like, to smoke and drink on the back porch and yabber on about her next big thing. I'm the one who's had to feed and dress him for the last two and a half years. What the hell do you think that meeting yesterday was, those forms we signed? One of your parties?" She laughed suddenly. "You weren't able to keep him for more than six months. It's a wonder you showed up at the woman's office yesterday." She fussed with the boy now, frenetic, combing his hair roughly with her fingers, her other hand still clenched around his glass. "He never was yours," she whispered. "You were always too busy being in love with yourself."

"Go to hell," Marie said. "You don't know anything about love. It's just hate turned inside out for you. You're so scared to lose him and you because lie to yourself that it's love that's keeping him with you because you know it's always been me he—" She broke off and gazed into the young man's eyes, which were now riveted on her. She quickly looked down at her hands. "Ah, fuck it," she sniffed.

"Who's *he?*" the wife said, suddenly turning to the young man. "Which *he* is she really talking about?"

"Don't," the boy pouted. "Daddy...don't..."

But the young man was still staring across at Marie. Her bangled wrists, her fair skin mottled from sun, the loud, unashamed dress. She caught his eyes and they hurt so she fumbled her sunglasses back on. She swilled back the last black puddle of her coffee as the boy started struggling back his juice. He sipped at it, but then let the liquid fall from his mouth as if a wad of gum. "Blecch!"

"You drink it all," the wife said. "Now."

The boy shook his head. Juice dripped sloppy from his chin.

"Drink it, I said."

Marie kicked back her chair and strode over to their table. She pulled some juice away from the boy's chin with her finger and licked it. Made a pleasant-surprise face at the wife. She picked up the kid's glass with both hands and raised it to her lips and began to drink, her elbows cocked up in the air. "Jesus," the man covered his face with his hands and laughed. Juice dribbled and ran out the sides of her mouth, down to her chin. It was sharp and sick tasting, but she gulped it back, ravenous. When she was finished she set it down slow and satisfied on the table.

"Mmmm," she smacked her lips. "Tha's good."

"There's your bus now," the wife said, without expression.

Marie started and looked out the window but saw only the yellow-and-black abdomen of a school bus rumble by. "Yeah. Thanks."

"No, really," the wife smirked, leaning across the man to peer out the window. "It's stopped right across from the Greyhound office."

"Bullshit."

"No," the man said, looking out through his fanned fingers. "She's right."

"Shit!" She made for her stuff, but the boy had grabbed a hold of her dress. "C'mon," she said. "Let go, little buddy." But he sat back, tie-dye bunched up tight in his pink fist. He kicked happily, all bright eyes, his face crinkled. She looked down at him and her eyes softened then broke. "C'mon," she said. "Please."

"Let go of her," the wife said. "She's got to go." She tried to pry the boy's fingers loose, but Marie picked up the chair, boy and all, and lifted it up over her guitar case and knapsack and away across the floor. She began to run, rocking the seated boy back and forth in her arms, leaning to his ear and going *vroom!* as she swooped between the tables, jostling chairs. The boy squealed with pleasure as he flew over the black and white diamonds. "You'll hurt him!" the wife cried. "Quit it!" She shook the man's shoulder. "Tell her to stop!"

But the man didn't seem to hear. "I give you six months," he said. "Tops. You'll still be the same person, you know. There, anywhere. It'll still be you." Marie made like she didn't hear him, but her head was afire. She circled the whole diner—doing figure eights here and there, speeding past the counter so the boy waved over the cash register at the girl as he floated by—before Marie finally tired and set him down gently in the middle of the floor. He enjoyed the ride. She ruffled and then found herself kissing his hair. It smelled sharp, of vinegar and bleach.

"See ya, little guy."

"Bye." But he was more interested in his own travels. His head lolled about, gazed all over the room from his happy new spot.

"I say it's just a change of scenery," the man said, his face red. The wife reached to stroke his cheek but he pulled away. Ignoring him, Marie strode back to her table and grabbed up her purse. She picked up the rest of her things and said bye again to the boy and lumbered out. The guitar case rattled the door as she shouldered into it, out of it. Yes, on the sidewalk she did turn, in spite of herself she looked back and saw, through the window, the man sitting alone at the table staring back at her through her own reflection. Her silly bulbous hat, her spectacled face in shadow, the jacket draped over her arm, a bundle of black gear about her body, as if she was a magnet for such stuff. There were things she could've said to him, redundant things. Behind him the wife was lifting the boy out of the chair and saying something, softer now, but neither the boy nor the man was listening to her as she jostled the chair back to their table. The boy twirled around under one of the ceiling fans, craning back his neck, entranced by the whirring blades. The wife grabbed his arm, her face drawn and pale. Ignoring them, the man rubbed at one of his eyes with heel of his fist. Marie imagined the salt working in there, how bitter that salt would be, and her own eyes started to work. When he took his hand away she half expected the eye to be gone, pushed back into the skull, but it was the same big, blue eye that stared back at her with its twin. The light, small scar on his upper lip. The wife said something, leading the boy toward the rear of the diner, then she suddenly stopped and petted the boy's hair, fawning over him, kissing him now, apologetic. Slowly, the young man turned and said something back to her. They picked up their things and walked back to the shaded half of the room where Marie could see them no longer.

She ran up the street as fast as she could, her dress billowing a hot, dry breeze about her legs, her feet slipping in her sweaty sandals. The school bus was sitting at the stop, the engine still running. She set down her things and wiped at her eyes, the sticky mess of orange on her face. The door was hinged open and when she stepped up to the bottom step the driver sat in his seat, a burly middle-aged man with dark three-quarter moons of sweat soaked through under his arms, shirt unbuttoned almost to the belly and hair stuck thick to his skin. His face a big bearded shine, rivulets of sweat caught in the laugh lines. He blew at his slick, matted-down bangs, glared dark at her and shook his head. "Fuck."

She had to bite her lip to stop from laughing through her tears at him when she handed him her ticket. "Hottest day of the year and my bus died on me," he said. "Just coming out of Port Dover. Nothing back at the shop. Had to go out to Blue Line Road to get one of these stupid things." He glared back at the regiment of green plastic seats, the black corduroy rubber floor, dust-caked windows in the back. He shook his head at her again. "Fuck."

There was no one else on the bus. Flies buzzed and razzled in the thick air. She walked up the wide aisle, wider than she remembered as a child, and dumped her baggage into a seat near the back. Her arms were light and hollow. A school bus, she thought. She just stood there a while, lost in a bubble of laughter, before she took her cap off and flung it onto the seat. She lifted her dress and let it fall, making a breeze. She began to turn around, once, twice, faster, until she was spinning now, twirling with her arms out like a helicopter skimming the tops of the seats, the skirt carouselling out all around her burgundy blue yellow green pink orange until it flew clear of her knees her thighs her underwear and swished over the dull green seats. "Hey, miss," the driver said. "Hey!"

She stopped in mid-flight, her blonde hair lashed across her face, in her smiling teeth. "What?" She punched the dress back down as an afterthought.

"You want to help me out with the windows? Might be easier for ya. You're liable to get dizzy by the time we reach Hagersville."

They went from one end of the bus to the other—she rear to front, he front to rear— opening the top windows and letting them clap down so that, little by little, hot outside air came slugging into the bus. When they were done the bus driver smiled, tired and painful, and sighed thanks. "Twenty years I've been working for this company," he said. "And *this* is the shit I have to put up with." For some reason this made her want to laugh all over again. She slumped into a seat across from her stuff, kicked her legs out across the expanse of green vinyl and leaned her head back against the glass. A maple's red leaves leaned into the window, rustled at her ear. Cool, insistent, knowing. The driver settled back in his seat and shifted the bus into first and pulled out onto the street and she watched as their yellow-and-black reflection sailed loudly across the Greyhound office windows, the fake plants reaching out of the dark, pawing the glass.

The bus rumbled out of town, past a strip mall, a car dealership, the OPP station. It clattered over the train tracks that ran diagonally through town and away across the flat countryside. Passing by the small grass-runwayed airport, she saw a skydiver float into view, swinging gently back and forth beneath a red-and-white-checker parachute. She watched the small figure land nimbly on a clearing of bare earth and come to a running stop as the huge silk umbrella crumpled in slow motion in his wake. A small crowd of people gathered on the surrounding grass, ready to greet him. The bus passed a Baptist church, its parking lot filled with the cars of afternoon worshippers. Soon the highway narrowed to two lanes. Buildings gave way to yellow birch, hickory, sassafras. Out by the Blue Line Road they passed a man at the side of the highway. He was shirtless and tanned and squinting into sunlight, thumbing for a ride. The bus driver laughed as the bus coughed a wall of dust at the man. "Now what kind of a person do you figure tries to hitch a ride from a school bus?" he said. "A *school* bus."

The heat was more bearable now, the sun behind them. They passed over a creek bridge, sped above treetops, leaves reaching up through the guardrails. And in the distance, on the lakeshore, she saw the steelworks, its blue-black riffles of smoke luminous in the sun. She took her sandals off, pulled her dress up over her knees and let the air through the windows cool her outstretched legs. She took off her yellow-tinted glasses too and suddenly the world was another, stranger and more real place. Tobacco fields floated past her bare toes, the new runt plants short and a pale, yellowish green in the sandy earth. On some farms tobacco had given way to ginseng. Kilns had been dismantled and where they once stood she saw hundreds upon hundreds of two-by-fours staked into the straw earth, propping up corrugated sheetmetal roofs fitted together so low that a grown woman had to stoop to walk beneath them. The sun caught the sheetmetal and glinted brilliant silver-white across the flatlands, so brilliant that for a moment she was blinded.

And she opened her eyes to an October afternoon almost four years ago now when the water glinted silver over the white pebble riverbed. And he stood before her, his face in shadow, breath pluming, and he said something about the light on her face. "I've got to get home," she said. And he said me too as crows lit from the branches overhead and he picked her up and set her on a graffitied rock and she wrapped her legs round his and the stone grazed her skin but it was good and they breathed into one another's mouth all teeth and tongue and she said, "I've dreamt about you, you know," and he said no and she said, "Yes, ever since, you know, that time," and he said you couldn't have 'cos there's only so many dreams to go round and I used them all up dreaming of you. She tugged hard on his coat lapels and his ear, translucent in the sun, tasted of cold smoke and she called him things she didn't mean, his hips viced between her knees. Her blonde hair was in his face between his lips the scarred one she licked and he said it meant one thing and one thing only and that was that they were soul-mates and she said, "You think?" And he said yes, he thought so, oh of course, yes, always. She looked at him suddenly, so close, his face loose and honest and pricked with cold. "You're such an idiot," she said. And she was laughing up into the sky then up over his shoulder his light brown hair the branches bared themselves grey in the sunlight and leaves fell in the shushing water like yellow and red flakes of rain and got carried away on the water that shivered over the white stones.

"No smoking, miss," the bus driver said.

"Not even cigarettes?"

He flashed a look at her in the large mirror. "Not even wacky tobacky."

She shrugged, flicked the cigarette out the window and watched it tumble and ricket into a bleached weed ditch. Then she took her whole pack out of her purse and threw it out of the window too. The little white sticks went laughing out in all directions. She smiled to herself, pictured kids happening upon the smokes sometime in the next few days, ecstatic, scrabbling about after them in the gravel as highway traffic whizzed by, and smoking each and every one of them down to the filter, one after the other, throwing up in a field on the way home, lit smokes dropped in a field of chaff. She saw these fields ignite behind the silhouettes of running children and saw the fire rage across the flatlands, burn up ribbons of trees like hair, the wildfires raging for days, flames licking the blue sky until it turned black, the outskirts of the town charred and deserted, smoke rising slow. And she saw two figures walking through the rubble, their faces blackened except for a ghost of orange around the smaller figure's mouth, and as he stopped to pick up some charred, wretched thing the man beside him said don't now, leave it alone.

So she found a new vision, and in this vision she saw herself out west. Smoke scrolling up from a hillside campfire. People dancing in colours and swirls and shared food and clotheslines and clean water lapping, blue-green from the trees surging down out of the mountains to the shore, cool air falling infinite from pine needles and arbutus leaves, and she would be sitting on a quiet strip of sand with the Pacific lapping at her feet and sand in her toes and there she would learn to play the guitar. Her name would be shouted and she would think of her name holding many things that it did not hold two, three weeks ago, before the three thousand miles of country she saw for the first time and drank in, drank up full.

The cottonball clouds hanging, almost within reach, over the first farmlands of Manitoba. The yellow yellow brown yellow of Alberta. The Badlands. The trail of rainbows in the Rockies. And here, on the edge of the world, there'd be a man walking out of the trees down to the water with a couple of cans of beer and she'd know already it was his step, by its weight and speed and music, and she'd smile and keep playing—maybe Neil Young, or Joni Mitchell, maybe even "Ripple" by the Dead—like she didn't know he was there so that he would touch her in a soft, hesitant, tender way sure not to alarm her, but she'd jump anyway from his cold beer hands and when she turned round his face wouldn't be movie- star handsome, no, that would be too much because with all his other charms it would just be too much. No, he wouldn't look quite like anybody she'd known before, no one from back home anyway, no, no one at all. And with her eyes closed but seeing him she smiled softly and, lulled by the heat and rhythm of the bus, drifted into sleep.

The old man locked the door behind the young woman and flipped over the sign. He walked back over the red shag carpet on his canes, which he had painted red some years ago in order to camouflage them against the carpet and give the impression, to any no-good who happened to be watching from the street, that he was walking of his own power and free will, and just fine thank you very much. Of course, this hadn't worked. He'd been robbed twice in the last year, which meant he'd been robbed three times since he opened the place thirty years ago. The world was going to hell in a handbasket and sorry, his hands were full up. He lifted the gate and squeaked past it and, stopping at the counter at the back, hung up one cane, picked up a thin sheaf of papers, flicked off the light, tucked the papers under his arm, then took his cane again and made his slow, inevitable way to a side door. Before passing through that door he saw the blurred form of the young woman still standing out on the sidewalk, looking in.

He shuffled into another room which held a stove and chair, a sink and fridge, a TV against one wall and bed against another, with a low drop-leaf table at the foot of the bed. He'd had these things moved downstairs last year, when he finally admitted to himself it was too much for him to traverse the stairs day in day out. The upstairs rooms were vacant now, save for unessential furniture and stacks of papers and magazines and the shuffling of something or other at night. But he wouldn't rent the place out to just any come-lately. He'd offered it to his granddaughter but something had gotten under her skirts and seeped into her brain since she'd left her mother's home and taken up with a lawyer in Toronto; somehow she'd gotten her nose lifted up so high she'd developed the notion that her shit didn't stink. Never came down to visit either. Not even when he was slated to get his cataracts done and they called off the operation last minute. Heart. Tests, they said. No, he didn't see hide nor hair of her. Just a telephone call, and not a word about what ailed him. "Get one of those motorized carts," she said. "They're cute." Dressed all in new ribbons and bows, she was, sitting pretty in the city, and still not believing in nothing. Sure, maybe she'll have that lawyer guy pay her way, but to where on God's green earth? the old man wanted to know.

It was then—a dull, aching ripple through his chest—that he realized the young blonde woman hadn't paid for her ticket. He stopped in his stuttering tracks. It was the third time in two weeks he'd made such a mistake. "That's all she wrote," he said, matter-of-fact. "All she wrote." He lit a gas burner and, hanging his canes over the lip of the sink, filled a kettle and set it on the stove. A dog whined somewhere outside, but the sound soon melded with the hissing water. The old man sat down in the chair in front of the stove, rested his chin on his hands and watched the water boil.

He drank two cups of coffee in the same chair. When he was done he got up shakily and swilled the cup under cold water and left it in the sink to dry. He took up the canes again in both hands and crossed the small room, past elaborate gilt frames that held portraits of men, women and children whose faces were no longer in fashion, pictures he had not looked at, not really, for some time. The white room was orange now, the ripe sun bouncing off the buildings across the street, its glow singing back through the small window in the wall. At the foot of the bed the old man slumped down, sighed, hung his canes on one of the hooks fixed here and there about the room's walls, sighed again, and withdrew the sheaf of papers from under his arm. He shuffled through them, found a Greyhound map of Canada, one he'd never opened before. He dropped the other papers on the bed and set the map on the drop-leaf table, unfolded it, spread it out and turned it over to the side that housed Ontario. He took a red pen from his pocket and began drawing, freehand, a thick heavy line from right to left along Highway 3 to Jarvis. Beside it, in the margin, he wrote down the highway kilometres: 18. His hands, old and driftwood coloured as they were, were steady, assured. Next he drew a line north along Highway 6, through Garnet, Hagersville, Caledonia, till he hit Hamilton: 58 kilometres. "The dead," he shook his head. "The dead. Now what in blazes..." He kept drawing the lines, complete with small detours for village stops, and wrote down all the corresponding numbers until he reached Toronto. He pictured the landscapes she would pass through, most of them changed, almost unrecognizable since he himself had last passed through them. Leaves and grass and water now steel and glass and plastic. She would change in Toronto. And there would be many more miles to go. The old man would wear out the first red pen, already on its last legs, before she got there. He'd write down a lot of numbers, add up a lot of numbers, making subtotals every ten numbers, so he could make list of the subtotals too, so that the sums curled around the map's margin. When it was time he'd turn the map over and start on the prairies, noticing how his previous red lines had seeped through the paper, and thinking how in all his days he could never sleep on a bus. He'd draw the lines with such care and purpose, all the way across Canada to the ocean.

Acknowledgments

The first epigraph is taken from Lady Charlotte Guest's translation of *The Mabinogion,* published by J.M. Dent and Co., 1906. The Andrei Tarkovsky epigraph appears in *Time within Time: The Diaries 1970-1986,* used with permission of Faber and Faber Limited. The epigraph for "Painter" is quoted from *The World of Icons,* Harper & Row, 1971. A short piece of Gene's dinner-table dialogue in "Painter" is quoted from *Inside Ethnic Families: Three Generations of Portuguese Canadians,* by Edite Noivo; permission granted from McGill-Queen's University Press. Pissarro's letter is quoted in *Post-Impressionism* by Bernard Denvir, published by Thames & Hudson, 1992. Short passages about the Azores and cement finishers were quoted and paraphrased from *A Future to Inherit: Portuguese Communities in Canada* by Grace M. Anderson and David Higgs, published by McClelland & Stewart as part of the Canadian Heritage-Multiculturalism Program. Reproduced with permission of the Minister of Public Works and Government Services Canada, 2000, and the Minister of Canadian Heritage.

I am grateful for the invaluable assistance of the Canada Council for the Arts and the Ontario Arts Council.

On the subject of wondrous things, big thanks to Madeleine Thien for everything from her great advance-editing talents to her love and endless support. I could never have finished this work without her. Thanks also to the following friends who generously offered their comments and helped me along the path of this book: Adam Schroeder, Kath Mockler, Christy Ann Conlin, Sioux Browning, Brad Cran, Melanie Little, Lee Henderson, Andrew Gray, Marita Dachsel, Geoff Dodd, Lucas Wright and Mary-Rose McColl.

Thanks to Nikki Barrett for discovering my manuscript at Knopf Canada and not throwing it away. Gratitude goes out to my editor, Diane Martin, who took the stories and showed them some secret moves, and for whose vision and hard work I'm super thankful. Thanks also to Noelle Zitzer for her tireless work. I'm indebted to Janice Kulyk Keefer ("If you don't finish this, I'll *keel* you!") and Linda Svendsen for their ongoing guidance and encouragement. Special thanks to Beth Wheatley. I also wish to express my gratitude to Audrey Thomas, Guy Vanderhaeghe, Paul Bowdring and Matt Cohen, for their insightful advice and yet more encouragement.

Thanks to Leah Postman, Sara O'Leary and all the *Prism international* folks. Thanks also to George McWhirter, Andreas Schroeder and UBC's Department of Creative Writing, Andris Taskans and *Prairie Fire*, Sabine Campbell and Ross Leckie at *The Fiddlehead*. Thanks to Kathryn Lewis and everyone at SOEH for their support. Thanks, Jon Wood and Palace Flophouse, A Western

Theatre Conspiracy, Denise Ryan and Ajay Heblé. Thanks to Rachel Wyatt, Edna Alford and everyone at the Banff Centre's Writing Studio, Fall 1999.

And finally, I wish to thank my family, who are the greatest.

RICK MADDOCKS was recently named by the *Vancouver Sun* as one of B.C.'s ten "most vaunted" writers. He has been published in numerous literary journals and anthologies, and was nominated by *Prism International* for the CAA/Air Canada Award for most promising writer under thirty. The opening story in *Sputnik Diner,* "Plane People," won *Prairie Fire's* Long Fiction Competition and was the winner of a Western Magazine Award. Rick Maddocks lives in Vancouver.